THE
WAR
CHILD

BOOKS BY RENITA D'SILVA

Monsoon Memories
The Forgotten Daughter
The Stolen Girl
A Sister's Promise
A Mother's Secret
A Daughter's Courage
Beneath an Indian Sky
The Girl in the Painting
The Orphan's Gift

RENITA D'SILVA

THE
WAR
CHILD

Best Wishes,
Renita D'Silva

bookouture

Published by Bookouture in 2021

An imprint of Storyfire Ltd.
Carmelite House
50 Victoria Embankment
London EC4Y 0DZ

www.bookouture.com

ISBN: 978-1-80019-145-7
eBook ISBN: 978-1-80019-144-0

*For the amazing women who have shaped and informed my life;
who've endured, survived and come through smiling – role models all.
My mother, Perdita Hilda D'Silva, whose love, generosity and
wisdom astounds, soothes and steadies.*

My aunt, Lucy Pinto – for her prayers, warmth and gentle kindness.

*My first teacher, Miss Tekla Pereira, who took a chance on a little
ragamuffin and instilled a lifelong love of learning.*

*My godmother, Irene Sequeira, for her steadfast love and prayers.
Devaki for selfless, loving care.*

*In loving memory of my grandmother, Mary Rodrigues, Baa, one
and only, beloved and very sorely missed.*

'We are plunged in slumber, we are the children of dust and ashes, until we love.'

– Leo Tolstoy, War and Peace

Prologue

Clara

1916, Monster

Clara is dreaming of a monster who growls and screams. 'Stop!' she yells, covering her ears with her hands. But it won't listen. 'Wooo, I'm coming for you,' it howls.

'Clara, wake up, my love.' Her mother's voice, soft but urgent.

Her mother is here. She's safe. She opens her eyes and is aware of noise. Whistling, shrill. She recognises the sound but can't quite place it, her terrifying dream disorientating her, pushing rational thought away, leaving a pulsing storm of residual terror.

'What's happening?' she asks, tasting panic, metallic blue in her mouth.

'Air raid, my love.' Mary smiles gently, reassuringly, but Clara reads the worry flickering in her mother's eyes. 'Come on, sweetheart, we need to get to the shelter.'

Clara rubs sleep from her eyes, as she and Mary pull on their coats and Mary opens their front door to join the crowd heading for the underground station, the frosty night whispering and rustling, pounding with the frantic footsteps of scores of people, the scent of broken sleep and interrupted dreams, the pungent reek of panic, the ominous rumble overhead, stalking them.

But they have barely stepped into the street when the loudest sound Clara has ever heard deafens her. There is dust in her eyes and when she rubs them clear, she cannot believe what she is seeing. Or rather, what she is *not*. Their street has houses on both sides – it's a sight as familiar to Clara as her mother's face. She blinks but the new vision doesn't go away. There is a huge hole in front of her. The house across from them is gone and with it so too is everyone who was running to the shelter. The street is eerily quiet.

Fear a physical thing, squatting on Clara's chest, alongside the lingering remnants of her dream. The monster weighing heavy upon her.

But Mary is already pulling her back into the house. 'Come on, my love, down to the basement. There's no time to get to the shelter now. The bombs must have come faster than they realised.' Her mother's hand in hers is comforting. She focuses on that touch – easier than remembering the horrifying reality outside.

'Zeppelins,' Mary mutters as they descend the stairs. Cylindrical balloons hovering ominously above. 'Monsters.'

Monsters. Clara's dream. Real. Here. Swooping overhead, casting a shadow over the dark night. *What about our neighbours? My friend, Tess, from across the street?*

Inside the damp basement, Mary lights a paraffin lamp and they huddle together under an old kitchen table. 'Here.' Her mother slips something metallic and heavy around her chest, even as she helps Clara upright. It smells silvery, it is weighted and grave. The necklace Mary is never without, given to her by *her* mother.

'My St Christopher medal. It will keep you safe,' her mother says, her eyes shining. 'It will make sure you come to no harm, I promise.'

A series of pops like fireworks. 'It'll be alright,' says Mary reassuringly. 'They never hit the same street twice.'

But then the cold darkness explodes in a fiery maelstrom of colour, which appears deceptively festive, before the rainbow is strung with smoke, raining debris, stinging and throbbing, stealing the breath from Clara with gusts of blazing smog.

It feels to Clara like their whole house is falling in on itself, on top of them, leaving mother and daughter trapped at the bottom. The only real things in the world are her mother's hand, warm against her palm, and the St Christopher medal, promising to keep her safe. And then her world goes black.

Part One

India

Tough

Chapter One

Indira

1995, Knock at the Closed Door

Indira is hosting the directors' board meeting and is in full flow, detailing her plans for the direction she wants the company to take in the next few weeks, when there is an unexpected, unprecedented knock at the closed door to the boardroom. Although piqued, she keeps her face blandly expressionless as she turns to address the intrusion, noting that Shankar is dozing, his head drooping upon the spreadsheets she circulated at the start of the meeting with the projections for revenue she wants the company to bring in.

He will have to go, she thinks, and is mulling on his possible replacement even as there's a second, more urgent knock. 'Come in,' she calls, only her voice, which is a notch sharper than usual, betraying her annoyance at this untimely interruption. No one, but no one, is allowed to interrupt these directorial meetings. They are sacred, *everyone* at the company knows this, which is why she's even more miffed when *her* PA, Nandita, pops her head around the door. Nandita should know not to disturb better than anyone.

At thirty-three, Indira is the youngest ever *and* the only ever female CEO of Telco Analytics (and possibly the youngest and only female CEO in India), promoted to the coveted position a few weeks ago in an announcement that shocked and ruffled everyone, especially the experienced veterans who were angling for the job. Only Indira was neither shocked nor ruffled – she had been working towards this goal since she joined the company straight from engineering college, where she was one of three girls on the course, which she had topped.

Indira makes it her mission to be tough and take no nonsense – it is the only way to deal with the older men she has bypassed to get to this position regardless of their years of experience and their entitled, chauvinistic superiority. She leads by example and takes no fools. She is more ruthless than any of them.

When she started rising up the ranks, almost from the moment she joined Telco, the lone woman in the cohort of men near and aiming for the top, they made jokes about her femininity and about women in general, but those dried up when she retorted with cracks about men and their incompetence. She knows they secretly hate her, but it doesn't bother her one bit.

'They call me ballbreaker and they're not wrong. I've earned the moniker and am proud of it. Are you still interested?' she'd asked Karan when he asked her out, a mere fifteen minutes after they met at a conference for industry movers and shakers – she was, as usual, the lone woman.

His expression never wavered. In fact, there was more admiration in his twinkling bronze eyes. 'I like a challenge.'

'You'll get more than you bargained for.'

He grinned. 'You can't scare me off.'

'Well, you've been warned,' she'd said.

Karan's response was to laugh delightedly, his mirth like ice tumbling into a glass, soothing a parched throat on a sweltering day.

Karan... A pang as she contemplates her husband, the distance that's crept between them lately that, preoccupied though she is, she can't help but notice and has no idea how to bridge. While she is extremely competent at her job, matters of the heart have her stumped.

'Good job that I'm the only one who gets to see your soft side,' Karan used to whisper when holding Indira in bed at night, in that deep gold voice like aged whisky that she finds irresistible.

But she cannot recall the last time he said so, or even spent the night in the same bed – Arun is going through a clingy phase and more often than not, Karan spends the night with him in his room so as not to disturb her as she has to be up early for work and, given the intensity and pressure of her job, she needs her rest to recharge.

Arun came along just as Indira was shouldering more responsibility at work, having been promoted to director, and Karan had suggested then that he'd assume the bulk of the childcare since he, while one of the founding partners at the start-up that he helped create, had more flexible working hours. His extremely progressive view had stunned Indira – despite having come to accept that Karan was one of a kind, she still kept waiting for him to show his true colours, disappoint her, reveal that he was in fact just like the other chauvinistic men she worked with every day.

But Karan *is* different. He's always treated her as an equal; always accepted her for who she is, all she is. Karan has never wanted her to be someone else, smaller, to fit into a mould designed by men for women. In this way he's completely different to any man she has known, including her father, whose every conversation with her is admonishment and warning: 'Career is well and good, but don't forget your duties as mother and wife.'

Although she'd never openly admit it, just once Indira would like her father to say he's proud of her and all she's achieved. She's still waiting.

But Karan, on the other hand, has always been proud of her, unashamedly, unreservedly so, and he hasn't changed in all their years of marriage.

In fact, it is she who is struggling to combine the demands of being CEO with mum and wife (another thing she won't admit – that there might be something to her father's gloomy proclamations) and it is her relationship with the only man she has ever loved, the only man who understands, cares, adores and respects her for who she is, that is the casualty.

'Ma'am,' Nandita says, 'please may I borrow you for a moment?' Although only her head is visible round the door, the usually composed PA looks troubled.

'Excuse me, gentlemen,' Indira says crisply to the assembled directors, all older than her, all of whom she bypassed to climb right to the top, to be their boss. 'I'll be back in a minute.'

The men stretch and sigh. Shankar gives up all pretence and drops his head among the papers, a small snore escaping him.

'Whatever it is, Nandita, couldn't it wait?' Indira can't keep the ire from her voice once she's pulled the door to the boardroom shut behind her and is alone with her PA. 'You *know* not to—'

'I'm sorry, Ma'am.' Nandita smooths the pleats of her sari, a nervous tic. 'Your husband has been trying to contact you…'

Husband. Indira's heart tattoos a frantic rhythm within the hemmed-in confines of her chest. In that moment she's no longer CEO and success story, just a woman fearing for her family. Karan understands that she's not to be disturbed when in the boardroom. If he called, it must be urgent.

'What did Karan want?' she asks, surprised that her voice is level, even though she's screaming inside: *Tell me.*

'You are to go to the hospital at once.'

Indira does not wait to hear more, although Nandita is calling, 'Ma'am, he said…'

'Tell the directors we'll reconvene later.'

'But Ma'am…'

She does not listen, she cannot, her heart thudding, *please not Arun*, even as she runs, Nandita's voice fading behind her, ignoring the looks she gets from those not senior enough to be at the meeting, curious and shocked, surprised to see their cool, unflappable CEO so flustered.

Part Two

England

Disappeared

Chapter Two

Clara

1916, Elevated View

When Clara is next aware of her surroundings, strong arms are pulling her from rubble. She is covered in dust, weak, disorientated, hurting all over.

'She's a real fighter, this one,' says a voice, as she is carried in arms that smell of smoke. 'I'd just about given up hope of finding anyone alive.'

She is dimly aware of a doctor checking her over, lifting a cup of watery soup to her cracked lips. As sleep takes her, she hears someone say quietly, 'She's the only one on the street who survived.'

Mother did too. Didn't she? Where are you, Mother?

Pain. Weighting down Clara's body, throbbing inside her head, pulsing under her eyelids even as she pushes them open, wanting respite from the horrific nightmare plaguing her – the world splitting open, inky night spitting sparks, slitting orange, erupting into a flaming fountain of peach, red and bright yellow, eye-burning, throat-gagging, ash-raining sparklers. She wants her mother's love-filled reassurance, her tender promise that all is well.

'Mother?'

'Ah, you've come round, my dear.' A kind voice belonging to a heavy-set woman wearing a uniform. *Not* Mother.

Clara blinks as she takes in her surroundings. Where is she?

As if the woman has read her mind, she says, 'You're in hospital, my dear. You took quite a knock.'

'My mother…'

'Ah.' The woman's gaze falters. 'She… she didn't make it, I'm afraid.'

Didn't make it.

And now she remembers. Her nightmare is real. The air raid. Hiding with her mother under the table in the basement. The explosion. Their building crumbling; a torment of bricks and debris. Fire storming in dazzling, devastating swathes…

No. Oh no. Mother…

The pain is a scald upon her heart. Burning worse than the wounds scorched upon her body.

'We've written to your aunt.'

Aunt Helen. Mother's sister. Clara only visited her once, with Mother, Father and Paul, back when they were a family of four, whole and hale and happy. Oh, how the memory hurts. She was only just six then and she barely remembers the visit. Her cousins were mean, she recalls, not wanting her to tag along, but Paul made sure Clara was included. She cannot picture Aunt Helen's face. She has no idea what her aunt is like.

'While we await her reply, you'll move to the orphanage on Burnham Road. We're pressed for beds here, you see.'

The woman smiles kindly at her, clearly expecting a reply, and so Clara nods, the lump in her throat choking speech. Tears sting her eyes; she blinks them away. She will not cry – it won't bring Mother back.

'Here, let me plump up your pillows, they're all squashed, pet. There you go.'

As Clara rests her aching head, heavy with grief, on the pillows, something pendulums against her chest.

Her mother's St Christopher medal.

She clutches it tight, drawing succour – this cold, hard coin that is all that is left of her family.

In the confusing welter of days that follow that traumatic night when she becomes an orphan, Clara goes over and over her memories of her family, trying to keep them alive in her mind, imprinting them upon her heart, a throbbing wound of loss.

A meagre cache of memories – ten years with her older brother Paul, lost to polio, twelve with her father, killed in action in France, fourteen with her mother. Not enough; not nearly enough.

Her happiest recollections, rainbow-tinted, are of Paul and herself each perched on one of her father's knees after supper, his beard tickling her cheek, her mother knitting beside them as Father regaled them with stories of growing up in India.

'It was quite something,' he'd say. 'There were snakes that would swallow a man whole.'

'Capital!' Paul's eyes wider than the pie they'd shared for supper.

'And the man still alive inside the python's belly!'

Clara shivered at her father's words, resting her head against his chest, revelling in his rumble of a laugh, how the words started there and exploded out of his mouth.

'Davy, you're scaring our Clara,' Mother admonished gently, smiling tenderly at Paul and Clara in turn before looking at her husband, her eyes shimmering green pools of warmth.

'She isn't scared. She's a brave thing, aren't you, Clara?'

'I am!' Clara piped up and her mother laughed, shaking her head, her laughter as colourful as the scarf she was knitting, a medley of fiery oranges, sunny peaches, blushing roses.

'You want to know how the python digests the poor man after he's been eaten?'

'How?' Paul whispered agog.

'They twist their bellies around a tree until their prey chokes to death.'

'Oh!' Awe and horror writ large on Paul's face.

Clara cosying up against her father, his scratchy clothes offering comfort, reassurance, safety, his smell: musk and cigar smoke and the gravy from supper. Familiar. Soothing. No snake could get her here, toasty in her family's bosom.

'There was a man who survived. The snake swallowed him while he was working in the fields, you see, and luckily, he had his scythe with him. Before the snake could digest the man, he sliced open its belly and escaped.'

'Ha!' Paul cried. 'I would do that.'

'Yes, son, when we go to India, remember not to go anywhere without a knife on you.' The sweep and tumble of laughter in her father's voice.

'We will?' Clara whispered.

'I'll take you all there one day.'

'Don't you go putting ideas in that child's head, Davy,' Mother grumbled.

But her father only winked, ruffling Clara's hair. 'Off to bed now, you two.'

'But what about the lions who can kill a buffalo and the elephants who are taller than a house and—'

Paul's usual, predictable protestations were interrupted by Father's firm, 'Tomorrow. Now, bedtime. Come on.'

'Will we really go to India?' Clara asked as her father tucked her in, his strong arms gentle as they made sure the sheet was snug around her, his tender smile, eyes mellow and glowing like golden embers of a dying fire.

'One day, we will, that's a promise.' His voice wistful, tasting of hope as he bent down to plant a kiss on her forehead.

*

Clara's impressions of her father: strong as he was tall; smelling woody, green shoots, autumn smoke and rich, loamy mulch; hairy, with a ginger beard; eyes that were always twinkling at her. Tree-trunk arms that would hoist her so very high, offering a different, elevated view, transforming her ordinary world into something new and wondrous, spread out for her perusal.

Picnics by the river, fish paste sandwiches and seed cake, the nectary gold of sun and sugar, feeding crusts to the birds, hide-and-seek among the weeping willows sweeping the water, Father's post-picnic nap on the grass of the bank, hairy arm slung carelessly across his eyes, ducks waddling up to him, curious, running away, quacking furiously when he started snoring. The sound of her mother's laughter.

Her brother, charm and mischief, clothes always torn from getting into scrapes and also somehow getting out of them unscathed, allowing her to tag along, always, even when his friends protested, defending Clara hotly when they proclaimed his little sister a terrible bore.

Eavesdropping on her parents' conversation when war was declared, the ghost of her big brother beside her – he had been dead nearly two years by then, the empty space reminding her sharply of all the previous times they'd stood there, side by side, his scent of dust and curiosity and enthusiastic, irrepressible naughtiness, that mischievous twinkle in his eyes.

Paul's absence a persistent, chafing wound, wishing she could discuss with him how this war everyone was talking about would change their life, how it would affect them. Paul had always patiently answered her every question, never getting impatient with her, or annoyed.

Later, she would discover that he had made much of it up, not knowing the answers himself, and yet he delivered them with such confidence and authority that she absolutely believed him.

'Where do you go when you die?' she'd asked when she recovered from polio only to find her vital, vibrant brother gone. Disappeared.

Mother had taken Clara's hand and placed it upon Clara's heart. 'He's here. He'll always be here. Look, you can feel it beating, once for him, once for you.'

When Father walked in the door and announced, 'I've signed up, my dear,' Mother had sent Clara to bed extra early, with only dry crackers for supper. But Clara couldn't sleep and when she heard Father and Mother talking, she'd tiptoed out of bed and eavesdropped on them, her nose pressed to the door, the scent of varnish and peeling distemper. The rumble of her father's earthy tones contrasting with the broody violet of her mother's softer cadence.

'I have to do this for our country.'

'I cannot bear to lose you too.'

'You won't be losing me. I'll come back. I always will return to you, my love.' Her father's tone soft.

Mother had believed him and so had Clara, snooping clandestinely on them.

Saying goodbye to Father, waving furiously as the train pulled away in a fug of smoke, her mother smiling fiercely, pride in her emerald eyes, and something else Clara couldn't quite place but later understood was a cocktail of worry and fear mingled with hope and promise.

Months later, the telegram fluttering from her mother's hand, her face blanched white…

*

The world around Clara, the orphanage, with others like her – stark-eyed and mute with loss (words seem superfluous when everything that matters, your family, your home, has been snatched from you in a burning instant) – appears bleached of colour. All she has left is the St Christopher medal, cold against her chest.

Chapter Three

Clara

1917, Connection

Clara fingers the St Christopher medal nestling against her heart as she looks up and down the deserted station. Her trunk with her few meagre possessions is by her feet. The lady at the orphanage had given her some new clothes and a toothbrush. She'd bought her a train ticket and taken her to the station, seen her safely aboard, but now Clara is alone and anxious. She has tried and tried but she cannot recall Aunt Helen's face or her last visit here in any detail. She does not remember what Aunt Helen was like. To take her mind off her worry, she focuses on the fields stretching wide and vast beyond the tracks, breeze rippling and sighing through emerald stalks, making them dance in gold-tipped waves. *It's so green here…*

The train, hiss and curdle, smoke billowing like a lady's skirt, burbling and bubbling like overflowing soup, dropped her here, at her aunt's village. It was full to bursting – families with dead eyes and missing or mangled limbs. They spoke in a strange language, unintelligible staccato words firing from their mouths like machine guns.

The woman sitting opposite Clara had shared her sandwiches with her and whispered conspiratorially, 'Don't mind them, my dear. Belgian refugees displaced by the war. Those blasted Germans occupied their country, made them homeless – these are the lucky ones, the ones who've managed to escape, come here. We've welcomed them with open arms.'

They didn't appear lucky. They looked weary, devastated, destroyed. *Perhaps I look the same*, Clara thought.

'Do you know, sixteen thousand of them arrived in Kent on a *single day* at the beginning of the war?' the woman had said, her voice low but eyes wide, as if imparting a great secret.

The stale bread she'd generously shared with Clara tasted heavenly – Clara had not realised just how hungry she was, assuming the cramping of her stomach was just another manifestation of the hurt, the ache, the sheer agony of missing her family and London, war-torn but familiar, witness to memories, childhood, innocence and its shattering. Her *home*.

'Clara?'

The voice so like Mother's. Hope buds, bright gold, once again refusing to listen to reason. She doesn't want to look, knowing it will be dashed, but her eyes are drawn upwards of their own accord. Green eyes, but not the bright green of spring shoots like Mother's. These eyes paler, with olive tones. This woman is her mother, but not. She is taller than Mary, thinner than her.

'I'm sorry I'm late. The bus was delayed. Our regular bus driver is fighting for king and country and the man who's taken his place – couldn't sign up because of his dodgy leg, he told me – is excessively chatty but does not know the route well.' A tone of censure in her aunt's voice. 'Ah well, I'm here now. Look at you, how you've grown. Last time we met, you were a scrawny little thing – I don't expect you to remember.'

It hurts so much to look at this woman, who is *so* like Mother. But *not* her mother.

'We meant to visit each other more often, your mother and I, but it just never happened, the years running away from us.' She sighs, a deep exhale. Then, briskly, 'Come on then.'

She walks in long strides without looking back. Clara hurries to catch up, the hand not lugging her trunk clutching her medal, this token from her mother, Clara's only connection to her absent family in a capricious, cruel, war-battered world.

Chapter Four

Clara

Lavender and Mothballs

Aunt Helen and Clara sit side by side on the bench seat of the bus as it trundles down the country lanes, so narrow as to almost make the thatch fly off the hamlets lining the road. It is a world away from the busyness of London, the shops and bustle, the markets, the noise. Grubby children wave from among green fields dusted with frost as darkness settles gloomy grey and cold, although it's still only afternoon, a dreamy shroud of fog gradually obliterating everything except what's visible in the immediate vicinity of the two yellow circles illuminated by the lamps on the bus.

Aunt Helen smells of lavender and mothballs, making Clara want to sneeze. She suppresses it, sitting rigid, hands on her knees. Her shoulders ache from holding herself stiff so she doesn't accidentally bump against Aunt Helen, her bony legs encased in stockings, her dress prim and pressed. Clara wants this stranger, her closest relative, who is now kindly taking her on, to be positively disposed towards her.

Aunt Helen sniffs and, with a sigh, stands, releasing a fresh wave of mothballs, sweat and a lingering hint of lavender. 'Come on, then.'

It is only then that Clara, lost to the dark haze through which the bus has been travelling, lulled by its soothing rumble, lamps cutting a buttery swathe through the icy blanket of dusk, realises they have stopped.

She blinks, pulling her coat closer around her, as fog smothers her with damp, moist fingers. The bus pulls away with a wheeze and a grumble and she is suddenly overcome. 'Wait,' she wants to call, 'Take me with you. I want to go home.'

Aunt Helen walks in long, determined strides and Clara stumbles along beside her, hurrying to keep pace, worried she might lose her in the mist, which thickens by the minute. It is a numbing, unnerving experience – the silence so absolute, although it can't be that late, barely teatime but it appears darkness comes quickly here – such a change from the city, where quiet just means a toning-down of noise, not the complete absence of it, where even that inky-velvet deepest part of night just before dawn is busy with rustle and hustle.

She cannot see where she is going, where she is putting her feet; the fog is all-consuming. She is so cold her teeth are chattering. But gradually, her eyes adjust to this alien world and she notices the spire of a church sticking out above the enveloping haze. A village green, given over to swirling mist. A couple of awnings – greengrocer, butcher, dancing pale gold under the dim glow of lamps barely piercing the ghost-grey curtain.

'Oh, hello there, Helen.' A rotund shape materialises from the misty murk, pink face wrapped in a garish orange scarf. 'My Eddie fancied liver for supper.' The woman nods at her covered basket. 'I didn't want to come out in this but after what he's been through, taking that bullet to his leg in France, well…' She shrugs.

'Hello, Edna.' Aunt Helen's voice crisp. Does this mean she doesn't like the woman much, Clara wonders, or does she always greet everyone in this way? Clara tries to recall how she had greeted her at the train station, but all she remembers is a rush of words, as if Aunt Helen had memorised them in advance and wanted to get them said and out of the way, and after that, silence that Clara didn't know how to fill.

'What are you doing out in this…?' The woman's assessing gaze resting on Clara's trunk and travelling up to her face. 'Ah, who's this?'

'My sister's girl. Clara, meet Mrs White.'

Mrs White nods at Clara and, to Aunt Helen, 'Your sister in London.' She says *London* with a mixture of awe and disdain.

'Air raid took her,' Aunt Helen sniffs. She says it in such a matter-of-fact manner that Clara feels winded. So she bites down on her lower lip hard. The pain helps to mask the other, deeper agony.

'I'm sorry,' Mrs White says, but it is perfunctory. 'I thought she had a boy? I remember him with your two raising merry hell when your sister visited last. Had old Ted after them, as I recall, for pinching his home-made apple cider.'

Aunt Helen lets out a startled bark of a laugh. 'I'd forgotten that.'

Paul. Clara can picture his cheeky smile as he egged his cousins on to steal cider from the farmer for a dare. She imagines his face as he took a swig and gagged on the acid sourness. Beneath the St Christopher medal, her heart burns and bleeds.

'Has he signed up, like your Johnny?' Mrs White asks.

'He died some years ago now. Polio,' Aunt Helen says in her brisk, no-nonsense tone.

'Ah, shame.' Mrs White shakes her head. Then with a nod at Clara, 'Another mouth to feed, eh?'

'She'll have to earn her keep, like the rest of us.'

Mrs White steps closer. She smells of raw meat, a sweet fetid tang, as she peers at Clara, looking her up and down. 'How old are you then?'

'I…' She clears her throat. Her voice is insubstantial in the filmy gloom billowing around them. 'Fifteen.' Her birthday the previous week while she was at the orphanage had gone unmarked – nothing to celebrate and no one to celebrate with.

'Old enough. They're looking for help over at Lord Howard-Wellesley's stately home on the far side of the green.' Mrs White nods in the general direction of the church spire sticking out of the gyrating screen of fog. 'He's opened it up; it's now a hospital catering to wounded soldiers. Scores coming over every day. I happen to know the matron, Mrs Redmond. I'll talk to her, if you'd like.'

'That'd be great, thanks ever so much, Edna.' Aunt Helen smiles, her teeth glimmering yellow in the gloaming.

'She can start Monday, all being well,' Mrs White says, nodding and disappearing, her orange scarf slowly fading into uniform white obscurity as Clara picks up her trunk, thinking, *Monday, that's two days from now*, and follows her aunt into a new life, the medal, her mother's legacy, beating against her chest with every step.

Chapter Five

Clara

Everyone's Business

Clara's cousin Danny barely hides his instant dislike of her when her aunt introduces them. His face takes on a mutinous expression, his voice a thundery growl: 'And how are we going to manage? We barely get by as it is.'

'We'll be alright, with you apprenticed to old George the greengrocer and Clara starting at the hospital on Monday.'

Danny raises an eyebrow. 'She's got a job already?'

'We bumped into Edna.'

'Who?' Danny scratches his head.

'Mrs White,' Aunt Helen clarifies.

'That woman has her nose in everyone's business,' Danny grunts.

Aunt Helen snorts. 'Well in our case, it's a good thing. She's promised to talk to Matron.'

'You've fitted right in, Cousin.' Danny smirks unpleasantly at Clara.

'You can have Danny's room in the attic – he moved into his brother's room when Johnny left for France,' Aunt Helen says.

Clara follows her aunt, lugging her trunk up into the tiny, draughty room under the eaves, barely enough room for her to manoeuvre in between the narrow bed and the chest of drawers. It is cold, even with the windows and door closed against the elements. The wind whistles and whines, rattling against the windowpanes, screaming to be let in.

Clara sets the trunk down with relief, turns round and that is when she notices the books in a rickety cupboard behind the bed. Almost without thinking, she picks one up. It is very worn, brittle orange and falling apart, smelling of damp and faraway worlds, ink and adventure.

'Danny hated having them here, but there's no place for them elsewhere in the house. My Tom doesn't hold with reading, says it fills your head with ideas above your station, and the boys are the same, but I cannot bear to throw them away,' Aunt Helen says, a faint note of embarrassment and apology colouring her voice. 'I used to love them; I know all the poems by heart.' Her voice softening, as if against her better judgement, becoming wistful and nostalgic.

And in this gentler version of her aunt, Clara is afforded a glimpse of her mother and it is searing pain and an unexpected gift, all in one.

'I was quite the romantic, once. Your mother was the practical one. But it was she who had her head turned,' Aunt Helen's voice hard again, sharp with disdain, 'by the chap from India, with his fantastic tales of adventure and action.'

'Father,' Clara breathes.

'When you visited last, your brother shared this room with Danny; you bedded with your parents. Your brother memorised the poems, would recite them to me, although he didn't understand much. He was a character.' A smile in Aunt Helen's voice, a shake of her head. 'A charmer, that one.'

'Paul,' Clara whispers.

'Shame what happened to him.'

In the dim shadowy light, hunched under the eaves, too tall for the cold, cramped room, her aunt's eyes sparkle with reminiscence. Then, sighing, her voice brisk again, 'But no use for poetry now, eh? Sentimental rubbish when there is a war on.'

After her aunt leaves, Clara, although wiped out from the journey and wanting bed, cannot resist leafing through the book she is holding, caressing each page reverently. Her brother had read these, liked them, although, at ten years old, he hadn't understood them. He had been so full of life, touching the lives of everyone he encountered so they all remembered him fondly, with a smile, even Aunt Helen.

Her brother, gone too soon. Clara falls asleep to the moan and grumble of wind, owls hooting mournfully outside, reading poetry, fancying they are the same words her brother had read all those years ago when he had slept in this very room, imagining his voice, reciting verses in a fancy accent...

Chapter Six

Clara

An Eye-Opener

Clara is jarred awake from a cosy dream in which she and her brother were ensconced in their father's lap, listening to his stories of a faraway country that came alive through his words, their mother knitting spools of kaleidoscopic yarn, by a shuddering boom on the door.

'Rise and shine!' A boy's voice, deep and throaty, just starting to break. A heavy tread thundering down the stairs, resonating in Clara's skull. She is *so* cold. Her knuckles are frozen numb around the medal. She blinks, slowly coming to as recollection catches up with sense and the last remnants of the dream fly away on a misty wisp of icy fog.

The kitchen smells of boiling oats and stewing tea. It is warm, more so than the rest of the house, which sits snug among a row of identical dwellings all on their own small plots of land, flanking the path that leads to the village green.

Aunt Helen is stirring porridge on the stove. 'Ah, there you are. You'll need to be getting up earlier, come Monday, to get your chores done before breakfast. We all chip in here. I'll drop you off to the hospital on the way to the post office, where I work. I start at eight sharp.'

Clara shivers, although the kitchen is toasty, doubt and worry assailing her. She will try her best to live up to her aunt's expectations, but what if she falls short? And this job at the hospital – what does it entail? Will she be up to it?

I will. I better.

Aunt Helen is looking at Clara sternly, clearly expecting an answer.

'Yes, Aunt.'

Danny barges in just then, the front door rocking on its hinges as it bangs against the wall, a gust of ice and wind, morning chill, wafting in his wake. 'No veggies, Ma. They're all shrivelled up and dead. I'm not green-fingered like Johnny.'

'You any good at growing vegetables, Clara?' Aunt Helen asks, waving a gloopy ladle at her niece.

'I can try.'

Aunt Helen nods. 'That'll be one of your chores then and while you're at it, you can see to the chickens. They're in the pen in the corner.'

'Yes, Aunt.'

On Monday, her aunt walks her to the hospital.

'If you get home before me, make a start on supper, scrub the tatties and see what you can do with them – not much else, what with the food shortages, unless you work magic on the veggie patch.'

Nothing can prepare Clara for the shock of working at the hospital. It is an eye-opener. A great leveller. It is incredibly humbling. It puts her loss into perspective, makes her realise she is not alone.

Although on some level she knows that almost everyone has lost someone in this war that has been dragging on too long, that nearly everyone has experienced pain, hurt, it has never been brought to her attention with such illuminating clarity as on her first day at work. Men with rotting limbs, broken bodies, broken minds. Men delirious from fever, driven insane by pain. The wounded, the stoic, the men who cry at horrors only they can see…

Matron is a no-nonsense woman who looks Clara up and down, rubs her palms together and declares, 'You're the new girl, are you? Well, come on then. No time to waste.'

The day goes by in a blink. It is horrifying, devastating, upsetting and yet, strangely, liberating. Clara has a purpose. She is doing something useful. She is needed.

'You're an angel, you are,' one of the soldiers says as she clumsily changes his dressing under Matron's watchful eye, trying not to flinch from the wound, Matron making sure to catch her every expression.

Angel. Her parents' nickname for her. But she has no time to indulge her grief, with Matron right there, supervising her.

'They're suffering enough, you are not to make it worse, you understand?' Matron says when Clara looks set to cry when she sees the stump where a leg should have been. She manages to run outside, where she retches.

'You'll get used to it. It's not so bad after the first time,' a kind voice says, its owner a girl about Clara's age, tall and exuding confidence and self-assurance. 'I'm Dolores. Dolly. You're the new girl.'

'Clara.' She manages a weak smile.

'It gets easier, believe me,' Dolly promises.

'Not bad for your first day, you'll do,' Matron pronounces at the end of the day and Clara smiles all the way back to Aunt Helen's. Dolly is keeping her company. As she was slipping on her too-big coat, a gift from the orphanage, Dolly had come up behind her, announcing cheerily, 'I'm leaving too. We'll walk together. I'm two doors down from you.'

'How do you…?'

'This is only a small village, you know. No secrets here.' And, lowering her voice, her breath icy sweet, 'Especially with a foghorn like Mrs White.'

Clara giggled. It felt like relief, a release.

Chapter Seven

Clara

Routine

Clara adjusts to her new life at her aunt's – she has a routine now, which affords structure to her days. Despite suffering from intense bouts of homesickness, feeling immensely lonely at Aunt Helen's, knowing exactly what to expect from each day is reassuring. Keeping busy stops her from living too much in her memories.

Clara's time at the hospital flies in a maelstrom of one emergency after another – there's never a quiet moment. It's grim, heartbreaking, but also rewarding when their care pays off and the ailing come through. Then walking back after work with Dolly. If Clara is home before her aunt, she makes a start on supper.

'Not potatoes *again*,' Danny complains, the tinny ringing of the bicycle bell and the rattle and clunk as he rests his bike, none too gently, against the outside wall announcing his return home. The whine of the front door opening, a draught reaching into the kitchen as he thuds and thumps his way indoors. Everything Clara's cousin does is noisy.

'He even came out of my womb wailing fit to wake the dead. That boy wouldn't know quiet if it hit him on the head,' Aunt Helen often complains, a fond note creeping into her brisk voice.

'There isn't anything else,' she says now, 'not with the food shortages; the Germans are bombing the ships bringing food into the country.'

Much as she hates to agree with her cousin, Clara is tired of potatoes, although between them, she and Aunt Helen try to come up with innovative ways of using them. Clara even made potato pudding the other day – Dolly's mother's recipe – and it wasn't half bad. She knows she mustn't complain. And yet… *Oh, what she wouldn't give for bread, milk, butter.*

Even the cakes her aunt makes every Sunday are dense with potato. Clara eats dutifully but Danny protests loudly and bitterly. Later, she wakes in pain, her stomach cramping, feeling as if it is being torn in two. Those times, night pressing dark and ominous outside, wind howling against the windows, weather insinuating indoors with frosty moodiness, cold indifference, Clara clasps the medal, which is also cold, with frozen fingers and tries to channel Paul, Father and Mother. But no matter how hard and fiercely she tries to keep them with her, her family members' features are blurring in Clara's mind and that hurts. Oh, how it hurts.

After supper, and once her chores are done, Clara reads in bed. Poetry, her friend and defence against loneliness, the torturous ache of missing. She imagines Paul reading these self-same poems and it is like communing with her long-dead brother. She falls asleep with sonnets ringing in her head, dreaming of her brother and happy times, Paul leading her into escapades, blissfully innocent of what was to come.

She's tried to get her aunt to open up about Mother, Father, Paul, but her aunt's mouth purses in a forbidding manner. 'No use dwelling.' And that's that.

She's mentioned Paul to Danny, trying to find some common ground with her cousin while also wanting desperately to discuss her brother with someone who knew him. But Danny only scoffs. He's hardly ever home and when he is, he grunts, shovels his food down and flies away again, to see his friends, or on errands for the Scouts.

Clara has started volunteering as a Girl Guide leader – Dolly is one too and she asked Clara if she'd like to come along one Friday after work: 'They're always looking for volunteers.'

Clara and Dolly help out during those weekends when they are not needed at the hospital – working on allotments and packaging clothing to send to soldiers, collecting scrap metal and, Clara's favourite, conkers to help with the war effort. Collecting them is of utmost importance, they've been told.

Clara loves being outdoors, beneath the horse chestnut trees – mulch and crunch, the rich brown fragrance of earth and mildewed vegetation, starlings and sparrows chattering and singing among the branches above – collecting conkers alongside the Girl Guides from where they are nestled among the bed of strewn yellow and orange leaves, like scattered fire.

These they will take back to the schoolroom – given over for this purpose – and shell, leaving just the nuts, which will be bagged and taken to the train station for transportation to top-secret locations. When in the schoolroom, Clara feels a pang of missing for home, for school, for what was. If things were different, she would have continued at school. She liked to learn, she was good at it. But she refuses to dwell. *This* is the new normal. And she is one of the lucky ones. The others at the orphanage had been envious when Aunt Helen wrote to say she'd take Clara on. And now, Clara has a vocation: nursing, which, despite its many heart-rending moments, she loves.

Dolly's hearty laughter echoes as they walk back together, clutching their bags of conkers, the earthy honeyed scent of autumn perfuming the gathering evening, the sweet, glorious taste of friendship providing solace when Clara is alone later that night in her cold room at Aunt Helen's.

Part Three

India

Family

Chapter Eight

Indira

1995, Culprit

In the taxi to the hospital, Indira tries to recall what she said to Arun that morning as she waved goodbye. She can't remember. They had had breakfast together before they left, Arun alternating between anticipation – they were all staying overnight at the hospital, Indira arriving there after work – and worry, asking question after question.

She hadn't paid attention – she was thinking about her agenda for the meeting. Karan as usual had patiently answered Arun's every query. Indira could afford to switch off because she knew Karan was tuned in to their son's every word. It was one of Karan's many strengths, making his family feel important, valued, loved.

'Arun tried telling you about his day but you were not listening,' Karan used to gently admonish when they were alone and Arun was in bed. 'He has me, but he needs you too.'

'I know but there's a report…'

'There'll always be reports but he won't be young always, Indu. Soon he'll stop needing you.'

'Tomorrow I'll listen, I promise.'

She can't remember the last time she properly listened or talked to either her husband or her son.

Since his infancy, Arun has been beleaguered by constant colds, his nose almost permanently leaking. It took years, but finally his paediatrician had realised that the culprit was his tonsils and recommended a tonsillectomy.

Arun had been excited to pack his bag for the overnight stay at the hospital. Karan had booked a family room for them. The hospital was overpriced but it was one of the best in the world.

'Mama, you'll come straight from work?' Arun asked at least three times, looking up at her, eyes bright.

'I promise. And I just might bring a treat for my brave boy.' He had glowed, clapped his hands.

Now, in the taxi, panic and worry overwhelming, she whispers quietly to herself: *It is the best hospital in the world.* So why is she not reassured? *Let it be nothing urgent, just Arun asking for me when he came out of surgery. Or perhaps the operation was cancelled or postponed because of some problem.* But she knows in her heart that it must be pretty urgent for Karan to call and ask for her to come to hospital at once… Karan understands how much she needs to maintain her standing with the all-male directors; if she'd interrupted the meeting, they'd have smirked: 'You're deluding yourself by thinking you can be a successful CEO. A woman's place is in her home with her family.'

Right now she couldn't care less what they think. She wrings her hands, willing the taxi to go faster in the stop-start traffic, wondering why she thought the board meeting so very important, why she set such store by her colleagues' opinions.

She wants to lash out, hit something. She wants to hear her son's voice, see him, touch him, make sure he's alright. She digs her nails into the soft skin of her palms until she draws blood.

When she gets to hospital, Arun will be asleep and Karan will say, flashing her a rueful smile, 'I'm so sorry for worrying you. It was a mistake. I forgot you had the meeting.' But he has always kept track of her schedule, has never forgotten once, in all these years. He didn't interrupt her a few months ago when

Arun's fever spiked to 101 degrees. By the time she got home, Karan was with Arun in hospital and she'd rushed straight there and they'd spent the night beside their fretful son. So why now? What could it be? It's just a routine tonsillectomy.

Isn't it?

Part Four

England

Problem

Chapter Nine

Clara

1918, Consternation

When Clara arrives at the hospital, it is to ambulances pulling up, although the sun is not yet out, the fields sequinned in a silky silver film, the village green dozing beneath a pearly diaphanous quilt, the sky a dull foggy grey. Scores of wounded being unloaded on stretchers, the white sheets bloodied from the weeping wounds of the men they are covering.

'Ah, there you are,' Matron says. 'About time.'

'Matron, I'm earl—'

'Where's your friend?'

'She—'

But Matron is not paying attention, her voice suddenly shrill, giving Clara pause. 'Who's this? Why is he *here*?'

'We were t… t… told to…' stutters one of the volunteers bearing the stretcher of the wounded man who is causing Matron such consternation.

'I thought *they* had their own hospital.' Matron's voice sharp as a butcher's knife slicing cleanly through flesh and bone.

Clara peers over Matron's shoulder.

The poor man's head is lolling off the stretcher, his eyes shut, face scored and bruised. But it is not that which is causing the other nurses who have gathered around – drawn by Matron's uncharacteristic high-pitched tone; Matron who is *always* calm – to gasp, as they nudge each other in excited stupefaction.

It is his colouring.

Chapter Ten

Clara

A Faraway Time

Dolly, who has only just arrived and is peering curiously, raises her eyebrows at Clara when she sees the man. One of the volunteers checks his chart, frowning, while those with him disperse to help carry other patients indoors. 'Says here he's a medic with the Imperial Service Troops. Was supposed to go to the Indian military hospital but ended up here. Sorry, Marm.'

Indian military hospital. Clara is transported, hearing her father in a faraway time, herself and her brother perched on his knees, the clickety-clack of her mother's knitting needles the soundtrack to her father's voice, Mother's smile the encore to the nostalgia colouring Father's tone as he recounted tales from his childhood and youth, his voice caramel gold as he talked with fondness of his regiment, the time they were patrolling near a forest and a tiger attacked.

'Now I was fast asleep, but woke to growling sounds, urgent and terrible and building in frenzy, louder than the cicadas. The tent reeked of festering meat, blood and danger. The campfire was almost out but in the light from the dying embers and the crescent moon, I saw silhouetted against the tent the long, sleek body of what could only be a tiger.'

'Oh,' Paul's eyes wide.

Clara buried her face in her father's shirt, his smell of musk and lemon, familiar and a world away from the peril looming over a defenceless tent in India.

'As I watched, too afraid to move, he hefted himself onto his hind legs and I saw his paws claw at the flimsy cloth of the tent.'

'No!'

The clicking sound of Mother's knitting needles had stopped. It was so quiet and still, only the sound of Father's heart beating loud and insistent, boom, boom, boom.

I am alive, it was saying. *I made it. It's only a story.*

Nevertheless, Clara kept her eyes shut tight, her face resting against her father's chest, love and reassurance.

'I was standing there, petrified, unable in my shock and fear to do a thing, even move, run for my life. It was my trusty subedar, Sundar, who burst into the tent and, pushing me out of the way, tackled the tiger.'

'Oh!'

'He saved my life with his quick thinking – he couldn't find a rifle, so he used a stick to attack the beast, ingeniously propping it between the tiger's jaws. The beast was furious but it did the job, held it off long enough for one of the others, roused by the noise, to get hold of a gun and shoot the tiger.'

'Your subedar was brave!' Clara muttered into her father's chest.

'He certainly was.' A smile in Father's voice. 'I'm grateful to him.'

And her mother had piped up softly, saying the words Clara wanted to, 'We are too.'

Now she looks at this man, his toffee skin wan beneath its garish greasepaint of dirt and blood, so far away from home, and hears her father's words: *He saved my life.*

'What are we supposed to do with him?' Matron is saying, her voice clipped and colder than the fog that is showing no signs of dispersing. 'Army protocol is that British nurses are not usually allowed to attend Indian soldiers in military hospitals, surely you know this?'

But Clara has resolved to heal, to use the gift of her life to save as many lives as she can, so that then her living while her family is dead is justified. *What if this is the man who saved my father's life?*

She clears her throat. 'I'll do it, Matron.'

Matron startles, then turns to look at her. 'I'd forgotten you were here, Sister Knight.' Matron addresses Clara formally in front of the volunteer she's just chastised. 'Are you quite sure?'

Clara swallows.

Behind Matron, Dolly is staring at Clara, bug-eyed, mouthing, 'Have you gone off your rocker?'

Clara stifles the sudden, irrational urge to laugh. Through it all, in the punishingly cold wind, the poor soldier lies, the casualty of a mistake by a tired, overworked person somewhere in the chain of command wrought by this terrible war, unaware that his fate is in the hands of people who do not want him. All the other soldiers have been taken inside and are at this moment being settled in, tended to.

'Sister Knight, are you *quite* sure?' Matron barks again. 'If not, I'll send him back.'

'It's a three-hour journey to the Indian hospital, Marm,' the driver ventures meekly. 'He may not survive—'

'That's not my problem, Sir, if you please,' Matron snaps and the driver flinches, looking suitably admonished.

It's what Father would want me to do. 'Yes,' Clara says even as, behind Matron, Dolly shakes her head and purses her lips.

'Very well,' Matron sighs. 'I hope you don't regret this, Sister Knight. I will not have you backtrack once…'

'I won't, Matron.'

'Good, that's one problem I didn't expect or ask for taken care of,' Matron says and, without a backward glance at either the sick man or his attendant, strides indoors, tossing over her shoulder, 'Well, bring him in then, what are you waiting for?'

And the stretcher-bearer snaps to attention in a hurry.

Chapter Eleven

Clara

Blood Will Out

'I didn't have you down as crazy,' Dolly hisses, pulling Clara back as she makes to follow in Matron's wake.

'He's only a man, a wounded one at that, injured in a war not his own, so far from home.' Clara shrugs with a nonchalance she is far from feeling.

The other nurses whisper, shocked awe, 'Rather you than me,' as she walks past them to the tucked-away alcove where Matron has deemed it fit to place the man.

'Have you gone quite mad, girl?' Aunt Helen has made an unprecedented visit across the green to the hospital to chew Clara's ear out, Mrs White, the bearer of all village gossip, goggling in her wake.

'She's agreed, she cannot go back on it now,' Matron says crisply when Aunt Helen takes her grievance to her. 'What will I do with him? I can't allow him to die, we have a duty of care.'

'She's only young, she—'

'She's sixteen, isn't she? And in any case, old enough to work here, old enough to make a decision.' Matron is brisk. 'Now if you'll excuse me…'

Aunt Helen is left gawping, mouth open, no words coming out. She cannot afford to have Clara stop working, of course;

they need the money her niece brings in, pittance though Aunt Helen might complain it is.

'On your head be it,' she manages to snap at Clara.

Mrs White throws Clara a disgusted look before saying to Aunt Helen, making sure Clara hears, 'Blood will out, as they say. You're a martyr, taking her on…'

That evening when Danny gets home, he smirks, 'Reduced to consorting with apes, eh? That's all you'll get with that face.'

Clara looks to Aunt Helen, who is wiping down the surfaces in the kitchen, pretending she hasn't heard Danny's slur.

'Just doing my job, Danny,' she retorts, coolly, 'which is more than can be said about you. Old George is thinking of letting you go, so I've heard, with you spending all your time at the public house.' Dolly had supplied this nugget of information during one of their walks home from work.

Now, at Clara's riposte, Aunt Helen's back goes rigid and if Clara hadn't been sure earlier that her aunt has heard every word, she is now. She refuses to feel guilty about calling Danny out – his drinking is not news to Aunt Helen.

'Shut your mouth, monkey lover,' Danny yells, storming out of the room.

She is tempted to go after him, give him a piece of her mind, but decides to tackle Aunt Helen first.

'Aunt, are you really going to let Danny speak to me like that?'

Her aunt's mouth sets in a thin line, her eyes so like Mother's and yet not, challenging Clara. Clara reads what she is not saying: *He's not wrong.*

She clenches her palms into fists, thinking of Father, his voice buttery gold as he recounted tales of his time in India.

*

'He's all yours,' Matron had said, leaving her to the soldier in his alcove. 'Dr Harrington will be over once he has seen to the others.'

Alone with the man, Clara experienced an overwhelming wash of panic, all the bravado she had affected in the impulsive heat of the moment leaving her. She heard Matron's voice in her head: 'I will not have you backtrack…'

What do I do now?

But then the man, lying unconscious on his pallet in that tiny space, twitched, emitting a small whine, and she was galvanised into action, the nurse in her taking over.

Nevertheless, when she sat down beside him preparatory to mopping the blood and dirt away, she had flinched, initially, upon touching him. But he had moaned quietly, restlessly thrashing, and suddenly it was like all the other soldiers she had tended to, *exactly* like them – when wounded, they were unhappy little boys, reverting to the young lads they'd been – and she had eased into the job. When she left after her shift he was lying cleaned up but comatose, wan despite his cinnamon skin, and dosed up on the medicine Dr Harrington had supplied.

'I'm not happy with what you've done, Clara,' Aunt's mouth is set in a thin line, 'and I don't feel like talking to you right now.'

'He's fighting for our country like Johnny and Uncle To—'

'Don't you dare use your cousin and uncle's name in the same breath as that—' Aunt Helen stops, takes a breath.

Clara barges right in: 'What did Mrs White mean when she said blood will out?'

'Oh…' Aunt Helen sucks her teeth. Then she appears to come to a decision, standing tall, chin up, looking right at Clara. 'Your father liked *them* too. Grew up with them.' She spits it out like it's the worst crime.

'That's—'

'Turned my sister's head with his stories of India. He whisked her away to the city and where are they now?'

'They were happy,' Clara says.

'Ha,' Aunt Helen laughs, a short, mirthless bark. 'She was, at first, perhaps. But she wanted to travel, see the world. That's what he'd promised her. The years went by and she was stuck in that crowded city, in that tiny house. She made do. But it wasn't what she wanted. It wasn't what he'd promised.'

Clara bunches her hands into fists, digging her nails into the soft flesh of her palms. She will not cry.

Aunt Helen is wrong. Mother was happy. *Wasn't she?*

But it is as if Aunt Helen's words have released something within her, for that night memories arrive of her and Paul hiding behind the door, huddled together, her brother's hand in hers, sweaty but not reassuring, not this time, the scent of sawdust and a splintering world, the raised voices of their parents reverberating harsh and bruising through the wood.

'You promised to take me away from all this.'

'I'm trying, Mary, love. I'm working on it.'

'I can't stand this cramped house, this smog-filled city. The children are…'

'I'm *trying*…'

The sound of something breaking. Clara flinching, shutting her ears and her eyes, hoping to hold her scream in.

Her brother leading her to their room, pulling her onto his bunk next to him, wrapping them in his blanket, whispering, 'They're just having an argument, like we do, sometimes. They'll be alright.'

'Promise?'

'I promise.'

Falling asleep with her brother's assurance ringing in her ears, his arms around her.

The next two days the silence in their small house ominous, their parents talking through each other, around each other, not *to* the other. Something thick in the air that makes Clara's heart beat faster, makes her cry for no reason at all.

Then the third evening returning home from school with Paul to their mother's tumbling laughter, Father's cheeky grin as he twirled Mother around and around, until she smacked him lightly on the cheek: 'Davy, the children are home.'

Father humming a tune as he set Mother down and lifted both Paul and Clara, one in each arm, Mother's skittering giggles resounding in their ears as they see-sawed in Father's roller-coaster embrace.

Chapter Twelve

Clara

Special Project

The Indian soldier is a medic, Clara has discovered, from the paperwork that accompanied him – just a small card with his name, Dr Anand Goel, and his battalion, the Imperial Service Troops. As Clara tends to him, she stops noticing his skin colour – he is just a patient needing care. *Her* patient.

Clara rejoices when Dr Goel's fever eases. His breathing comes back to normal and he's no longer wheezing asthmatically, although he's still unconscious. When Clara relays this to Matron, despite all her warnings against Clara changing her mind, she says, 'Now that he's well enough to travel, I can make arrangements for him to be transferred—'

'Matron,' Clara counters, firmly, 'I said I'd look after him and I will, until he recovers completely.'

'You're a nurse through and through.' Matron's voice thrumming with a rare note of approval.

The praise from Matron, the awe from her fellow nurses, gives Clara confidence. Standing up to Aunt Helen and Danny, doing something they disapprove of, makes her feel important, instead of feeling small all the time, beholden, despite the money she earns working at the hospital, all of which she gives Aunt Helen, despite the vegetables she's managed to grow in the small patch of garden, the chores she does, more than her fair share, as Danny does not pull his weight.

Clara stumbled into nursing, but she has discovered she is good at it. And in giving, she finds solace. In helping others heal, the wound of loss she permanently carries eases. Seeing the suffering of others puts her own in perspective, makes her understand she is not alone and that there are always others much worse off, that she is lucky to have a home with relatives, that she is blessed with good health and food to eat, a friend in Dolly, a profession she loves. She believes her mother saved her by bequeathing her the St Christopher medal – it kept her safe just as Mother promised. In saving others, she is repaying that debt.

'What's that you're giving me? Ether? Morphine?'

Clara startles, almost dropping the syringe with the cocktail of medicines Dr Harrington prescribed that she was about to inject into her patient. He is awake. His voice is deep and smooth, like flowing chocolate, and cultured; he speaks beautiful English with only the barest hint of an accent – if she is honest, she wasn't expecting that.

His eyes are sparkling gold, like pools of water holding the sun within them, and bright with intelligence. He is a medic, of course he'd be interested in the medicines she is feeding him.

She's taken too long to answer, for he says, '*You* have been taking away my pain. I didn't dream you.' He shakes his head and winces. His face is pale, the effort of speaking wiping him out, sweat beading on his forehead. 'What *is* this place?'

'Oh.' She finds her voice. 'You're in…'

'A cupboard?'

A startled laugh bursts from her.

He smiles and it is like the sun emerging from clouds. 'In any case, it is an improvement on the icy trenches. It's warm. And I have an angel tending to me.'

Angel. Like a blessing, she hears her parents' voices, 'You are our angel.'

His eyes close. But, his voice barely above a whisper, 'You have a beautiful laugh, like a rainbow after a storm.'

When she's bitten her lip furiously to stop her heated cheeks from giving her away and turns back to him, he is asleep.

Chapter Thirteen

Clara

Intense

'He's conscious,' Clara tells Matron.

'Oh, is he? Well done, Clara.' Matron addresses her by her first name in private, but when there's someone about, she's briskly professional and Clara is 'Sister Knight'. Now she adds, 'That's our job done then. I'll send word to his regiment and they'll have someone collect him.'

'But he's still…'

Matron glares at Clara. 'We've done our bit, nursed him back from almost certain death.'

I *did that*, Clara thinks, but knows not to say.

'He was brought here by mistake but we've gone out of our way to do our best by him.'

I've *gone out of my way.*

'He's had his own dedicated nurse…'

Because nobody else wanted to tend to him.

'…even though we couldn't really spare you. None of the other soldiers have that privilege. He can go back to his regiment knowing that he had the best possible care. And, now,' Matron's stern features relax into what for her amounts to a smile, 'we can have you back. About time, I say. Clara, you've proved yourself an invaluable addition to our team, dedicated enough to give the best care even to a coloured man. I *am* impressed.'

*

After that, things move quickly.

Dr Harrington signs off her patient, who, once he regained consciousness, has recovered in leaps and bounds.

'Sister Knight, I'm a medic charged with saving lives, but you are the angel who saved mine. I am eternally grateful to you,' Dr Goel says, the day he is due to depart.

Clara cannot keep the embarrassment from igniting her cheeks, setting them ablaze. Dr Goel is prone to these extravagant statements.

'I told him his new lease of life was thanks to you,' Matron had declared the previous day. 'And do you know what he said?' Matron put her hands on her hips. '"I agree wholeheartedly. She's my guardian angel here in England."'

'Oh.' Clara dipped her head to hide her blush.

'Such an *intense* way of putting things.' Matron tutted.

'You have a real gift, Sister Knight, and I'm the grateful recipient of it. If you ever need anything, at any time, please do not hesitate to write to me, care of the Imperial Service Troops. I owe you my life.' And with these flowery words, delivered so earnestly that she believes every one, his eyes sparkling with sincerity, Dr Goel walks out of Clara's life.

'As if you would want anything from *him*,' Dolly sniffs, linking arms with her.

But Clara is not listening; she's watching him go, thinking, *my purpose is gone*.

Part Five

India

Imperative

Chapter Fourteen

Indira

1995, First

In the taxi they'd all taken together that morning to the hospital, Indira's son had wound his arms around her, planting wet kisses on her cheeks, his little-boy scent of mischief and innocence. *What did she say to him? Did she kiss him back?*

Was she as usual, preoccupied, as Karan gently disentangled Arun from her and took him into hospital, Indira leafing through the papers spread on her lap, going through the projections again? She hadn't even watched her husband and son go in.

Had her son waved? He must have, and said, 'Bye, Mama.' He did that every morning. She can't remember and, for some reason, it is now imperative that she does. For her heart is hammering in her chest, even as the taxi inches forward and the hospital comes into view.

She thinks, *If I remember what he said, the look on his face when I left him, all will be well.*

'Here we are, Ma'a—'

Before the taxi driver has finished, she flings money at him – almost double the fare – and is out the door and running up the steps of the hospital, elbowing people out of her way.

From now on, she resolves, she will give Arun her complete and undivided attention, like Karan does. And she will rekindle the passion in her relationship with her husband, she will work at their marriage. She will try more, not take them for granted.

When Arun asks her to play with him, she will not say, 'Ask Baba,' or, 'In a minute,' hoping that he'll get absorbed in something else. He will know how much she loves him.

'Mama belongs to her office first. Then to me,' he had once said and it had broken her heart. But not enough for her to tear herself from her work.

From now on, I will make sure you know you are first, she promises her son in her head as she runs to the paediatric unit.

Part Six

England

Reverberations

Chapter Fifteen

Clara

1918, Church Bells

They are at the hospital when the church bells start ringing, loud and long and sonorous, their brassy reverberations jolting Clara and her fellow nurses out of their mid-morning rounds and the ill and wounded from their pain or rest.

Clara is in the general ward, bandaging a soldier's septic wound. *What now*, she thinks, as the morning is burst wide open by the prolonged, golden thrumming of church bells. She catches Dolly's eye across the patients' beds – Dolly is at the other end of the room – and raises an eyebrow in question. The room is alive with nudging and whispering: 'What's going on?'

Urgent patter of footsteps and then Matron bursts in, panting, nose pink with excitement, her usually neat uniform awry, sweat beading the top of her lips.

'It's over,' she yells – Matron, who is usually the very picture of decorum – and, as all pairs of eyes in the room fix bewildered upon her, 'The war's ended.'

The room erupts in commotion, fear and illness shrugged away, tossed aside by elation. A profusion, cascade, waterfall of joy, glorious, kaleidoscopic as ringing bells. The soldiers' light-hearted laughter briefly renders them carefree boys again.

Dolly throws her arms around Clara, her friend's whisper hot and sweet with anticipation and coloured bright with hope: 'This means Pa will be home soon. Ma and I have been missing him ever so much.'

Clara clasps her medal close even as she hugs her friend, trying to contain her tears, salt and celebration, bittersweet, joy and sorrow: that her parents and brother never got to experience this jubilation, the culmination of the collective effort, sorrow and sacrifice of an entire nation; that she will have nobody coming home.

Chapter Sixteen

Clara

1919, Poise

Over the next few weeks and months, the soldiers who've survived the war return. But there is no sign of Uncle Tom or Johnny. Danny has taken to coming straight home each evening, skipping his daily detour to the tavern. 'Any news?' he asks Aunt Helen, hope shining in his hollow eyes, creaming his voice.

It makes Clara warm to her cousin, despite his meanness, his surliness towards her. He is human after all and looking forward to his brother's and father's return home. Perhaps he too, like her, doted on and looked up to his older brother…

Aunt Helen and Danny sit facing the door, their glances skimming it now and again. Both of them waiting, and, as the hours and days go by, veering between impatience, hope, anxiety, despair. Clara watches them and is assaulted afresh by hurt and loss. *I wish I had someone to wait for too.*

I am lucky, she chastises herself, then. *I am not destitute.* And yet…

But she has no time to dwell. She is busier than ever at work. It is incredibly humbling, caring for soldiers enduring the unendurable with such poise – trench foot, limbs that have rotted right off, trench fever, typhoid. As if war hadn't claimed enough lives, the Spanish flu has afflicted the suffering and wounded, broken and battered, severely dwindled population. It has been horrible and heartbreaking watching the soldiers who survived the war succumb to the flu.

There are funerals daily and the grave-diggers are exhausted, the cemetery running out of space. Every day as Dolly and Clara walk to work, more funeral cortèges pass by, the mournful hymns wafting from the church ringing in their ears as they reach the hospital. On the wards, there's the worry of infection – each day there are more deaths, both patients and staff. The Spanish flu is highly contagious and it doesn't discriminate.

'Everyone I speak to has a different cure that they swear by. Camphor, iodine, the list goes on,' Dolly says. 'But none of them seem to work. *All* the soldiers in Cypress ward succumbed to the flu this week. Ideally, Ma would like me to stop working at the hospital until this epidemic has passed but we need the money I bring in. And if we give up our jobs, we won't find work anywhere else. Have you seen the queues of men returned from war lining up for jobs?'

They wait with placards begging for work: 'Will do any job, big or small'; they line up outside the butcher, the greengrocer, the post office, the newsagent. These men who were hailed as heroes, who fought for their country, gave it their all, now desperate and destitute.

'Whatever the risks, I don't want to stop working. I *will* do my bit.' Dolly is fierce. 'Anyway, Ma's cure of choice is brandy. A small swig every night is the thing to keep this horrid epidemic at bay, she insists. I don't mind, I quite like it.'

'Lucky you. Mrs White has convinced Aunt Helen Oxo is the cure for this dreadful Spanish flu,' Clara sighs, 'so we have potatoes doused in gravy every night.'

The following week, Dolly's father returns home. 'He's not the man he was, Clara,' Dolly cries. 'He startles at loud noises. He refuses to get up from bed some days and moans as if he's in pain. Others he sits by the fire and stares into it, shivering. He can't seem to get warm, no matter how many coats he wears, how many blankets Ma and I wrap around him.'

'Oh, Dolly...' Clara wishes there was something she could do to ease her friend's pain.

'The nights are the worst. He screams, "No, No, No!" over and over. Oh, Clara, it's terrible seeing him like this. Broken.'

Clara's friend's eyes shimmer with bemusement and hurt.

'When we attempt to help, he lashes out. There's nothing but to try and ignore it. I... Even though I cover my ears with a pillow, I can't block him out.'

'He'll get better, he's just getting used to home.' These tired platitudes are the best Clara can offer her friend, knowing they're not enough but not knowing what else to do, except listen, let Dolly know she's here for her.

'That's what Ma says. But I don't think she quite believes it herself.' Dolly's voice breaks. 'You know the worst thing? I hate myself for it but some nights when he screams and cries, tormented by the horrors he endured, I... I wish Pa had not returned.'

Clara holds her friend as she sobs, sobbing along with her, both of them casualties of a war that has stripped her of family, rendered her an orphan and returned to her friend a father she doesn't recognise, devastated and tortured by what he has experienced. On the horizon, behind the neat rows of red-brick cottages, the sun sets in a blaze of defiant orange.

Chapter Seventeen

Clara

Awful Din

The men keep coming, trains full of them. Having left body parts behind but lugging hearts full of torment, a nightmare cache of horror. Wounded eyes that have seen too much, that yearn to forget, but cannot. But no uncle and no cousin. No news either. 'This waiting is turning my hair grey,' Aunt Helen says with a sigh.

Dolly's father is not getting any better. Her mother is working long hours as a charwoman. In the evenings, once all her chores are done, Clara walks over to her friend's house, knowing she'll appreciate the company. She's taken to doing this since she dropped round once, with a slice of a cake she'd made after having saved up rations for weeks.

The slice she'd salvaged for Dolly was half of her own serving. She wanted to gift it to her friend, who loved cake and who had been so glum lately. And so she'd carefully wrapped the piece and knocked on Dolly's door, imagining the smile on her friend's face.

Nobody answered. She knocked again, and again and then, tentatively, pushed the door open. It was dark inside and there was the most awful din. An anguished keening. A man wailing, 'No, no, no, no.' Tears stung Clara's eyes and the hand not holding the cake crept to the medal nestling against her chest.

'Dolly?'

Dolly was huddled in a corner of the dark room, her hands covering her ears, silent tears coursing down her face. She gasped when she saw Clara, her eyes shining with shame and hurt.

'Ma's working late. He will not accept help, he lashes out when he's like this.' A sniff. 'And lately, he's *always* like this. I feel so… *impotent*. I am a nurse, I should be able to help my own father, but I can't…'

Clara had set down the cake, sat beside her friend, put her arms around her and held her as she wept for a father who could not be comforted, whose tortured cries went on and on and on.

After that, Clara made it a habit to drop in on Dolly after supper, that weary twilight time before her mother came home when her friend was at her wits' end with not being able to console her father, when her patience was frayed thin.

'How brave they are, how stoic!' Dolly marvels of the soldiers at the hospital. They are sitting on the garden wall, the sun tinting the sky the fiery red of rage, the smell of ripe berries and evening primrose, lavender, honeysuckle and friendship. 'All some of them want is a kind word, a smile. But there are others like my da who are locked in their own private world of pain.' Her eyes pools of empathy, shining with anguish.

'Dolly, it's not that he won't accept help, but that he *can't.*'

Her friend's voice when she speaks is hoarse, marinated in tears. 'Yes, but I wish I could help.'

'I know.'

One day, Clara is cleaning a soldier's wound when he moans shortly, jerks suddenly and is still. It takes her a moment to realise that he is dead. She has lost patients before, they all have. Although each one is a painful shock, she has managed to take it in her stride and move on.

But not this time.

She is inconsolable. All the tears she has been holding back, all the fear and the pain and the loneliness, the upset on Dolly's behalf, and the anger and frustration at herself for being miserable when she is lucky – hale and whole, in body and mind, when compared to these soldiers – comes out in a seemingly endless gush.

Dolly holds her. Afterwards, Clara says, 'Thank you.'

'Clara, it is I who thank *you*. I've complained, moaned and groused and you've listened. I've told you my worst secret – confided in you that I sometimes think my father was better off dead – and you didn't judge me.'

'There's no need to sound so surprised.' Clara jogs her friend's elbow.

'I *am* grateful Pa is alive. I'm happy he's home. It's because I know he's safe that I can afford to think such things. But I shouldn't have said them to you.'

'I don't...'

'I know how much it must hurt when your own family...'

'Oh, Dolly.' Her friend gets it. She *understands*. Clara is overcome.

'And yet, you listen. You do not judge. Thank you, Clara.'

'Oh shush, that's what friends are for, to share our feelings and be done with them.' Clara smiles weakly.

'You're wise, you know. Your parents and brother would be proud.'

They walk back from the hospital in the surprisingly mild winter evening.

'Do you know what I'd like the most?' Her friend's voice faraway, looking beyond their little village, the cottages stained crimson, a rare, glorious winter dusk unmarred by fog or frost, the fields beyond, scented with witch hazel and arrow wood and nostalgia for a happier time that they cannot quite remember or grasp for all they've known these past few years is war and illness, death and devastation, ruptured families, the broken, the wounded and the lost.

'Yes, I do,' Clara says, lightly – Dolly has shared her fantasy with her many times since they became friends. 'You'd like to go somewhere exotic, as different from here as possible, a place untouched by war.'

When Dolly had first said this, Clara had heard *exotic* and thought: *India*. And when she looked at her friend's face, soft and shining with hope, she had thought, *Mother must have felt like this, when Father told her stories of India and promised to take her there*. And so she makes it her job to try to bring Dolly down to earth; she doesn't want her friend to be like Mother must have been – the unfulfilled woman dreaming of something better and unhappy with what she had – whose despair Clara, with the naivety of childhood, didn't see until Aunt Helen pointed it out to her and the memories she'd repressed of her parents arguing flooded back.

'But you do know there's no such place, Dolly? Every country in the world has seen its share of war,' Clara says now, gently.

A boy comes whizzing past on his bike, almost grazing Dolly's cheek, ringing his bell furiously as he calls, 'Watch out, Miss.'

'I can dream,' Dolly says jauntily.

Clara nods. Much as she tries to be the sensible one, she is not immune to dreaming herself, especially after another heartbreaking day at the hospital.

As they approach Aunt Helen's, they stop, stare at each other, then they're running. The whole village gathered at the gate. Clamour. Commotion. And... her aunt's voice. Clara elbows her way through the crowd.

Her aunt. *Laughing.* She turns and Clara's heart jumps. Joy and disbelief.

Could it be…? But of course it isn't. For a minute there… Her aunt's smile, so wide and unusual, transforming her, making her look like a much younger woman. Like Clara's mother.

'Clara, there you are. You'll never guess. Your uncle and cousin ended up in the same convalescent hospital and travelled back together!' Her words tumble out in an exhilarated gush completely unlike her. 'They are home.'

Chapter Eighteen

Clara

Answers

Uncle Tom is a small, squat man, quite bald. He is a stranger to Clara; she does not remember him at all from her one visit here when she was six. He is sitting by the window looking out at Clara's veggie patch and beyond that, the road, as if it holds answers to questions only he knows. He does not look up when Clara enters in Aunt Helen's wake, does not give any indication of seeing or knowing anyone, hearing anything at all. He is seemingly lost in a world of his own.

Clara recognises it – she's seen it in some of the soldiers she tends to – a dissociation from the world around them, caused by whatever they experienced in the war, as if by doing so, they can keep the horrors at bay.

'Tom, would you like to go upstairs, have a rest?' Aunt Helen prompts.

But he sits staring into the distance, giving no indication of having heard. He doesn't respond, doesn't utter a word.

'His hearing wasn't great to begin with and the artillery shells must have damaged—' Aunt Helen's words are cut off by an almighty crash from upstairs.

Aunt Helen and Clara exchange horrified looks – Uncle Tom is unaffected, calmly gazing out of the window – before charging up the stairs, Aunt Helen nearly stumbling in her haste.

A tall, thin man is flinging Danny's clothes, his chair, the trunk containing his prized possessions out of his room, his face contorted in fury as he mumbles to himself.

'Johnny, what are you…?'

'Why is this in my room?'

'W… we… Your brother…' Aunt Helen stutters.

'I want this out, all of it…' Johnny screams, his rage seemingly uncontrollable.

'But Joh—'

The front door bangs and Danny thunders up the stairs, calling, 'Ma, I got whatever I could with the ration books—' And, stopping short upon seeing his belongings strewn on the landing. 'Wh… Why are my…'

He doesn't get any further, for Johnny slams the door in his face.

'Ma, what's going on?' For a moment, Clara's cousin, lower lip trembling with upset, looks like the little boy he must have been once.

'Johnny wants his room back.' Aunt Helen sounds tired.

Clara feels for her aunt, this woman who had waited for her husband and son to return and who just a few minutes ago was so happy they had that she had transformed into an entirely different person altogether. The person she must have been, the poetry-loving, starry-eyed romantic, before life wore her down.

'Well,' Danny's lip curls as his bravado returns, his gaze landing on Clara, cruel and alive with meanness, 'I'll just have to take my room back then.'

'Clara, we'll sort something out for you,' Aunt Helen says and goes down the stairs. All the empathy Clara was feeling towards her disappears as she leaves her to her cousin, who says, with unabashed glee, 'You have ten minutes to move your things from my room or I'll do what my brother has done.'

After supper, Uncle Tom once again ignores all Aunt Helen's gentle persuading, coaxing and cajoling to go upstairs. He sleeps sitting in the chair by the window, which Aunt Helen fortifies with cushions and blankets, placing a little footstool in front of it so he can stretch his legs. He thrashes restlessly through the night, letting out little whimpers, sorry moans.

Clara is downstairs on spare bedding masquerading as a make-shift bed, unable to sleep for being cold, upset and now constantly disturbed by her uncle. Just as she is drifting off to sleep, someone thunders down the stairs and opens the front door, letting in a draught of freezing air – as if the house wasn't cold as a mortuary already. Johnny, muttering, 'I can't stay in here a moment longer.' The door slams, hard, shaking the whole house – but not Uncle Tom, who, waking, just stares unfazed out into the night.

Johnny returns as dawn is breaking, ushering in a gust of icy breeze, the frosty shiver of outdoors. Clara has endured a sleepless night counting down the interminable hours. Shivering inside her blanket, which does not keep the cold at bay, she thinks, *If Johnny isn't going to spend the night in his room, what does he want it for?*

As she rolls up the bedding, frozen numb, heartsick and even more tired than when she went to bed, she decides, *I cannot stay here, where I am not wanted.*

The next evening too, once everyone has settled for the night, Johnny goes out, returning just before dawn. On the third evening, Clara decides, on impulse, to follow him, figuring that the wintry chill will not be that much worse than the cold indoors. She's worried about him. He's so highly strung, any little thing, and often nothing at all, making him lash out – she wants to make sure he's alright.

Uncle Tom is awake, Clara notes as she leaves, staring out into the dark – he does not give any indication of having heard her, does not flinch at the blast of wintry air blustering inside although Clara is careful not to open the door too wide. His eyes blank and empty.

What is he thinking? Is he thinking at all? What happened to him?

The window faces her vegetable patch and Clara wishes it was summer so Uncle Tom could experience hope in the ripening tomatoes, the lanky beans dangling from the vines, the fat green marrows, but all there is to see is his own face reflected back at him in the shadow-rife gloom.

In any case, Clara knows that he is not looking at the present but into the past, what he endured, the horrors he cannot escape, that dog him with the unrelenting persistence of pitiless nightmares.

Johnny cuts a solitary figure, hunched against the icy wind, but nevertheless navigating the darkness with single-minded purpose. He is tall and he is walking very fast, great big strides, and Clara, blinking as her eyes adjust to the frost-edged dark, taking care to stay in the shadows, loses him once they get to the woods behind the village.

She enters the woods, meaning to look for him, but the trees that, during the day, are shady and verdant and welcoming, now loom tall and dark and forbidding; the rustling and hissing of the nocturnal animals is sinister and vaguely threatening.

She is just about to give up, turn back, when she startles at the sudden piercing keening – human, raging yet mournful, oozing pain, brimming with anger and ache – jarring, out of place in the night-shrouded woods.

She follows the sound, parts the vegetation, dark velvet, brushed with dew, and sees him. He is squatting on the mulchy ground, sobbing, a prisoner to his fiery grief, which he can vent only here, ensconced in nature's embrace, in the anonymity of the woods at night.

Clara walks back, swiping at the pain that leaks from her eyes, for him, for all the dead and the dying, for Uncle, who is lost, for Dolly's father and for Dolly, who is unable to help him, for all those young men, who were so excited to go to war and have come back broken, in body and mind – those lucky enough to have come back at all, that is – for Paul and for Father, for Mother with her rainbow laughter, her crushed dreams, for all the mothers and sisters, wives and daughters.

Part Seven

India

In Charge

Chapter Nineteen

Indira

1995, Lethargy

'I'm sorry, Ma'am,' the receptionist at Paediatric ICU says, 'Arun Bhat is not here.' Indira did not think to ask after her son at the hospital's main reception desk. She had rushed straight here, knowing this was where he would be brought after his surgery.

'I don't understand.' Indira manages to keep her voice level although her heart is clenched with panic. She wants to shake this woman, make her disclose the whereabouts of her son. She wants to shriek, into these hushed confines, 'Where is my son?'

'I'm checking for you.' The woman, with what appears to Indira to be extreme lethargy, picks up the phone.

'Arun Bhat, yes.' A glance towards her. 'He was supposed to come in here after his tonsillectomy, his mother says.' A long pause. Then, 'Oh.'

She looks at Indira – is her face blanched or is Indira imagining it? Indira opens her mouth but the woman's gaze flusters away.

'Okay, yes.' The woman carefully replaces the receiver.

Come on, Indira thinks, shifting from foot to foot, wringing her hands, breathing in the scent of antiseptic, phenyl, urgency and despair. Why have they given this woman this job, facing anxious parents, when she has no people skills, for heaven's sake?

If Indira was in charge, she would…

'But you are not in charge here,' she hears Karan's voice in her head.

Karan. *Where* is he? Where on earth is Arun if not here?

The worry is back, taking centre stage again, and it makes her sharp. 'Why is my son not back here?' The panic she has been keeping a tenuous hold on spilling out of her in a shrill bark, 'Look, whatever it is, I'd rather know than not!'

The woman stares at her, clearly startled. 'Ma'am, it's n…'

'Indira!' Karan's voice saying her name. 'They told me you were here.'

Part Eight

England

An Adventure

Chapter Twenty

Clara

1920, Next Step

'Matron, can I have a word?' Clara asks.

It has taken a while for Clara to come up with a plan of escape, her fear and worry about managing on her own holding her back. She has tried to tell herself she is strong, brave – she had stood up to her aunt when Dr Goel was admitted to hospital, after all. She had cured him. And yet… taking the next step, starting again somewhere new all on her own was terrifying. She had a job she cherished and was good at. And at Aunt Helen's, although she wasn't welcome, she was tolerated. If not exactly homely, it was the only home she knew. But, as weeks rolled by with nothing changing, she knew she had to do something – she couldn't sleep downstairs on makeshift bedding forever.

She would move to London – it was where she had grown up after all. But the thought of the big city after the relative safety – albeit often the claustrophobia – of the small village, where everyone knew everyone else, was scary. As was the thought of giving up the job she adored.

Then one day when the hospital was packed and they were rushing from one patient to another, one emergency to the next, one of the nurses had complained and Matron had snapped, 'If you think this is busy, my dear, you should hear the tales my friend tells of hospitals in London. Packed to the gills, she writes, and never enough nurses…'

And that was when it came to Clara. She needn't give up the job that, even at its busiest, messiest, most heartbreaking, she *loved*.

Now, Matron: 'Yes, my dear, what is it?'

'Matron, I… since my uncle and cousin returned from war, there's no room for me in my aunt's home…'

'You're looking for a place, are you? Well, I heard that since she lost her sons to war and husband to the Spanish flu, Mrs Rhodrin is looking for lodgers.'

'I… I'd like to move back to London, now the war's over.'

'Ah…'

'Do you know of a hospital where I could work?'

'Well, my friend Alice is matron at St John's House, which is merging with St Thomas's, so I've heard. I'm sure she would be very glad to take you on. They're always looking for good nurses. But, my dear, can't I convince you to stay here? It would be a shame to lose you.'

'I… I'd like a fresh start.'

Matron looks keenly at Clara, then sighs. 'I remember what it was to be young, just about. But I consider it my duty to warn you: London may not be better than here, in fact it might be worse. Do you still want to go?'

Clara thinks of enduring another cold, sleepless night listening to her uncle toss and turn, whimper and cry.

'Yes.'

'I'll write to Alice.'

'Thank you, Matron.'

Chapter Twenty-One

Clara

Responsibility

The city Clara encounters is a sorry cousin to the one she left. There are holes where houses should be. Ruin and devastation everywhere she looks. Queues snaking out of and around tumble-down shops looking the worse for wear. Broken, wounded men with haunted eyes holding placards bearing the legend: 'Don't pity a disabled soldier, find him a job'. Knots of women hold placards declaring, 'We want our say. We want the right to vote'.

Memories swamp her, glorious times with her brother, father and mother and, later, waving Father off to war, bursting with pride; and later still, buildings crumbling like hazy mirages, Mother slipping the medal around her neck...

Matron's words ringing in Clara's ears, 'London may not be better than here, in fact it might be worse.'

However it turns out, this new stage of her life, it is *her* decision, like the time when she chose to look after Dr Goel, and she will accept responsibility for it. She is nearly eighteen years old and steering her life, its architect; she is determined that she will succeed.

Aunt Helen's mouth had set in a thin line when Clara told her she was leaving for London. 'Just like your mother,' she had sniffed, 'running away in the hope of a better life.'

'What's wrong with wanting a better life?' Clara wanted to ask, but her aunt was in full flow. *I'm certainly not wanted here.*

'She did not understand and neither do you that you have to make the best of the chips you are dealt. Always angling for something more, different, grander will bring nothing but unhappiness.'

I will prove you wrong. Clara stood up straighter, opened her mouth to speak, but her aunt beat her to it.

'That is why I stopped reading poetry; those books in Danny's room that I know you enjoy. Poetry is not real life and the sooner you understand, the better.' And with this, Aunt Helen had turned away, Danny smirking from the doorway. Uncle, unresponsive, taciturn, was looking out of the window at a world only he could see. Johnny was locked away in his room, as ever, until after everyone was in bed, when he would escape into the woods to sob his pain away.

'Don't come running back if it doesn't work out,' Aunt Helen said, with her back still turned.

I will not. I will work hard, continue to use my profession to make a difference. I will put this life of mine to good use. I have my family living on in me and I have my medal – I do not need nor want anyone else.

Chapter Twenty-Two

Clara

Small Slice of Heaven

Matron Alice Andrews is a small, rotund, fiery bundle of dynamite. 'Ah, Sister Knight, you come highly recommended. Are you tired from your journey? No? Capital! We're completely swamped. Wash up and we'll get you to the wards. Don't worry about your trunk – I've instructed the porter to leave it in the staffroom. You can pick it up later. Now let me explain what's what.' And with that, Clara is inducted into her London life, and, at the hospital at least, it is just the same as in the country, if busier.

Afterwards, when Clara is exhausted in that exhilarated way of having done a job well, Matron introduces her to Meg.

'Meg is sharing with you – and as luck would have it, she's also finishing her shift, so you can get acquainted while she shows you to your accommodation. Now if you'll excuse me…' And with this, Matron disappears.

Meg is tall, red-headed and cheerful. She beams at Clara and chatters all the way to the nurses' quarters, which are in an annexe accessed from the hospital via a maze of corridors. 'You must be dead on your feet. Not far to go, thankfully, and we're a friendly lot, as you can see. Can you believe how busy it is – not a moment to spare. We're grateful to have you join, I can tell you. Now, these are the bathrooms and this is the kitchen – hello, Annie, Eve, this is Clara, she's sharing with me.'

Clara manages a smile and a wave at the two girls, not much older than her, one of whom is chopping vegetables, the other brewing tea before Meg urges her on. Both call hello as Clara is rushed past by Meg, who is saying, 'Would you believe, Matron put her straight to work as soon as she arrived? I'll show her to our room.'

The room is serviceable, with a wardrobe and a writing desk for each of them beside their beds. For Clara, it is her own small slice of heaven. That night, she lies down on a proper bed, *her* bed, and it feels glorious despite the footfall in the corridor, the whispering and soft giggles of nurses coming off shifts, despite the clatter of carriages, neighing of horses, calls of people and drone of sirens filtering in. The sounds of the city deeply, comfortingly familiar – she fell asleep to them every day of her childhood. Meg's soft sighs from the bed beside her hark back to happier times when Paul, her big brother, was in the bunk below her. Although Meg warned that their room was never quite warm enough, Clara, used to lying on the makeshift bedding downstairs at her aunt's these last few weeks, blasted by cold draughts and never feeling warm, is cosily snug. She sleeps through the night, deeply and heavily, unperturbed by either dreams or nightmares, for the first time in weeks.

Chapter Twenty-Three

Clara

1925, Proposition

'Sister Knight, do I really need to be in hospital? Can't I recover at home?' Clara's patient, Captain Adams, asks, his brow furrowed.

'Sir, Doctor Stern is worried about that infection in the leg you injured in the war; he thinks it might turn septic. We cannot in all good faith discharge you.'

'But my wife… She needs me. Our son…'

'I'm sure your family would rather you were healthy.'

Captain Adams nods bleakly.

Clara goes over her schedule in her head. She has to check the nurses' rota – Sister Lewes is ill and Clara must make sure Sister Partridge knows to take her place. Then there's the patient in bed seven…

But Captain Adams needs sympathy and a listening ear; they will do more good than all the medicines Doctor Stern prescribes. If there is one thing Clara has learned in her career it is that mind and body are intricately linked and that often, a healthy, positive frame of mind will go a long way towards mending even the most broken of bodies. And so, despite not having the time to spare, she sits down beside Captain Adams and says, gently, 'Do you want to talk about it?'

Captain Adams begins hesitantly. 'My son, Henry. He's five. He was born late in life, our post-war miracle. But he's sickly, prone to colds and coughs and fevers, anything going really.' Now that he's started, the words come in a gush, 'Thankfully he's been spared the horrid Spanish flu – we've made sure to keep him closeted away. But he's growing quickly, a smart little boy, cheeky too…' A smile softening the worry lines on the captain's face. Then, his face creasing with anxiety again, 'My wife… she worries awfully, you see. When I came in for a check, Henry was enjoying one of his rare good spells, which is why Pat, that's my wife, urged me to get my leg seen to. But we didn't think I'd be admitted into hospital, that I'd have to stay over.' His voice clipped with upset. 'Pat… she's of a nervous disposition. She wrote to say Henry's ill again, his fever has spiked alarmingly. I can't be here, he… They need me there.' Now his voice rising in agitation.

'Captain,' Clara says, gently, 'this is exactly where you should be. You are of no use to them ill. And with regards to your son, can I make a suggestion?'

'Please do,' Captain Adams says, curiosity mingling with the anxiety clouding his face.

'From what you've said, it appears the weather does not suit him, or perhaps his body is reacting to something in the air. Have you thought about moving to warmer climes? My father was brought up in India. He used to boast that no disease dared touch him, for the scorching heat he experienced during childhood had burrowed within him and would burn away any infection.' Clara smiles at the memory, hearing her father's beloved voice in her head.

Clara was afraid she was losing her family – their features, the cadence of their voices – and so she had started opening up about them with her patients, sharing her precious, treasured reminiscences with them; and, like her mother had promised when they grieved Paul together so very long ago, talking about them did bring them briefly back to her.

She leaves Captain Adams busily contemplating what she has said, his upset momentarily pushed aside.

*

A month or so after Captain Adams is discharged from hospital, his leg healed of infection, he comes back: 'Sister Knight, may I have a word?'

'Captain, you're not ill again, surely?'

'My dear, on the contrary, thanks to you I'm fit as a fiddle.'

'Come now…'

'I'm here with a proposition for you.'

'Oh?' Clara is intrigued.

'I took your suggestion on board and I…'

'*My* suggestion?'

'Regarding my son Henry; you said his health might improve in warmer climes. I consulted his doctor and he agrees. I'm blown as to why he didn't suggest it himself! You truly are a gem, Sister Knight.'

'Oh, I'm so pleased to have been of help.'

'I requested a transfer to India and it's just been approved. It is initially for a year but if Henry and my wife take to it, and crucially, if it suits Henry's health, then we will stay longer. Sister Knight, you haven't even met Henry and yet you divined what might help him. I know you love your job here but I thought I'd put this to you.' Captain Adams clears his throat, knots his palms together. 'Would you consider travelling with us as Henry's nurse? My wife and I would be very much at ease if you were to accompany us to India.'

India. The land her father loved, where he had wanted to take his family. Clara's happiest memories – sitting on his knee, her brother perched on the other, listening to him recount tales of his childhood, Mother knitting beside him, a wistful smile upon her face.

Mother, who in marrying Father hoped to travel, experience the world and especially the country that her beau described in such vivid detail. That magical place that held such sway for her parents and to be honest for her too, because of which she had decided to look after a brown-skinned soldier, which gave her confidence when she needed it most and belief in herself.

She's been at this hospital in London for five years. She's worked hard, risen up the ranks, been promoted to senior nurse. She has her own room in the nurses' accommodation, no longer sharing with Meg.

Meg fell in love with Fred, an ambulance driver, who'd returned mostly unscathed from the war – he had been shot in the belly but thankfully, the bullet missed all the crucial organs. Meg still works at the hospital but moved out of the nurses' accommodation and into a flat two streets away, with Fred, when they married two years previously – Clara was their bridesmaid.

When she visited Meg and Fred for Sunday lunch a few weeks ago, Meg had announced, cheeks ruddy and glowing, one hand on her stomach, the other piling Clara's plate with roast potatoes, 'Get that down you, you're looking peaky. My babe doesn't fancy a skinny auntie.'

Clara had set her fork down, staring at Meg.

'Yes, I am! A winter baby, this one,' stroking her stomach fondly, Fred looking on proudly. 'I'm thinking of stopping work when she comes along.'

'He, you mean,' twinkled Fred.

'But as *her* auntie,' Meg continued, swatting her husband lightly, 'we'll see you often, Clara – you'll visit not only on Sundays like now, but midweek too, once you finish your shift; so you won't miss me even if I'm no longer at the hospital.'

Dolly corresponds with Clara regularly. A few months after Clara arrived in London, Dolly's father contracted and succumbed to the Spanish flu, her mother meeting the same fate soon after.

Dolly wrote,

In many ways, death was a relief for Pa. I think he felt guilty for living when his fellow men had died at the battlefield, for returning home when they were buried in an alien land. When he died, his face held an expression of release at odds with the haunted one that had graced it since he came back – I believe he found peace at last, the peace he had been seeking since he arrived home broken. As for Ma – after Pa, she was too weary to go on. She had not known what to make of the man who returned from war, mournful and lost, so very different to the husband who had left.

A year after her parents' deaths, Dolly fell in love with a Canadian soldier in her care, married him and moved to Toronto. She is mother to one-year-old Rosie, with another child on the way, and is, judging from her letters, blissfully happy.

Remember how we would sit on the mossy cemetery wall, watch the grave-diggers try and find space among the crowded headstones, as the hymns from yet another funeral drifted over to us? We'd look over the green, the neat rows of cottages, the woods beyond, and dream of escape, yearn to experience the world. Well, now we are! Isn't it splendid, Clara? You an independent woman of the world and a senior nurse to boot. Me in Canada with Ed and Rosie and a new babe on the way! Who would have thought it, eh?

Indeed. Who would have thought it? Here Clara is: happy, busy, all her time accounted for. In the little spare time she gets, when not visiting Meg, she is involved in the suffragette movement. She has found her place.

'Find a beau, Clara,' Meg prompts, patting her bump, glowing, content.

'I'm quite happy as I am,' Clara responds. 'I do not need a man to complete me, define me.'

'It is a partnership,' Meg insists.

But Clara sees how Fred takes all their earnings and metes out Meg's allowance. Clara is determined that she will not depend upon a man, upon anyone. She loved and lost and although time has formed a scab over the wound, it still hurts dreadfully. At the hospital she encounters death and its effect on the living: loved ones devastated, crushed.

Love is a trap. Its legacy – precious few glorious years to create treasured memories and a lifetime of pain.

Which is why she has danced with a few men, flirted with others but has not gone any further. She hasn't wanted to, although they have – she values her independence too much. Clara will make her own choices, orchestrate her destiny.

'You should stop associating with those suffragettes, they're filling your head with nonsense,' Meg grumbles.

'They're saying women have rights. Our own minds.'

'I agree, but Clara, tell that to yourself when you're lonely at night.'

'I'm not lonely, I'm happy.'

But she has to admit that at times, when she struggles to fall asleep, when she can no longer conjure her brother's face and his perpetually teenage self seems far removed from her life, when memories of life with Mother and Father and Paul feel as if they happened to someone else, when she aches for something she cannot name, she asks herself, *Is this it? Is this all I want from my life?*

*

'Sister Knight, would you consider it?' Captain Adams is saying.

There's nothing holding her here. There are enough nurses now to take her place – there is no dire need like during the war, or just after it when the country was reeling from the Spanish flu. She is free to leave if she so wants.

India. Clara tastes the tropical feel of the word, its exquisite, remote promise. She touches her St Christopher medal as she entertains this glimmering, tantalising notion, suddenly within reach. She thinks of the suffragettes, their bold disregard for rules, their desire to break free of the constraints by which women are bound.

'It's for a year initially but if you don't like it, we'll arrange for your passage back,' Captain Adams says.

Only for a year. An adventure. What do I have to lose?

'Think about it and if you are agreeable, come to tea with myself, my wife and Henry on Friday. I know it is your afternoon off – I must admit I wished Fridays away when I was here, the ward wasn't the same without Sister Knight,' Captain Adams says.

'Ah now, Captain, flattery won't work with me, you know,' Clara laughs even as she considers. *My family lives on in me. If I take up this offer, I'll be doing what they wanted to, taking them to the place they yearned for, each in their different ways – Father wanting to return to his childhood home; Mother and Paul spurred on by his stories, wanting to see this magical land that had such an effect on Father. This opportunity to go to India, perhaps it is destiny.*

Chapter Twenty-Four

Clara

Pearls and Black Leather

'Miss Knight, my wife, Patricia,' Captain Adams beams. And, turning to his wife, 'My dear, this is the admirable Miss Knight, who saved my life and diagnosed Henry without even meeting him.'

'Captain, you exaggerate greatly.' Clara laughs.

But Mrs Adams steps forward, takes her hand in both of hers. 'Miss Knight, I thank you.'

Mrs Adams is attired in a dazzling turquoise silk crêpe dress that brings out the aquamarine of her eyes. She has accessorised it with pearls and black leather shoes. She is nearly as tall as her husband and very slender.

Like Captain Adams mentioned, Clara notes that Mrs Adams is of a nervous temperament, her eyes worried and hands fluttering anxiously as she says, 'Come and meet Henry. He's been suffering from the flu this past week.' She wrings her hands together in distress. 'But fortunately, he's better today and out of bed.' She smiles weakly.

When Clara found herself seriously considering Captain Adams's invitation, she had asked Matron's advice – over the years she has come to respect and admire the woman greatly.

Matron had smiled. 'I wondered if you'd come to me. Captain Adams already has.'

'Oh.'

'Although I'd rather you stayed on here for purely selfish reasons, this opportunity is too good to miss, Clara. I'd go, but they want *you*.' Matron smiled. 'You've been around death and suffering long enough. Looking after a child will do you a world of good. How old are you, twenty?'

'Twenty-three.'

'You're only young once, my dear. And when, *if*, you come back, your job here will be waiting for you.'

Henry is in his nursery. He is small for his age, his face peaky, complexion wan. He's on his knees, playing with his train set, which runs on tracks weaving around the entire room, but stands when his mother enters, Clara in her wake.

'Henry, this is Nurse Knight.'

Clara can see he is poorly; she noted the wince as he got to his feet, the feverish flush creeping up his cheeks, the redness tinting the whites of his eyes.

'Won't you say hello, Henry?' his mother prompts.

His eyes, although ringed with dark circles, are alive with curiosity – and is that a mischievous twinkle? – as he politely holds out his hand. 'How do you do?'

She takes it – and stifles a scream as the slimy thing concealed in his palm makes contact with hers. She grabs it and holds it by her side, her hand fisted around it even as it squirms, nodding gravely, 'Pleased to meet you, Master Henry.'

'I'll leave you two to get acquainted. Come and join us in the morning room for tea.'

As soon as his mother's footsteps recede, Henry flops onto a chair. It is as if he was holding himself together for his mother's sake and it has exhausted his store of energy.

'Please give Bess back, will you?' he says to Clara.

'Bess, is she? Nice name for a frog.' She winks at him before depositing the small green creature in his palm.

'I grew her myself – from a tadpole!' Pride coating his voice and shining from his red-rimmed eyes. Then, excitement taking over the fever-flushed features: 'I've heard there are snakes in India even taller than I am. You're not scared of frogs. Are you scared of snakes? I bet you're not.' He scrunches his nose, assessing her.

'Well, you can be afraid of one and not the other.'

His face falls.

'But… I'd like to think I'd be brave if I encountered one.'

'India has spiders as big as your hand, Father says.' His eyes wide with marvellous wonder, at odds with his illness-plagued face.

She is reminded of her brother, gloriously and painfully – Paul was also fascinated by tales of Indian wildlife and, like this endearing boy, not a bit scared. She fingers her St Christopher medal, swallows down the sorrow that is now a part of her, along with happiness at this unexpected reminder. 'Goodness!'

Henry laughs. A glorious tumbling waterfall of a sound. In Henry's laughter, Clara hears an echo of her brother's.

'I like you.' Henry grins.

'I like you too, Master Henry.' In him she sees her brother and while it hurts, it also brings Paul vividly alive for the first time in years.

Part Nine

India

Without Reservation

Chapter Twenty-Five

Indira

1995, Puzzled

Indira struggles to make sense of the words her husband is saying. 'Your mother has been trying to contact you. When she couldn't get through to you, she called home. Thankfully I'd nipped back to get Arun's Lamby – he realised he hadn't packed it and was tearful, so I promised to get it for him – and took the call. That was fortunate. If I'd been any earlier or later…' Then gently, 'Indu, your father…'

'But what about Arun?'

'Arun?' Karan appears puzzled.

'Our son,' she snaps, her voice shrill.

The receptionist looks up sharply, 'Ma'am, I must ask you to…'

But Indira ignores her, her focus on Karan. 'Is Arun alright?'

'He's fine, he's asleep.'

Sweet relief floods her body but her mind takes its time catching up. *Arun is alright. My boy is safe.* 'So why isn't he here?'

'He came to quite quickly and wanted to move into the room we've booked. But once he got there, fatigue caught up. He's asleep.' Karan smiles. 'But there are nurses checking up on him so I was able to leave him to come here. He'd been asking for you before he fell asleep. He is very proud of himself.' His smile falls. 'I'm sorry about your father, Indu.'

And now fear, once again taking her heart captive.

Her father, whom she has also taken for granted. *When was the last time she visited?*

'He's not…?'

'He's at Mahatma Gandhi Hospital in your hometown. He suffered a massive heart attack. I told your PA to tell you to go to the hospital at once, that you were not to worry about Arun, that he was okay, that once he was signed off, we'd join you there. Why are you here?'

And *now*, she understands.

It isn't Karan's fault, it is hers. As usual she was rushing, impatient – she only heard part of the message: 'You are to go to the hospital at once…' before she was off. She recalls now that Nandita had called after her, but she hadn't waited to listen. She had asked Nandita to fob off the directors in the boardroom with an excuse and had rushed straight here.

Now, relief that Arun is okay mingles with worry and anxiety about her father.

'I will look in on Arun and then leave,' she says to Karan.

He extends his hand but she is rummaging in her bag for her purse, checking if she has enough cash for the journey, and when she looks up, it is to see his hand drop to his side.

Once, he would have hugged her, without reservation. In fact, he used to be very demonstrative and she had quickly got over her initial hesitation and begun to enjoy and expect his affection. He's still that way with Arun. *But with her…*

When did it stop? Perhaps when she stopped noticing, too busy to acknowledge his affection. Perhaps he tired of always having to initiate contact. When did this reserve come between them, this lack of intimacy? Never mind sleeping with her husband, when did she even hug Karan last?

She has tried to do *everything* but she is realising that she hasn't been doing anything properly. She looks at her son sleeping peacefully, a half-smile on his face. She drops a kiss on his cheek – he smells of hospital, medicinal, and yet there's that sweetness, the underlying candy and mischief scent that is uniquely her son.

And then, telling herself it is time to re-evaluate her life, assess what's important, to start honouring the promises she made when she was out of her mind with worry just now, to not take her family for granted, to put them first, she leaves her husband and son and rushes to her father's bedside, Karan reassuring her that he will follow with Arun as soon as the hospital gives their son the all-clear.

Part Ten

En Route to India

Miracle from Another Life

Chapter Twenty-Six

Clara

1925, A Bejewelled Throne

'Nurse Knight, let's go see the maharaja.' Henry tugs at Clara's hand, his eyes sparkling mischievously. Only two days into their journey and already the boy looks so much healthier, his cheeks aglow, his complexion not quite so pale. It appears all he needed was a change of scene, new experiences to look forward to, instead of being closeted away in his home for fear of infection and illness.

Henry had been so excited – as had Clara – when, as they were about to board the ship, an officious man in a turban had asked them, none too kindly, to 'please make way for the maharaja.'

Captain and Mrs Adams, Clara and Henry had watched agog as a veritable army of turbaned, silk-clad men had carried a bejewelled throne, draped in colourful, mirrored silks, up the gangplank. This was followed by more men carrying another three, not as elaborate as the first, but grand nonetheless. 'The maharanis,' a woman to Clara's right whispered, straightening her hat.

'Maharani*s*?' Clara couldn't help asking.

'Well, my dear, these Eastern kings are not content with just one wife, I'm afraid.'

Clara has loved every minute of their voyage so far. Although she adores nursing, like Matron said, she's also enjoying the break from the grievously ill and the dying, the wounded and the afflicted. Her charge is different – he's a brave little boy and, despite the limitations of his body, very enthusiastic, full of life.

Despite having promised herself not to care too deeply – and she *won't* – she adores Henry already, his positivity and warm embrace of every experience, his sickliness not holding him back one bit. He allows her to wrap him up warm – they are yet to cross the seas into warmer climes – and he tires easily but he does not let that stop him. He's a delight, marvelling at everything, eternally curious and extremely bright.

'We'll miss you, Baby and I,' Meg had said, eyes shining, when Clara had gone round to say goodbye. 'But a year will fly by. And when you're back, your godchild will be here.' Throwing her arms around Clara, her bump between them, her scent of roses. Then, with a mischievous sparkle in her eyes, 'And you just might meet someone special, given the dearth of eligible young men here after the war. I was lucky to meet Fred when I did.'

I don't need nor want anyone, Clara thought quietly to herself – it was no use protesting out loud. Happy in her marriage, with a baby on the way, Meg could not see how anyone could be content on their own and took Clara's assertions as excuses because she hadn't yet found someone.

Her friend meant well; she wanted Clara to be happy. Clara would miss her. 'I'm sorry I won't be here to welcome your baby but I'll be back before you know it,' she told her.

Now, 'Nurse Knight? Please can we see the maharaja?' Henry pleads.

They've just finished breakfast – the children's sitting. The dining room busy with chatter and cries, infectious giggles, chubby cheeks smeared with marmalade, cherubic faces sporting moustaches of cocoa; nannies' murmurs, both the musical cadence of Indian ayahs in their colourful saris and their creased brown faces and the crisp voices of British nannies in starched dresses. The delicious scent of toast and fried bacon mingling with the acidic pungency of juice and the honeyed aroma of porridge.

Clara smiles down at the boy, taking his hand in hers. That cheeky grin of his is irresistible. 'Come on then.'

Henry watches the maharaja order his huge retinue of servants about, his favourite pastime. Clara stands on deck savouring the seaweed and salt taste of adventure, the dazzling gold thrill of possibility, and watches the sea, midnight blue mingled with starry green, capped with playful frothy wavelets, its undulating translucent calm a front for the thriving life within. Every so often it affords a glimpse into the secrets it slickly conceals – a fin slicing the water, sparkling silver; a bird swooping low, a flash, a skirmish and then rising again with a fish flapping desperately within its beak. The sky above, vast and wide and palest blue like the soothing memory of a calming dream.

She cannot quite believe that she is, at twenty-three, travelling to an exotic country on the opposite side of the world. She touches the St Christopher medal – it will keep her safe like her mother promised.

The maharaja's harem has commandeered almost the entirety of the women's first-class cabins, much to the consternation of the other ladies in first class. They sniff, annoyed, complaining to anyone who will listen, 'Do you know it's just three of his wives who are travelling with him, his current favourites? Rumour has it he picked one at Aden, the other in Suez. Only one came with him from India. The rest of them are *servants*.'

The maharanis never come out of their rooms, their maids flitting between cabins, carrying platters of food and gossip, their scent of rosewater and spices wafting through first class, their faces hidden by veils, their gold-threaded saris glimmering in the corridor, glorious and tropical as exotic birds showing off their plumage.

As Clara passes by on the way to her own modest second-class cabin, she hears them giggling and chatting in their musical language, their anklets chiming a musical melody, and misses, acutely, the warm comfort of female companionship.

Chapter Twenty-Seven

Clara

A Zoo on Board

'Is it true there are lions and leopards that come up to the villages?' Henry is quizzing one of the lascars – the ship stewards – about the animals in India. With every day that passes, he is getting better, no longer wan, healthy colour staining his cheeks. Clara surmises that all Henry, a child born just after the war, in a city irrevocably changed by it, has known and breathed is smog and rubble-infested air and it has wreaked havoc with his lungs.

Now, as they journey on the open sea, the salty air, fresh and bracing, seems to be doing wonders for the boy. She's tried telling Captain and Mrs Adams as much, but they are convinced his recovery is down to her.

'I told you Miss Knight was a miracle worker, Pat,' the captain had said.

'She definitely is,' Mrs Adams, who is also much changed, no longer anxiously fretting about her son, nervously wringing her hands, smiled. Clara privately thinks that this too might have contributed to Henry's improved heath – the fact that his mother is no longer watching his every breath and worrying about it.

Now, the lascar smiles at Henry, his eyes twinkling at the boy's obvious awe and enthusiasm. 'Lions and tigers come for the cattle but sometimes end up eating humans.'

'Capital!' Henry exclaims, his eyes shining. 'I do hope I see one.'

'You most likely will do. Just take care not to get eaten, will you, young sir?' Then, 'Have you visited the zoo on board?'

'There's a zoo *on board*?' Henry's voice is a screech of pure excitement.

'The maharaja is an avid collector of strange and exotic species. You'll need to seek his permission to visit his zoo, but when he sees how much you love animals, I'm sure he—'

Henry is already standing, galvanised into action before the lascar has finished speaking, tugging urgently at Clara's hand. 'Come, Nurse Knight, we need to see the maharaja.'

'Henry, I don't think we can visit the maharaja without an appointment,' Clara demurs gently.

'How do we get one?' Henry asks, looking at her with huge, hopeful eyes.

'We'll find a way,' Clara says with all the conviction she can muster.

The next morning, as Clara is on her way to meet Henry, walking past the first-class cabins that house the maharaja's wives and their coterie, she is aware of a commotion. Footsteps scurrying up and down the corridors and in and out of rooms, silver anklets chiming a frantic melody. The maids clustering together, talking rapidly, frowns puckering their eyes, the only part of their veiled faces visible.

They rush about like flustered birds, their voices ringing anxious, although still musical. As she steps onto the deck with Henry for the children's breakfast service, one of the maids darts past her and towards a man who is standing by the stairs that lead down to the cabins. His face is in shadow, but there is something familiar about him.

The maid converses intently with the man. She's looking down, away from him, even as she talks, the sea silhouetted, a bright dreamy blue set aglow by the morning sun, behind him. The man listens, nods. *Where has Clara seen him before?*

If only he was not in shadow, haloed by the coppery teal of the sea, the gold of the rising sun dancing upon the waves.

'This way, Nurse Knight,' Henry's little hand tugging at hers.

'Nurse Knight?' The man turns abruptly to look at her.

The maid keeps on talking, sounding more urgent by the minute, but he is not listening, his gaze, which like the rest of him is in shadow, trained on Clara's face.

But his voice, the way he said *Nurse Knight*... So familiar. *It can't be...*

'Nurse Knight!' he exclaims, sounding so very thrilled, and then he steps into the light and she gasps in stunned surprise, for she is looking straight into a vision from her past, a miracle from another life.

Chapter Twenty-Eight

Clara

Transfixed

Before Clara can say a word, Henry steps protectively in front of her, hands on hips, regarding the man sternly. 'How do you know Nurse Knight?'

'Ah, young man, Nurse Knight saved my life when I was wounded during the war.'

'Dr Goel, you exagge…'

But Henry nods vigorously and sounds marginally warmer when he says, 'She saved Father's life too and she's now my nurse.'

'Well, you are very lucky indeed, young sir, to have the best nurse in all of England looking after you.' He smiles at Henry and then turns to her, his chocolate gold eyes shining. 'Miss Knight, what a great pleasure it is to make your acquaintance again. You're travelling to India?'

Clara has stood all this while transfixed – one hand upon her disbelieving, wondrous heart – at finding the man who helped her to find herself, here aboard the ship, looking fit and fine. She has been trying to suppress her pride: *If he's looking well, it's partly down to me.*

Now, upon being addressed by this apparition from her past, she gathers her wits about her, clears her throat. 'Hello, Dr Goel. As Henry said, I'm accompanying him as his nurse for the year his father is posted in India. And you?'

'I'm the maharaja's physician. As you know, I served with the Imperial Service Troops, the forces raised by the princely states, and after the war I was taken on by the maharaja of Phulgarh as his royal physician.'

'*You're* the maharaja's physician?' Henry pipes up. He can barely contain his excitement. 'I'd like to visit his zoo. Can you get me an appointment?'

'Henry…' Clara cautions at the same time as the veiled maid, tired of waiting, pipes up, her voice high-pitched, a continuous, seemingly unstoppable tirade – evident even to Clara and Henry, who exchange alarmed looks; they do not understand a word but know a scolding when they hear it.

Even as she is speaking – yelling – apparently without pause, another maid arrives, anklets chiming, bangles tinkling, and she too joins in, their words staccato and urgent, shrill as parakeets.

Dr Goel manages to say, 'Excuse me, please,' to Henry and Clara before turning to give the maids his complete attention. He appears unsettled by what he's hearing, rubbing at his chin, his eyes troubled.

Clara and Henry are about to walk away when he calls, 'Miss Knight!'

'Yes.' Clara turns.

The troubled expression has left his face and he is smiling. 'You have the knack of appearing just when I need you. Are you sure you're not an angel?'

Clara raises an eyebrow, even as Henry asks, 'What do you mean?'

A seagull squawks above them, a shadowy arc against a gold-splashed sapphire sky.

'I'm in something of a quandary, you see. One of the maharanis is taken ill.'

Ah, that explains the commotion in the first-class cabins.

'But no man except the maharaja is allowed anywhere near the maharanis…'

'Oh?' Clara says.

Henry is open-mouthed.

The ship rocks severely and an arc of froth splashes them. Crockery crashes in the dining room and a child wails, others joining in, a mournful chorus. The scent of bacon wafts on the honeyed, salt-speckled breeze.

'I've tried to assess the problem from the maids' account but they can only provide a vague explanation – not enough for a proper diagnosis. They say she is experiencing severe pain in the general abdominal area but they cannot narrow it down. I'm not allowed to go near her, or see her, so I definitely cannot examine her. And now, here you are. If the maharaja gives permission, would you be willing to examine the maharani?'

'I...'

Henry is nodding vigorously even though Clara is sure he does not fully understand what's going on. He tucks his small hand in Clara's and tells Dr Goel, 'Of course she will.'

Chapter Twenty-Nine

Clara

Royal Insignia

The maharaja is lounging on the choicest part of the deck, the whole section cordoned off for him and guarded by his vast retinue of servants, clad in long silk tops, elaborate pleated trousers and matching gold-lined turbans bearing the royal insignia in jewels that wink and shimmer in the sun.

The servants part for Dr Goel, their reverential gazes turning curious as Clara and Henry follow in his wake to where the maharaja is reclining on his cushioned and bedecked throne-like seat. As Dr Goel approaches, the maharaja sits up, his gaze swivelling towards Clara and Henry. There is a sudden hush, even the ocean seeming to quiet its burbling, mischievous swell and rise. The servant fanning the maharaja stops momentarily before resuming with gusto.

'Who are they?' the maharaja asks Dr Goel in English, in the polished tones of British aristocracy. He is a short, squat man, appearing overwhelmed by his dazzling robes, his squeaky voice, while carrying in the solemn silence, matching his small stature.

'Your Majesty, may I present Miss Clara Knight, whom I discovered just now is travelling on our ship, an incredibly devoted nurse who saved my life when I was serving with the Imperial Service Troops during the war, and her charge, Master Henry Adams.'

The maharaja's gaze roves over Henry and settles upon Clara, his bulbous eyes glinting with something she does not recognise.

Clara is aware of the silence stretching, taut, all the servants waiting, rapt, for the maharaja's pronouncement, her heart beating a wild tattoo within the confines of her chest. The sea breeze brushing her flushed cheeks is pleasantly warm, salty and charged with intrigue.

The maharaja smiles. It is as if the entire entourage lets out a collective breath.

Chapter Thirty

Clara

An Urgent Message

The jewels adorning the maharaja's head, his arms, his chest, his elaborate robes twinkle and shimmer as he addresses Clara, 'It is a pleasure to meet you, Miss…'

'Miss Knight,' Dr Goel prompts.

'The woman to whom my physician owes his life. Well, well…'

She can't decide if he is being complimentary or derogatory.

'Your Majes—' Clara begins, but the maharaja cuts her off, his gaze shifting to Henry, who is skipping with excitement and impatience beside her. 'So, you're travelling to India with this young man?'

'My charge, Henry Adams, Your Majesty.'

'Pleased to meet you, Your Majesty,' Henry says gravely.

The maharaja inclines his head regally, acknowledging Henry.

A bedecked and bejewelled courtier approaches the maharaja, bowing deeply. Perhaps in deference to Clara and Henry, he too speaks in English, although his vowels are pronounced, his message at odds with the halting syllables – it's evident he's translating each word in his head before uttering it. 'Sorry to interrupt, Your Majesty, but I have an urgent message.'

At this, Dr Goel says, 'Ah, is it about Maharani Maya Devi?'

The man nods.

The maharaja looks from the messenger to the doctor: 'What about my favourite maharani?' His face darkens into a scowl.

Clara notes the fearful hush that descends upon the assembled courtiers. Henry picks up on it too, for he sidles closer to her.

'She's ill, Your Majesty,' Dr Goel says, his voice calm, not betraying any of the anxiety the courtiers wear so palpably and the sight of which is sending chills down Clara's spine. 'Her maids brought word to me.'

'Then why are you here instead of doing something about it?' the maharaja roars.

Clara bites her lower lip to stop from flinching. Henry shrinks beside her, clinging to her. Seagulls perched on the rails startle and squawk, flying away in a breezy swoop. The sea grumbles and roars, smacking their faces with salt-slicked spray.

Only Dr Goel is unperturbed, as he says, in the same soft voice, 'This is why I introduced you to Miss Knight, Your Majesty. From the maharani's symptoms as described by the maids, I am not at liberty to determine quite what is the matter without exam…'

At this the maharaja scowls even deeper, his face darkening to an alarming red.

The messenger next to him stiffens. The courtiers' faces are pale and contorted in varying degrees of apprehension.

'I know it is not possible for me to visit the maharani,' Dr Goel says and as the maharaja leans forward in his chair, his face now puce, a gasp of collective panic weaves through the courtiers as they wait for the axe to fall.

'…which is why I'm here to ask your permission, Your Majesty, for Miss Knight to examine the maharani and report to me.'

Clara is in awe of this version of that sorry-looking Indian soldier she nursed, wondering how Dr Goel can remain so steady in the face of such concentrated wrath.

A beat. Two.

The courtiers have given up all pretence of working. A dreadful chill is in the air. Even the sun has slipped behind clouds and appears to be frowning.

Then the maharaja's face clears. 'Well, there's no harm, I suppose.'

The courtiers' shoulders relax and they go back to their duties.

The maharaja fixes Clara with his beady gaze, his expression sombre and voice carrying a hint of threat: 'Miss Knight, I trust you will do your best by my *favourite* maharani.'

She opens her mouth and discovers she's lost her voice. She clears her throat and there it is: 'I will, Your Majesty.'

He waves his hand, rings twinkling in the sun, and they are dismissed, the courtiers' sweet sighs of relief following them.

'Nurse Knight,' Henry whispers as they walk away, Clara's legs, her entire body, shaking so much she doesn't know if she is holding Henry up or the other way round, 'you better cure this maharani. It will please the maharaja and he'll let me visit his zoo.'

And Clara feels all the tension ebb away as she laughs.

'Your laugh really is like rainbows in a festive sky,' Dr Goel says, smiling at her, and her face blooms with colour.

Chapter Thirty-One

Clara

A World Apart

The first-class cabins housing the maharanis are extraordinary, a world apart. Each cabin is almost obscenely spacious, branching into interconnected rooms – a reading room, a lounge, a dressing room, washroom and bedroom. But, Clara notes with awe, even this is not large nor grand enough for the king's consorts – for each of the maharanis has a *suite* of cabins to herself, alongside a myriad of personal maids to tend to her every whim.

The cabins have been furnished lavishly with ornate furniture and plush carpets, but what stands out are the personal touches the maharanis' maids have added – the opulent silk tapestries showcasing intricate etchings in a spate of shimmering colours, the jewellery boxes spilling gems and trinkets that twinkle and shine with a secret tantalising light competing with the glitter of the sea through the portholes. The bejewelled throws carelessly scattered, the sequinned draperies. Small, patterned lamps lit around the rooms, orange flames darting from wicks dancing in fragrant oil – eucalyptus? Sandalwood?

Bowls of nuts and sweetmeats, candied fruit and translucent gold and cream globules drowning in syrupy nectar, chocolate boxes and snacks Clara has never laid eyes on before that smell spicy and exotic, making her nose itch and her stomach rumble. They obviously haven't heard of rationing in this opulent, extravagant, cloistered environment.

Clara only has a glimpse of the endless rooms, so casually luxurious, spilling with maids who polish and shine, sweep and dust, perusing her curiously from behind veils, looking away when their eyes meet hers.

The maid leading her stops at a door, knocks. The door is opened by another maid, whose eyes widen at Clara, as out of place in her plain cream dress as a dove in a cluster of brightly coloured parakeets.

The room Clara enters is huge, and very dark, all the portholes covered by heavy velvet draperies. It smells of incense, nutty rose, and when her eyes adjust to the darkness, Clara locates the source as a small lamp in a lotus-shaped brass holder, fragranced oil scattered with rose petals, no flame, the wick smoking, dispersing sweet-scented wisps into the close air.

In the centre of the room is a vast bed, draped with sari curtains, which the maids must have rigged up. They stand reverently beside the bed, from within which emerge moans at periodic intervals, and speak softly. After a bit, they gently part the curtains aside.

What surprises Clara, at this first glimpse of the maharani, is how very *young* she is. When Clara and the Adamses were rudely pushed aside on the gangplank to allow the royals to be carried onto the ship, the palanquins had been covered with silks, so mere commoners and, especially, no men would be allowed sight of the maharanis.

Barely sixteen, Clara surmises, at most a few months older than Clara herself when her mother died and she came to live with Aunt Helen and Danny. Tears have pooled around the maharani's huge eyes and freckled her cheeks, Clara can see as she turns her tormented face towards her. Despite the opulence in which she is clad, the sari she is wearing setting the dark room alight with the jewels encrusted upon it, she looks so small and vulnerable in the huge, grandiose bed. Just a girl, in pain, more than a little lost and out of her depth.

Clara's surprised heart goes out to her. She bows, and as she opens her mouth to speak, she realises something she should have thought of earlier: 'Do you speak English, Your Majesty?'

'I understand well. And I can speak, but not...' the girl flounders, then smiles weakly as the word comes to her, '...fluent.'

Thank goodness for that, Clara thinks. 'That will do very well.' She smiles. 'Please could you show me where it hurts?'

As Clara conducts her examination she forgets where she is, who she is tasked with examining and what rests upon it. She becomes what she is most comfortable as – a nurse, doing what she does best. She pokes and prods, all the while keeping a soothing banter going, apologising when she touches a sore spot and the maharani winces.

Afterwards, she holds the maharani's hand and says, 'I promise, Dr Goel and I will try our best to make the pain go away.'

The maharani nods, her beautiful eyes sequinned with tears, and Clara thinks of the maharaja, that small, rotund man, with this slip of a girl and shudders.

Henry is with Dr Goel, the two of them chatting away, the lascars spraying the deck with water around them, the sea showering them with salty benediction every so often.

'And what happened to the tiger?' Henry's voice agog.

As is the case so often when she is with Henry, Clara is transported to her childhood, sitting on Father's knee, hiding her face in his chest as Paul plied him with breathless questions, and it is joy and heartache, bittersweet.

'Oh, it's still terrorising villages nearby, I imagine.' Clara can hear the indulgent smile in Dr Goel's butterscotch voice.

She luxuriates for a moment in the whisper and swell, wink and froth of the sea, the call of seagulls, the twinkling gleam of flying fish, the soothing murmur of Henry and the doctor's voices, tasting of nostalgia, inducing an ache for a time long gone, a country and family not yet ruined by illness and war.

'I'd love to see one!' Henry says to Dr Goel.

Clara clears her throat. They both look up.

'Nurse Knight! Did you cure her?' Henry asks.

Clara smiles at her eager charge. 'Not yet, but we will.'

'What's your diagnosis, Miss Knight?' Dr Goel fixes his gaze upon her.

'Acute gastritis, caused by change of diet aboard ship, I suspect.'

'Ah, I thought that might be the case.' He smiles. 'I've just the thing for it, I'll have her maids administer it at once. Thank you, Miss Knight.'

'Will she get better soon?' Henry queries.

'In the next day or two, I should think.'

'Nurse Knight, when she does, we can…'

'Ask the maharaja's permission to visit his zoo,' Dr Goel finishes for Henry, his laughing eyes the sparkling gold of water in rock pools rejoicing in sunlight.

Chapter Thirty-Two

Clara

Python at Feeding Time

Two days later, as Clara sits on a chair, cheering Henry on – his health continues to improve the further they move into the tropics – as he slips and slides on deck, which the crew are washing with water, his laughter ringing like festive chimes, she is approached by one of the maharaja's courtiers, the jewels on his turban rivalling the silvery sheen of the frolicking waves.

'The maharaja requests an audience with you,' he says solemnly in very good English.

Henry comes up to Clara, dripping water everywhere, unabashedly perusing the courtier, at once curious and suspicious. 'Where's Dr Goel?'

'He's with the maharaja already.'

Neither Clara nor Henry have seen the doctor since Clara diagnosed the maharani and all has been quiet in the first-class cabins when Clara has walked past – rather more often than strictly necessary.

Henry slips his hand into Clara's, clasping tight as they follow the courtier to the maharaja, and Clara tries to ignore the misgiving in her heart as she offers her charge what she hopes is a reassuring smile.

The previous day, Sunday, she had attended church alongside Henry and his parents. It was a makeshift church, set up each weekend in the ballroom, the previous night's dancing couples sitting sedately on chairs, looking a little worse for wear as they tried to pay heed to the vicar's sermon. Waves crashed against the ship as it swayed. Hymns sung gustily, if not quite in tune, rose up to the rafters and travelled on, into the sky all the way to the heavens. Clara had sought refuge in God and prayer, haunted by the maharani's soulful eyes, taut with pain: *Please let her be cured.*

The maharaja reclines on deck, his entourage in obsequious attendance, the ocean framed behind him, stretching to infinity, a glassy plate of shimmering aquamarine. Flying fish skitter and dart on the surface of the water, playful silver shards. The sky above, a dreamy blue that is almost white, scissored with clouds.

Dr Goel stands facing him, his back to them. It is the maharaja who sees them first, his entourage parting to let them through.

'Ah, Miss Knight and young…'

'Henry Adams, Your Majesty,' Henry says gravely.

'Master Adams.' The maharaja inclines his head, setting the myriad of jewels on his ostentatious turban a-clinking.

Dr Goel turns and beams at them.

Does this mean…?

The maharaja addresses Clara. 'Miss Knight, not only are you beautiful but you are a skilled healer as well.'

A sudden breeze tasting of the sea flings salty wet droplets on her face even as her heart sings, *the maharani is well.*

'My favourite maharani is quite restored.' A pregnant pause while he regards her speculatively. 'But I lie.'

What?

Even Dr Goel appears shocked – this is news to him too.

'Pardon me, Your Majesty?'

'She is no longer my favourite, Miss Knight, for *you* are.' The maharaja's eyes glint appreciatively. 'I have a proposition for you.'

'Your Majesty?'

'Would you be my mistress?'

Has she misheard? Surely he's not saying what she thinks he is? And in front of Henry too? A sharp intake of breath from the servants who understand English and furious whispering as they translate the maharaja's unprecedented request to their non-English speaking peers. Everyone looks to Clara, Henry and Dr Goel included. Her charge's mouth is open. Dr Goel's expression is inscrutable, his eyes the deep gold of tree bark.

'I can't offer marriage, it wouldn't do, with you being British.' The maharaja is matter of fact – he might as well be discussing the weather.

Is he quite mad?

Judging from the expansive smile directed at her, it is as if he is bestowing a great honour.

He is a man used to getting his own way, convinced his every whim will be indulged. Clara swallows, the hand not holding Henry's reaching for the St Christopher medal anchoring her frenetic heart. Summoning all her inner strength, she smiles brightly (she hopes) at the king, praying this is the right strategy: 'I am honoured, Your Majesty.' She is pleased that her voice does not betray the turbulent turmoil and anger raging in her chest. How *dare* he put her in this position? And in front of her charge too. 'But I must respectfully decline. I have been hired as nurse to Henry here and his parents would be sorely disadvantaged if I were to take up your offer.'

The maharaja's posse look nervous even as they appear poised to deal with the fallout of this heathen woman daring to stand up to their king. The moment stretches, endless, elastic, Henry's hand sticky in hers, the medal slippery in her clasp. Dr Goel is standing very still.

Then the maharaja's face is contorting, his features twisted in… a smile.

A smile!

His eyes sparkle even more appreciatively than before, admiration glowing in their nutty onyx depths. 'I do appreciate your loyalty and sense of duty towards your employers. However, you need not worry your pretty head. It's a trifling concern, easily resolved.' He beams, displaying a crowded mouthful of teeth. 'One of the maharanis' maids can take your place. They're all very good with children – I trust my own with them. That should be endorsement enough for your employers.'

As Clara grapples for an answer, Henry speaks up, his voice an octave higher than usual but ringing clear as sunlight on a cloudless summer afternoon. 'I'd like Nurse Knight to continue as *my* nurse, Your Majesty. In any case, she doesn't own a sari.' Henry is earnest. 'And she can't even speak your language.' Here, his voice rises in indignation.

Clara clutches her medal with one hand while the other squeezes the small, precious, sweaty palm of her charge.

We are in trouble.

The servants appear to be of the same opinion. They are standing to attention, ready for the fallout from this flouting of the maharaja's offer. The few out of the maharaja's eyeline are shaking their heads soberly, their kind faces green with worry, eyes fixed on Henry. Even Dr Goel appears troubled.

The maharaja throws back his head. His stomach moves. He appears to be convulsing. The servants exchange alarmed glances, even as Dr Goel hastens towards him. A choking sound escapes the maharaja, followed by what sound like rapid-fire hiccups. It is only when Clara notices Dr Goel return to where he was standing, and the servants relaxing visibly, their colour returning to normal, that she understands: the maharaja is laughing.

After a time, the maharaja wipes his eyes, the hiccupy chuckles stopping as suddenly as they had started. His attendants, Dr Goel included, beam in reciprocal, relieved mirth.

'Young man, I like you.' The maharaja addresses Henry. 'You've alleviated some of the boredom of this journey. How would you like a pearl necklace as a gift for making me laugh?'

'No, thank you,' Henry says. 'Instead, could I visit your zoo?'

'Permission granted, young man.' The maharaja smiles, teeth flashing. 'Don't get too close to the python at feeding time is my advice.'

'Thank you, Your Majesty.' Henry bows ceremoniously before turning to grin cheekily at Clara.

'Miss Knight, I thank you for curing my maharani of her ailment. If you change your mind about becoming my mistress, the offer is open. In the meantime, a pearl necklace for you. It will complement your English rose complexion perfectly.'

She does not want his pearls but she knows that refusing this too would be a step too far. He plucks a velvet pouch from beside him and hands it to her even as the courtiers ogle and Dr Goel smiles.

Even long after they've walked away, Clara can't stop shaking.

Chapter Thirty-Three

Clara

A Character

Since the maharaja granted permission, Henry has been spending all his time at the zoo, Clara accompanying him while Henry quizzes the minders about each animal's characteristics and feeding habits. He is now so conversant in the animals' care that the minders have entrusted him with the feeding and handling duties of the smaller, less dangerous animals. Clara has never seen Henry happier than when he is helping with the animals.

After his first visit to the zoo, Henry had beamed. 'Thank you, Nurse Knight, for curing the maharani. It made the maharaja happy and now I get to visit the zoo as often as I like!'

'Ah, there you are,' Dr Goel has come to find Henry and Clara.

Henry is absorbed with the animals, so the doctor joins Clara, where she is sitting a safe distance from them but near enough to keep an eye on her charge.

'The king is in a terrible mood. He has a headache and will not rest until the rest of us get one too,' Dr Goel sighs.

The sea grumbles and tumbles, whispers and agitates. The ship sways gently and the air caressing Clara's cheek is pleasantly warm, tasting of brine and contentment, burnished gold.

'Doesn't he scare you?' she asks.

'He did at first.' Dr Goel twinkles. 'But now I'm used to his blustering.'

'Nurse Knight, I fed bananas to the chimpanzees,' Henry calls, and then, 'Oh, hello, Dr Goel.'

The doctor and Henry have become fast friends, Dr Goel at ease with the young boy as they discuss the animals in the maharaja's zoo and the ones they might encounter in India, Henry treating Dr Goel like the authority on this subject.

'He's a physician, not an animal expert,' Clara once joked when Henry's questions kept on coming.

Henry shot her an annoyed glance while Dr Goel laughed, his chuckles like spilling gold, liquid warmth. 'I don't mind. Fire away, Henry.'

Now, Dr Goel says, easily, 'Hello yourself, young man.'

'It's feeding time for the snakes. Are you sure you don't want to come and see, Nurse Knight?'

'Quite sure,' Clara says.

'Would you like to watch, Dr Goel?'

'I'll pass, young man.'

'I'll see you later then.' And with that, Henry skips away.

Dr Goel smiles. 'He's a character, your charge.'

'So is yours,' she says.

He throws his head to the heavens and laughs, exploding fireworks.

'What did you give him?'

He looks at her, his face bright with mirth. 'Pardon me?'

'For his headache.'

'A placebo.'

She sits up in her chair, stares at him. This man she first saw on a fog-doused morning in a war-torn country, which seems so very far away now, his features obliterated by dirt and blood, head lolling off the stretcher, quite unconscious. Whose face she'd gently cleaned until his chocolate skin shone through. Who is now smiling at her, amusement igniting amber sparks in his caramel eyes.

'The maharaja is bored and so he dreams up illnesses. Head-aches and muscle pain, back spasms and cramps. Nothing that can't be cured by a little less eating and a little more movement. But who's to tell him?' Dr Goel shrugs. 'We can't all be like you, spurning him and getting away with it. I, for one, don't have the looks to pull it off.'

She blushes, sitting back in her chair, and Dr Goel grins wider. 'Therefore I have to be less obvious, more underhand.' He shrugs.

'But what if it really is a headache?'

'Then it's off with my own head tomorrow.'

The sea flings a spray of brine into her eyes. She blinks. 'You're joking, of course?'

She can't help her voice rising in question as she thinks of the short man, power exuding from him, his palpable wrath when informed of his favourite maharani's illness, his eyes darting venom as they fixed on Dr Goel.

The doctor sighs, his laughter disappearing. 'If it really is a headache, he'll be in even more of a mood tomorrow. I'll deal with it then.' Smiling again, 'But I'm certain it's not. I know him well enough now to gauge when he's really ill and when it's just lethargy. But never mind him.' He beams at her. 'Tell me about you, the story behind the amazing nurse.'

And again, her cheeks on fire.

The next day, when he comes looking for them, Clara is in the same spot.

Dr Goel queries, 'Did you return to your cabins at all or was young Henry here all night?'

She smiles. 'Did your placebo work?'

'The maharaja complimented me on its effectiveness. "You're a true physician," he said. "Not like the quacks I employed before. Their pills were bitter as an enemy's ire and didn't work, while yours are sweet as sugar cubes and do." I had to bite my tongue not to say, "They're sweet as sugar cubes because they *are* sugar cubes."'

She laughs.

The days get hotter the further east they travel.

Henry spends every moment he can at the zoo, on first-name terms with the animals and their keepers. Dr Goel keeps Clara company after he has tended to the maharaja's – mostly imaginary – ailments. They sit companionably, sometimes talking, sometimes not, enjoying the sunshine, the gentle lull of the waves lapping against the ship.

'I notice you stroking that medal often. Does it have a special significance?' he asks one day. She is touched that he has noticed; he is the only one.

She is hesitant, at first, to talk about the air raid. But he is looking at her with soulful eyes, this man with whom she has a connection going back to those anguished years just after she was orphaned. His eyes glimmer with sadness when she tells him of Mother gifting her the medal on the last night of her life.

'She saved you and you saved me. It is destiny,' he says, 'that led me to you.'

'Yes,' she whispers.

The air tastes sweet, the sun on her face is warm as a caress, the medal smooth to the touch.

He understands.

*

'Can I visit Maharani Maya Devi, just to make sure she's alright?' Clara asks Dr Goel, even as she thinks: *Such a grand name for that slip of a girl.*

'I'm afraid not.' His eyes glow caramel with regret. 'This maharaja is obsessed with privacy and allows very few outsiders, if any, access to the zenana – the maharanis' quarters. Your visit was a huge concession for him.'

'He acquires all these women and then they are tucked out of sight, sequestered in their wing on board the ship,' she says tartly. Then, noting that he said, *this maharaja*, 'You know many maharajas, do you?'

'I got to know a maharaja and prince or two during my time at the Imperial Service Troops,' he twinkles. 'Some of them were quite modern, limiting themselves to two or three wives only…'

'Only!'

'And not even insisting their wives remain veiled. But this maharaja, he collects wives only to keep them hidden like secrets.' Dr Goel sighs.

'What about you? Are you quite modern too?' Clara asks.

'I like to think so.' He smiles.

'How many wives is modern for you?'

'Miss Knight, I'm not royalty, so I've just the one.' He chuckles.

He is married. Why does she feel light-headed suddenly? Perhaps she's caught the sun, which she's been unabashedly courting since they sailed into more tropical climes.

Dr Goel's gaze is soft and focused east, upon the horizon beyond which India and his wife await. 'And she's more than enough for me.'

His demeanour changes when he talks of his wife, he sits up straighter, his gaze narrowing even as it shines with a secret light. Clara sits up too, moving imperceptibly away from him. An unfamiliar ache deep within her. She feels tired, trembly.

'Her name is Rathi and she will want to meet you – the woman who saved my life.' A smile in Dr Goel's voice when he says his wife's name.

'Rathi.' The syllables like pearl drops. 'A lovely name.' Her mouth is bitter, throat hoarse.

'She *is* lovely.' Again that smile, that glow to him.

The ache has spread to her whole body now. Is she coming down with one of those dreaded tropical fevers?

Dr Goel is saying, 'And although we've been betrothed since childhood…'

'Since childhood?'

'It's a Hindu custom. I know it sounds strange.'

She thinks of her parents then and her memories of their arguments and Mother's unhappiness and disillusionment. 'No stranger than falling madly in love with a man who woos you with false promises.' It felt disloyal to Father, even if it was, she understood now, the truth.

'Ah, Miss Knight, you are not only an incredible healer but wise with it. My parents were too. They chose my wife for me when I was a toddler and she just an infant, the daughter of their family friends. I don't know how they knew we were suited but we are – very much so.'

The pain is intense, all-consuming. Suddenly she longs for someone to speak of her like Dr Goel does of his wife, with love and admiration, his face lit up with an inner joy he can't contain at the mere thought of her.

I don't need anyone. My family, living within me, is enough, she reiterates in her head as she clutches the medal. But the words feel hollow and the medal slips from her sweaty grasp.

'They chose well,' she manages.

Dr Goel nods. 'I married her two years ago…'

'After you had served with the Imperial Service Troops?'

'Yes.'

She feels relieved, vindicated. It matters to her that when he was in her care he wasn't married. *Why? What on earth is wrong with me?* And again her hand seeks her medal, as it always does when she feels upset or troubled. But the cool metal is not a comfort. *Why do I need comforting? I am on my way to India, the adventure of a lifetime, something Father, Mother and Paul yearned for.*

'I'd just started working for the maharaja. I lost my parents soon after to typhoid.' His eyes shining.

'I'm sorry.'

'Rathi was wonderful through it all. Then just as we were getting onto an even keel, the maharaja decided on this trip and wanted me to accompany him. I must say, I *am* looking forward to going home.'

'I'm sure.'

And again that peculiar, all-consuming ache accompanied by an uncalled-for stab of hurt. *Stop this whimsy now.*

'I do hope you get to meet Rathi,' Dr Goel is saying. Then his eyes sparkling like the sky lit with stars, 'But I'm afraid the only way you'll get to visit the maharani is by taking up the maharaja's offer.'

Afterwards, she cannot stop thinking of the way he said, 'I *am* looking forward to going home,' his golden eyes aglow. She bats away the hurt that prods and pokes with fiery darts, thinking, *Home. I haven't found mine yet.*

But I will.

Chapter Thirty-Four

Clara

Bombay Port

Clara wakes to excitement, bustle, busyness, coloured with a palpable energy and excitement. Lascars calling to each other. The rumble and thud of trunks being dragged. Someone knocks on the door to her cabin. She checks she is respectable before calling, 'Come in.' A lascar pops his head around the door, nods at her: 'We'll be docking at Bombay Port soon, Memsahib.'

Bombay port!

The Adamses are already on deck, Henry hopping in anticipation, rubbing his palms together. 'Nurse Knight,' he exclaims. 'We're nearly there!'

Clara can hardly contain her excitement. And alongside it, a lance of pain. *I'm carrying you within me, Father, Mother, Paul. But I wish you were actually here, experiencing this charged atmosphere, this electric anticipation with me.*

Instead of dwelling on the past, she throws her head to the heavens, the light: blinding, buttery white. *And oh, the heat!* Thick and moist and pressing. Although it is only morning, steam rising from the water that is splashed onto the deck by the lascars.

The maharaja reclines as usual on the sizeable portion of the deck marked out for him, flanked by his myriad attendants, his bejewelled robes shimmering and dazzling in the blinding sunlight.

'He must be so hot, I am just looking at him,' Clara muses, Henry nodding assent.

It is only when Dr Goel approaches, smiling, and Clara feels her heart settle that she realises she was scouring the king's entourage looking for him. The doctor looks dapper in Indian clothes: a long silk shirt, silver threaded with gold that ripples in the light, and matching, flared silk trousers. He is beaming. *In anticipation of seeing his wife*, Clara thinks and the happiness she was feeling seeps away like water through a sieve.

Dr Goel greets Captain and Mrs Adams and Clara before grinning widely at Henry. 'So, young man, are you looking forward to the exotic wildlife in India?'

'I am,' Henry gushes. Then, 'You look nice, Dr Goel.'

Dr Goel's amused gaze meets Clara's over her charge's head.

Clara looks away, across the water, at the horizon, willing the port into view. Sea spray slicks her face with salty, velvet-warm caresses.

'Thanks, young man.' She hears the smile in Dr Goel's voice. The water sparkles silvery blue, surge and swell.

'Do you think the maharaja will get another wife in India?' Henry asks.

Dr Goel throws his head back and laughs, syrupy gold, and Clara thinks, *I will miss this*.

A cheer goes up among the passengers clothed in linen suits and gay dresses in summery colours, wide hats resting at jaunty angles, replacing their bright, anticipatory chatter.

Clara stumbles into Dr Goel. He puts his arms around her to steady her and she experiences an electric jolt. It is disorienting and she immediately pulls away, even as she fights the perplexing instinct to stay in those arms, to experience that thrill again. She looks to him but he's looking away, across the water, his expression hopeful and joyous.

She follows his gaze and is transfixed by the strip of red-dusted land flanked by palm trees coming into view over his shoulder.

They have arrived.

This is my *life. I'm in* India, *Father, Mother, Paul!*

Part Eleven

India

Adrift

Chapter Thirty-Five

Indira

1995, Divine Intervention

A second hospital in the space of a few hours. The same fever-blue scent of desperation and disinfectant, a bitter tang that catches at the back of Indira's throat and reeks of helplessness.

Her mother is sitting on her own, appearing lost and adrift despite being surrounded by a sea of people. A tiny woman, looking as if she has shrunk from worry, kneading the pallu of her sari as she does when she is anxious. Indira's heart goes out to her mother – why hasn't she come to see her parents before? *Why has she left it so long – too long perhaps?*

She has been juggling too many balls, work commanding all of her attention and time so everything else has slipped, been taken for granted.

'Ma,' Indira says.

Her mother looks up at her and her face lights up and falls at the same time. Tears erupt soundlessly as her face crumples. She appears so vulnerable suddenly. Indira is surprised by an impulse to hug her, to give and receive comfort in this way. But they are not that sort of family, although Indira often had the impression growing up that her mother would have loved to cuddle her and that her father wouldn't have minded either. But she was fiercely independent even as a child and while her parents respected this, overbearing relatives never did and she would endure their cheek pinches and wriggle out of their fleshy, talcum powder and sweat embraces as fast as she possibly could. Now she wishes she could take her mother in her arms, wishes the action would come easily for her. Instead, she settles for awkwardly patting her mother's hand.

'He's having heart bypass surgery,' her mother whispers, fear pulsing off her in frantic waves.

Indira is used to managing everything, to getting her way with persistence, hard work and sheer, stubborn determination. But this, she can't fix. This, she can do nothing about – and it chafes as much as it scares her. Her father is only sixty. He has many years left yet. *Hasn't he?*

Indira's parents are both quiet people. Her father has worked at the same bank all his life. Not ambitious, but rising up the ranks when it was required, when his bosses urged him to. Her mother is content to be a homemaker.

Her parents – especially her father – have never understood her ambition, her need to excel, to rise to the top of a male-dominated world.

'But why?' her father asked often, in turn perplexed and irritated. 'How will you get a husband if you insist on being smarter than all the men?'

'Why should I have a husband?' she'd retorted. 'I'm doing it for me and no one else.'

Her parents' lack of drive, their befuddlement at her own had irritated her. Almost as much as her own refusal to conform to their idea of how a woman should be had upset them in turn.

Her disinclination to even consider an arranged marriage had spawned heated, fiery arguments. When she told them she was marrying Karan, they were relieved. By that time they had given up hope that she would ever settle down.

'Now you can concentrate on building a home and family,' her father had beamed.

'I'm not giving up my job – Karan knows and accepts this,' Indira retorted.

When she was pregnant with Arun, her father tried again: 'When are you giving up work?'

'Karan has said he'll handle the childcare so I can concentrate on work.'

A part of her had enjoyed seeing the horrified shock in her father's face, while the other was hurt, wanting her parents to be proud of her, a woman succeeding in a man's world, instead of expecting her to adhere to their narrow ideal of what she should be.

She has never told them she loves them, their too-brief conversations usually escalating into argument.

'He'll be alright,' Indira whispers.

Please, she prays with all her might, to a God about whom she has always been on the fence, having never needed divine intervention before. *If you make him better, I will focus on what is important, get my priorities right, not take family for granted any longer.*

Part Twelve

India

Mystical

Chapter Thirty-Six

Clara

1925, Turbans and Skirts

Clara watches the ship dock at Bombay harbour, clutching the rail to steady herself, excitement overwhelming her as she finally finds herself in India – mystical land of her father's stories. Hungrily, she surveys the exotic vista, the squat buildings carpeted in a layer of red dust, the colourful people: men clad in multicoloured turbans and *skirts*, torsos bare and gleaming burnished ebony, women clothed in saris from head to toe glimmering in the hot, bright sunshine.

Is this what her father saw and experienced, the essence of this vibrant land furled into his very being? So much so that, when far away, desire and yearning bloomed hot and vivid and inviting, so charmingly incessant, so thoroughly tantalising that it cast a spell not only on Father but his entire family through his glorious, sun-spangled memories.

People waiting in welcome, their bright, eager faces contrasting with the yellow water, men bathing, their brown skin glittering with sun-glazed droplets. Dark-turbaned boatmen rowing colourful dinghies grin as they call out to each other, their language musical and hypnotic, teeth glittering yellow in leathery faces. The air sizzles, tasting of spices and saffron, burnt sugar, caramel gold.

Animals mingle among the crowds, cows, horses, dogs, even a hen and some pigs. A snake charmer, the snake writhing to his haunting tune. Dancing monkeys and performing bears.

'Look, a camel train.' Henry tugs eagerly at Clara's hand, his voice burnished with awe.

It is fiendishly hot, sweat beading Clara's face even though it is shielded by her hat, vigorous strokes of her small fan hardly displacing the heavy, humid air. Beside her, Henry dances from foot to foot, unable to contain his delight at the sheer array of exotic beasts.

Clara is overcome by fondness for this boy, his boundless love of animals, his avid curiosity and zesty enthusiasm, who brings to life, vividly, the brother she was worried she was beginning to forget.

The ship gently nudges into their berth at the pier to another great cheer – this time the throng waiting on shore joining those on deck in applause and celebration.

'Home at last,' Dr Goel breathes.

Clara fingers her St Christopher medal and thinks of her brother and mother, who had both hoped to come here one day, her father who'd yearned to return to his childhood home.

I will cherish every moment, live it for you as well as for myself. It promises to be every bit as magical as I'd come to expect from your stories, Father. The amalgam of languages, strange and melodic, the noise, the chaos, the aromas, spicy sweet, the dramatic heat, the colourful attire, the orange-red dust…

She closes her eyes. Feels the sun on them, beating white gold.

'Miss Knight.' Dr Goel.

She opens her eyes. A courtier is standing next to Dr Goel, looking at her but talking to him in the native language.

'Yes?'

'The maharaja wishes to offer you the use of one of his cars for your onward journey as thanks for your help in curing his maharani.'

Above her, in the wide, cloudless, unfamiliar sky, the sun shines. People laugh, converse, greet their loved ones in a welter of languages, bursts of sound and colour. Dr Goel smiles radiantly at her.

Chapter Thirty-Seven

Clara

A Sleek, Purring, Gleaming Machine

The maharaja's car is a sleek, purring, gleaming machine.

'I say, the latest model Rolls-Royce, with custom-made gold plates!' Captain Adams exclaims in delight, 'You did well, Miss Knight.'

Clara can't help but revel in the Adamses' pleasure. Her time in India is off to an adventurous, glamorous start. If only it didn't involve saying goodbye to Dr Goel, who has, over the course of the journey, become a good friend to both her and Henry.

'I'll be in touch once you're settled in, Miss Knight,' Dr Goel, who hasn't stopped smiling since they docked at Bombay port, glowing at being reunited with his wife, reiterates, prior to parting ways. 'My wife will want to thank you for saving my life.'

My wife. The palpable joy humming from those syllables in his musical voice makes her ache.

'This is *not* goodbye, Miss Knight,' he adds as he hands her into the car, his touch igniting sparks upon her skin. 'Until we meet again.'

And with a nod and a smile, he shuts the door and steps away, leaving her with an impression of caramel eyes and butterscotch voice soothing as a lullaby, her arm thrumming where he touched it.

She and Henry wave until Dr Goel disappears in the haze of red dust displaced by the car. He is a friend. Like Dolly, like Meg. So why is his image blurring long before the screen of dirt obliterates him, why is her mouth bitter with brine, her heart heavy as if she has lost, why is she hurting when she should be excited, on the cusp of the greatest adventure of her life?

This new, vastly different country, decked out in beautiful red and green and gold colours, flashes past as the car picks up speed. Veiled women in colourful saris, anklets chiming, balancing baskets upon their heads and carrying infants on their hips with apparent ease. Men, only a small loincloth covering their hips, their brown bodies gleaming. Emerald fields capped with dust. Bright white sun.

The hot sweet scent of baked earth, potent with spices. She can taste the air, heavy and humid – it should smack of possibility, but instead it is weighted with loss. *I am sad Father, Mother and Paul are not here. They are in my heart but I'd rather they were actually experiencing this with me.*

So why, when she closes her eyes, is the image that rises in front of closed lids that of a man waving at the car, receding further and further into the distance in a film of salt?

Out of the city and onto unpaved roads. Villages – mud huts squatting, burnished amber, shimmering in the heat haze. Children clad in only a sheen of dust, orange bodies and faces, even their dark hair dusted saffron, yellow teeth in grinning mouths, shining black eyes, jumping out of the way of the car while waving frantically at them.

Sometime during the journey, Clara must have fallen asleep, for she is jolted awake by Henry's voice, bright with delight: 'Nurse Knight, we're nearly there.'

They're passing a hamlet, as quaint as it is tiny: thatched cottages flanking dirt roads so narrow the car can barely pass through. A bullock cart coming from the opposite direction has to wait in the ditch, the bullocks shaking their great heads, their horns almost scratching the maharaja's car, earning an indrawn breath and muttered incantation from the chauffeur and exclamations of ecstatic delight from Henry.

Once he is reassured that the bullocks will not damage the car, the chauffeur asks the bullock cart owner for directions. He nods vigorously, gesticulating towards the hill looming behind the village. They pass a tented shop selling saris and another hawking bangles, glass jewellery and trinkets, glittery dazzle. A bakery, the scent of spicy dough, all manner of sweetmeats in gaudy colours, the owner gathering yellow globules with a slotted spoon from a sizzling vat, which he drops with a sticky splash into a vat of syrup. The tantalising aroma of spun sugar and caramel, cinnamon and mixed spice.

They turn the corner and see, rising atop a hill, a mansion, breathtaking, all lit up and haloed by the sun. The car climbs the hill, overtaking women in saris the colours of earth and rust, sun-splashed water, sequinned with glittering stars reflecting the sky. Their faces covered, anklets and bangles jingling, balancing pots of water on their heads while carrying more on their hips, mud-clothed children hanging off their sari skirts.

They turn another corner and stop for a man herding goats off the road, a cacophony of bleating. As with the bullocks, Henry is absolutely riveted. He pushes open the door, skips out and asks the goatherd, 'Can I touch them?'

'Henry!' His mother is shocked. 'I don't think it's…'

But Henry's attention is fixed upon the man, whose face is scrunched in incomprehension even as he gently pushes away the horns of a goat that is butting his hip. Henry imitates the action and somehow the man understands. He nods, flashing Henry a gap-toothed smile, almost all his teeth missing and the few that are left rotting away. He is wearing only a loincloth and a turban, both soaked through with perspiration, which runs in rivulets down his hairy torso.

Henry squints against the sun as he tenderly strokes the goat nearest him. It is the same height as him and when it butts him, his mother flinches, as does Clara, but Henry beams as if he's been bestowed the greatest blessing.

Captain Adams laughs. 'I do believe this country is going to be good to our boy, Pat.'

The women whom they had overtaken moments ago pass in a musical mass, expertly gliding through the herd of goats, their children gawping at the car and at Henry, pale among the goats and the tanned goatherd, Henry's mother watching anxiously from the car, her hands clasped together, knuckles glowing white.

The goats are impatient, shaking their horned heads and stamping their hooves. The driver of the maharaja's Rolls grimaces; in all this time, his eyes have never strayed from the herd, one hand on the steering wheel, poised to move the car if any of the animals so much as takes a step closer to it. The goatherd clicks his tongue at his butting herd of unruly goats and off they go down the hill in the sweltering heat, the turbaned, bare-chested, toffee-skinned man and his animal train.

Henry climbs back in the car, looking fatigued but elated, the skin on his forehead where the goat butted him a little red and sore. As the car starts, Clara stares at the mansion up ahead, shimmering like a mirage. Her home for the next year. *I will be happy here*, she promises herself, breathing in the hot, spiced air, pushing away the heaviness weighing down her heart.

Chapter Thirty-Eight

Clara

1926, Siesta

'One more lap,' Henry commands, hands on hips.

'Not another one,' Clara remonstrates.

Henry has thrived in India, his asthmatic wheezing and sickliness a thing of the past. He is glowing, growing, happy. He loves to read and learn – he asked his father for a tutor to teach him Hindi and Captain Adams was only too pleased to oblige.

Every afternoon when, as per the tradition here, everyone has their siesta, from Henry's mother – who has enthusiastically embraced this aspect of life – to his tutor, from the sweeper to the head servant, Henry undertakes to teach Clara the Hindi he has learned. There's a hierarchy to the servants, Clara has come to understand, the lower castes doing the lowliest jobs, the Hindu chef not touching beef, his Muslim assistant shying away from pork, each of these cuts of meat being cooked in a different annexe of the kitchen – yes, the kitchen has several annexes in this vast mansion.

She can speak Hindi nearly fluently now, thanks to Henry's exhortations. If she gets something wrong, she has to run laps of the grounds in front of the house, up to the gate and back again.

'To make it fair, I will run too, after you've finished.'

'Why can't we run together?'

'Because I'll beat you, of course and I don't want to shame you, Nurse Knight.' He grins mischievously.

'Cheeky boy,' she chides and he grins wider.

Secretly she's pleased. He's not making an empty claim – he will beat her hands down and it is *wonderful*; when they first arrived, he couldn't manage a lap without collapsing in a wheezing fit. He has fallen in love with India, as have the Adamses, and they are looking to extend their stay.

'Would you stay on, Miss Knight?' Captain Adams asked her, his gaze grave. 'We will understand, of course, if you want to leave.'

I don't have anything, anyone waiting for me in England. And she loves this country too.

'Please stay, Nurse Knight,' Henry pleaded.

'Henry…' his father admonished.

'Of course I'll stay, Henry.' Clara smiled. 'I'm not fluent in Hindi yet.'

Henry's laughter incandescent in the fragrant evening.

'You didn't say the last sentence properly, you mixed up your tenses so you have to do your lap.'

Clara sighs loudly for Henry's benefit, although she doesn't mind at all. She quite likes running in the fragrant courtyard, shady with fruit trees, Henry cheering her on from the veranda, almost everyone else, including the gardeners, slumbering in the golden afternoon sunshine.

Clara loves this time and so does Henry – they get up to all sorts, playing hide-and-seek, finding and cataloguing animals and insects (Henry's favourite activity, and if left to him, it is all they'd do), exploring the house's many hidden corners. With Henry, Clara is discovering the joys of childhood, which she missed when she had to grow up too quickly after Paul's death and the advent of war.

If there is a cloud that has marred her stay, it is memories of a certain medic, which intrude into every day and even inveigle themselves into her dreams. *He's so close*, her heart sighs, *and yet he might as well be on the moon. He said he'd be in touch but he hasn't been.*

Of course he hasn't, her conscience retorts. *He's married, he has commitments. He's just a friend whose company you enjoyed on board the ship. Just a friend.*

She closes her eyes, lifts her face up to the gilded rays, tasting of nectar and exertion, baked dust and hot earth, revelling in the rhythm of her footfall, sizzling air rushing against her body.

'Watch out!' she hears and her eyes fly open even as she collides, headlong, into a human wall, the embrace of solid arms. The thud, thud of a heart beating against her face. Enveloped by the ginger and sandalwood scent that wafts through her dreams. An electric jolt travelling through her. She pulls away, nonplussed.

'Running away already, Miss Knight?'

'Dr Goel!' Her voice is breathless. It comes out a squeak. 'Welcome.' Better.

'Are you sure?' he twinkles. 'Or shall I give you a lift to the port?'

She laughs. So happy to see him again.

'I've missed your laughter, like glorious bells ringing in celebration.'

I've missed you. The thought in her head, wrongfooting her.

She strokes her medal. It will ground her. *And yet…*

Even before she saw who it was, she had known him. In his arms, she felt secure, charged, heady. She wanted to stay in them forever even as she pulled away. She already misses that sensation: intoxicating, thrilling. She wants to touch him to see if she will feel it again.

Stop.

'Nurse Knight,' Henry calls, 'why have you stopped?'

And again, she is disorientated. Has Henry read her mind?

But Henry is squinting, a hand shading his forehead: 'Oh!' Running up to join them. 'Dr Goel! It's lovely to see you. Are you still the maharaja's physician? How is his zoo? I've heard the one at the palace is—'

'Henry!' Clara admonishes, smiling. She can't stop smiling. 'One question at a time. And perhaps after the doctor is settled indoors with a cold drink?'

Dr Goel chuckles. 'I've missed you, young man.'

Have you missed me?

'And how you've grown. Look at you, quite brown too, nearly my colour.'

Henry laughs with delight and immediately holds his hand against Dr Goel's, comparing skin tones.

Dr Goel laughs. She breathes in the glorious sound, silver bright, infectious. *Why have you stayed away?* Out loud, she asks, 'To what do we owe the honour of your visit?'

'Ah,' Dr Goel beams at Henry and Clara in turn, 'now that's a story and a half.'

Chapter Thirty-Nine

Clara

Reason

'You look well, young man,' Dr Goel says to Henry as they amble up to the house.

Clara studies him. She can't look away. He is the one who looks well. India and married life suit him. She wonders at the woman who has a right to those arms (does she experience a thrill at his touch?), whose name – *Rathi* – he says with such love, that secret glow.

She swipes aside these involuntary thoughts that keep on coming and concentrates instead on guessing at the reason for the doctor's unprecedented visit – that look he gave her when he said, 'a story and a half.' Does he have need of her services as a nurse? Is it to do with the maharanis, like on board the ship, perhaps?

Did he miss her like…

She's had a wonderful time here this past year, there's never a dull moment with Henry around, but with her charge's health on an even keel, and even with looking after and sorting the medical issues of the household, she's still not doing much nursing. And although she hasn't missed it *that* much, she wouldn't mind helping Dr Goel at all if that is the reason he's here. That's why she's happy. *That's all.*

As they approach the veranda, Henry pipes up, 'I've started a zoo here. Would you like to see it?'

'Henry,' Clara interjects, 'perhaps once Dr Goel has had some refreshments…'

'It's alright, I'm not tired.' Dr Goel smiles at Clara. Then, to Henry, 'Lead on, young sir.'

Henry beams. Then, turning to Clara, he asks kindly, 'Would you like to join us, Nurse Knight?'

Yes, I don't want to spend a minute away from him now he's here.

Firmly, she pushes the inclination away. 'No, thanks. I'll let your mother know Dr Goel's here.'

Clara makes her way indoors to alert Mrs Adams to Dr Goel's presence and inform the servants that there will be a guest for tea. She can hear pots clanking, giggles and chatter, the music of anklets, the scent of onions sizzling, brewing tea, sugar caramelising, honey-sweet – siesta is over, the servants are awake.

Captain Adams returns just as tea is served alongside fruit cake rich and dense with dates, raisins and cashew nuts, cucumber and mint chutney sandwiches, spicy samosas, creamy laddoos and nectary jalebis.

'I say, Dr Goel, what a pleasant surprise!' Captain Adams beams. 'Tuck in, do. The food in this country is capital. Have another slice of cake, man.'

Henry talks non-stop about his zoo, picking Dr Goel's brains about how to acquire more animals and where from.

'Don't pester our guest, old boy,' Captain Adams is moved to say fondly.

'It's an exchange of ideas, Father,' Henry protests hotly.

Clara and Mrs Adams hide their smiles behind their cups of tea while Dr Goel says, gravely, 'I quite agree with Henry, sir.'

Henry grins happily at the doctor through a mouthful of cake.

*

Afterwards, they retire to the veranda, the adults reclining on cane chairs with Henry in the hammock, jasmine- and earth-scented breeze caressing their cheeks.

Dr Goel says, 'Thank you for making me so very welcome. I have a favour to ask.'

'Yes?' Captain Adams queries, taking a sip of the lime juice he adores, very strong, with a pinch of sugar and lots of ice cubes, made from limes from the orchard, poured into a tall glass that is dotted with condensation from the gently melting ice.

Dr Goel clears his throat. 'I'm afraid I need Miss Knight's help again. One of the maharanis is about to go into labour and the wise women the maharanis consult have declared she'll die and there's nothing they can do…'

'They've told her she'll *die*?' Clara is shocked.

'I'm afraid so. Given your track record with maharanis, the maharaja asked if you could kindly help.'

'I say, the poor maharani! We have no objection, if you're willing, Miss Knight?' Captain Adams says.

'Of course,' Clara says.

'It's a matter of some urgency – the maharani has had a difficult time of it and her maids report that her condition has worsened this morning. I think her body is readying for the birth; I suspect she'll go into labour in a day or two. The maharaja would like you to come as soon as possible.' Dr Goel pauses. Then, 'If it's not too inconvenient, we can set out today. It will be too late to seek an audience with the king – even though he's sanctioned your visit to the zenana, he'd never agree to allowing you in after dusk no matter how much pain his maharani is in. My wife and I would be honoured if you would stay with us tonight and we can visit the palace together tomorrow? She is looking forward to meeting you.'

My wife. That inflection – love, joy, admiration – when he speaks of her.

'I'm looking forward to meeting her,' Clara manages.

Henry, who has been listening with great concentration, asks, 'Can I come too?'

His parents exchange glances.

'Please, Dr Goel, I'd like to visit the maharaja's zoo. I heard from the courtiers that it is at least five times the size of the one on the ship.'

'Well…' his mother dithers, wringing her hands as she looks at her husband, who says to the doctor, 'Be straight with me, sir. If he accompanies you, will he be too much of a nuisance?'

'Nuisance, Father!' Henry is shocked.

'On the contrary,' Dr Goel says sincerely, 'it will be a great pleasure. The maharaja likes you, young sir, and it will be my absolute honour to have you visit my home.'

'That's settled then,' Captain Adams says, and patting his wife's hand, 'My dear, as you well know, Miss Knight will ensure Henry is looked after and comes to no harm.'

'I will,' Clara reassures Mrs Adams and she smiles, her furrowed brow clearing, even more so when Henry jumps off the hammock and throws his arms around her: 'Thank you, Mother.' His whirlpool of delighted laughter perfumes the air, heady sweet.

Chapter Forty

Clara

Hallowed Space

'Thanks for coming to our aid again, Miss Knight,' Dr Goel says as they set off.

'I'm looking forward to visiting the zenana, the hallowed space where no male is allowed.' *And to my time with you.*

'And I,' Henry pipes up, 'cannot wait to see the zoo.'

Dr Goel and Clara exchange a smile over Henry's tousled head. She has missed this gentle companionship she had shared with him on board the ship, which they have slipped back into as easily as a beloved coat. He is her friend and she is happy to be with him.

That is all.

Their journey is punctuated by stops and starts as, to Henry's delight, the road seems to hold a strange fascination for all manner of wildlife. They congregate right in the centre of it, the driver cursing as he brakes sharply: cows, dogs, hens, bullocks, a gaggle of peacocks showing off to their mates, their kaleidoscopic fans shimmering gloriously, and a troop of dancing, entirely unconcerned monkeys who take their time getting off the road, despite the driver shooing, sounding the horn and shaking his fists – they shake their fists right back at him, chittering and grinning, wildly amused.

When, from the top of a hill they spy a felled tree, thick and very long, straddling the road, the driver sighs deeply as he comes to another weary stop.

'Right, Henry, I think we'll have to help the driver move it. Coming?' Dr Goel says, his hand on the door of the car.

'Or perhaps it will move by itself,' Clara breathes in awe and incredulity, as the log undulates lazily.

'I say,' Henry is beside himself with astounded delight, 'a real, live *python*!'

It is huge and seemingly endless. They watch breathlessly as it gracefully makes its way off the road, Clara reminded, with a bittersweet pang of nostalgia, of her father's stories a lifetime ago.

Often the disconnect between where she is now and that family sitting in the small but cosy living room of their house in London, the sounds of the city filtering in, alongside the scents of the supper they'd just had, gravy and boiled cabbage, is too huge. There was no war then, no indication of what was to come. It feels as if it happened to another person altogether, a different, naive child who listened to her father's stories nestled securely against his chest, unable to imagine the country he was describing with its potent sun and animals that sounded like fairy-tale monsters.

The python is still going, the many folds of its magnificent body unwinding sinuously.

'Can I touch it?' Henry asks.

'Absolutely not,' Clara says at the same time as Dr Goel murmurs apologetically, 'I'm afraid that's a bad idea, young man. It could swallow you in a gulp and still have space for me too.'

Clara shudders.

Henry's eyes are fixed on the python's long yellow body, unblinking, greedily taking in every detail. He sighs sadly when its tail finally disappears into the foliage of the forest beside the road and the driver starts the car with an assertive vroom.

*

'So, what do you think is the matter with the maharani?' Clara asks, gritty air tasting of adventure stroking her face. Henry has fallen asleep, tired out from all the excitement.

'It is the youngest of the maharaja's wives who needs expert help, his favourite of the moment.' Dr Goel smiles warmly at Clara when he says 'expert help' and she glows. 'She's had a difficult pregnancy and the last time the wise woman whom the maharanis usually consult visited, she prophesied that the maharani and her child would die. That terrified the maharani, of course. Her maids summoned another wise woman. She too spoke of bad omens and forecasted doom. The maharani was inconsolable and the maharaja, who cannot stand fuss and hates being bothered by womanly matters, so he says, when he has a kingdom to run—'

'She's his favourite maharani,' Clara interjects. 'Isn't he worried?'

'He abhors anything disrupting his peace of mind,' Dr Goel says. 'He gave me unprecedented permission to visit the ante-chamber to the zenana to consult with the maharani's maids. The first man to be allowed anywhere near the zenana – other than the maharaja himself, of course.'

'No need to sound so smug,' Clara teases.

He chuckles.

She realises that she is completely happy in this moment. Her charge asleep and her friend beside her, his laughter like flowing nectar, his gaze warm as it settles on her. 'What happened next?'

'The zenana, as you will see for yourself, is located in the interior of the palace, a whole, vast section set apart for the ever-expanding coterie of the maharaja's wives and guarded even more securely than the palace itself. I was met at the forecourt to the zenana by a eunuch called Shalimar. The courtier who had accompanied me wilted under Shalimar's disapproving glare and the words, "I'll take it from here," uttered through gritted teeth.' Dr Goel chuckles. 'Eunuchs are the only non-females other than the maharaja to have access to the zenana, but even they are not allowed into the living quarters.'

The scented breeze whispers silken secrets, laced with intrigue.

'From the forecourt, there were even more maze-like corridors. I tell you, the zenana is better fortified than any prison! Finally, after it felt like we had been walking forever, we came to the cloistered-off section. There was a gate and a grille. If it was a prison, it was a sweet-smelling one, perfumed with roses and incense.'

'And?' Clara is breathless.

'I was issued instructions by Shalimar: "The maharani herself is being brought here, despite her very delicate state. Don't look at her. Speak to her, if you must, through the grille, with your back turned to her." "But how do I make a diagnosis if I can't even look at her, let alone examine her?" I asked. "You're the doctor, it's your *job*," Shalimar's voice sounding deeper the more annoyed she got. "But I need to…" I protested. She cut me off with, "No examining. No looking. And *definitely* no touching."'

Clara laughs. 'What happened next?'

'There was a very long, and on my part, anxious, wait. Shalimar did not attempt to make conversation. I could smell her sweat although she had liberally doused her sari in perfume. The small room we were in felt claustrophobic. Just when I was getting desperate for fresh air, the clinking of anklets indicated that the maharani had arrived with her train of maids.' He pauses. 'I was facing away, like Shalimar had instructed. I asked what problems she had been experiencing in her pregnancy. Shalimar looked at me as if I was crazy. "You can't ask that! It's too personal." So

I asked, "What did the wise women say the problem was?" Of course, Shalimar had a problem with that too.'

'She did?'

'"You're supposed to diagnose the maharani, not ask her about the wise women's diagnoses and upset her more."' Dr Goel's voice throaty as he imitated Shalimar.

'And?'

'I was at a loss as to what to do so I asked Shalimar to ask the maharani if anything hurt. "Of course she's hurting, that's why she's come to you!" Shalimar retorted. It was the last straw. "You're supposed to translate my question, not question me," I snapped. "I don't know why the maharaja keeps you on," she muttered, but she did relay my query to the maharani. The maharani made a sound of pain. A wounded whimper.'

'A whimper?'

'Which Shalimar replicated and by this time I didn't have the energy to protest that a whimper didn't need translation.'

Clara can't help it; she bursts out laughing. Beside her Henry stirs, his hot little head resting against her arm.

'You really have a wonderful laugh.' Dr Goel's voice is admiring as Clara wipes her eyes with her handkerchief.

'So what happened next?' she asks through her blushes.

'They went back and forth.'

'The whimpers?'

'The whimpers.' Dr Goel sighs.

Clara chuckles.

'It wasn't funny then, I assure you.'

'I imagine not. And definitely not for the maharani.'

'In desperation, I repeated my question, "Where does it hurt?" The maharani cried out, "Here." I turned and immediately Shalimar's hand shot out and pushed my head back. She said if I looked again, I would be shot.'

'No!'

'She said, "The maharani is in excruciating agony, both physical and mental." As if on cue, the maharani cried out. "She has come to meet you despite it, for you are her last chance. She's the maharaja's favourite wife, as you know. You *must* cure her." And then she grumbled under her breath, "Although I don't hold out much hope."'

'Oh!'

'The maids are experienced at pregnancy and childbirth, having guided the other maharanis through theirs, but they're at a loss. There must be something the matter if the wise women predicted death – I have a suspicion the baby's breech.'

'Oh.'

'She needs someone trained with her to help, which is why I thought of the best.'

Even his glowing smile cannot ease the trepidation creeping up on Clara and she says, 'It will be a difficult birth.'

'Yes, but I've absolute faith in you, Miss Knight, as does the maharaja. When I reported back to him that the maharani would need an expert present at the birth, he yelled at me for five whole minutes, at the end of which he cried, "Since you're not doing what I pay you to do, why don't you find the nurse who cured my maharani Maya Devi during our voyage from England and bring her here to help my maharani, Usha Devi?"' Dr Goel twinkles at Clara. 'Miss Knight, as I said, I've the greatest faith in you. That said, I've warned the maharaja of the risks involved. I promise, if he rages, I'll take the punishment.'

'And what will it be?' she whispers.

'Off with my head.'

She shudders.

'I'm joking, of course. He's all bluster. And in any case, he likes you – I seem to recall a certain proposition he made.'

'I'd rather be swallowed by a python.' Clara grimaces.

Henry stirs as if knowing, even in sleep, that she's mentioned something that interests him enormously.

Dr Goel smiles at her, his eyes glowing in the gilded, rose-tinted evening.

Chapter Forty-One

Clara

A Lovely Surprise of Green

'Welcome to my home, Miss Knight, Master Henry.' Dr Goel beams.

Dr Goel's house is colourful and sprawling in the exotic Indian style. A festive celebration of flowers trail down walls painted in bright, cheery hues. It is as if the house is smiling at them in warm welcome.

It is built around a central, vast, inner courtyard – a lovely surprise of green, boasting a fountain and plant beds profuse with roses, marigolds, jasmine and hibiscus in vibrant hues. Fruit trees are heavy with produce. Peacocks roam, calling out in their shrill voices, their fans shimmering violet.

A sari-clad, veiled maid leads them through the tastefully furnished rooms, her anklets tinkling a merry tune with every step, the marble floor polished to shining. In the courtyard, a woman sits by the fountain, her hand dangling in the rainbow-freckled water. She is small, covered head to toe in a dazzling sari the glinting navy of starry midnight, sequinned with secrets.

'I'll let my wife know you're here,' Dr Goel says, nodding at the woman.

Clara looks towards the door through which they entered the courtyard. 'Shall we wait inside?'

'If you would, please. We'll be along shortly.' He smiles.

As Dr Goel approaches his wife, she turns, pulling her veil back to reveal her face. She is stunning. Clear skin. Rosebud lips.

Her silken ebony hair pulled back into a plait. High cheekbones, chiselled perfection. Dr Goel's eyes never leave his wife's face as he speaks. He tenderly tucks the stray strand of hair dancing upon her forehead behind her ear.

She smiles at him, an exotic flower unfurling in the caress of sun. An intensely private moment – Clara feels she is intruding upon them. But she can't look away, even as something hot and bitter floods her chest.

'Nurse Knight, this is quite an adventure, isn't it?'

Caught up in watching the doctor with his wife, she has forgotten about Henry beside her. A burst of warm breeze carrying the scent of roasting spices and sweet tropical fruit chides Clara even as it gently strokes her cheek.

Dr Goel brings his wife over to them. Her face is covered again, only her eyes showing. Huge, almond shaped, beautiful. They flit animatedly between Clara and Henry. She joins her palms together in welcome, arcs of water spraying dazzling rainbows, complementing her dancing, starry gaze.

'Namaste, Miss Knight, welcome! I am so very grateful to you, my husband's guardian angel.' She speaks perfect English and her voice is as beautiful as her eyes.

Clara feels colour flooding her cheeks. 'Oh, he exagger—'

'Miss Knight,' she waves her hand, bangles tinkling in musical medley, 'I know that if it wasn't for you, he wouldn't be here.'

And before Clara can interject, she turns to Henry and her eyes twinkle gaily. 'And you must be Master Henry, the world's greatest animal lover.'

'I don't know if I'm the world's *greatest*, but I am an animal lover, yes,' Henry says gravely. 'Pleased to meet you, Mrs Goel.'

'An absolute pleasure to make your acquaintance, Master Henry.'

Henry is charmed by her, Clara notes.

Dr Goel is looking at his wife with affection and pride.

Nobody has ever looked at me that way.

He very tenderly takes his wife's hand. It ignites an ache deep within Clara. She is overcome by the urge to weep. Her hand snakes to her St Christopher medal. The metal is unforgivingly cold and hard; it does not offer the solace she suddenly, desperately needs.

Chapter Forty-Two

Clara

Feast

Mrs Goel has arranged for a feast in their honour. The dining table is swamped with food, maids arriving with more dishes, different varieties of rice and bread, curries and sweetmeats, every morsel perfectly spiced.

After dinner, they sit in the central courtyard, twilight settling fragrant around them. Dark, shadow-dusted flowers dance in the fruity breeze, the pale cream blooms of aromatic jasmine painted velvet navy by encroaching night.

'Can you say, "What is your name?" in Hindi?' Mrs Goel is testing Henry, at his request, on his fluency of the language.

Clara chastises herself for the pang of jealousy that stabbed her heart when Henry insisted upon sitting next to Rathi. This charming, beautiful, entertaining woman is, Clara can see, the perfect companion for Dr Goel. His eyes follow his wife, glowing with a secret, sultry light.

'That's too easy. Ask me a hard one,' Henry cries.

Peacocks spy upon them. A cat jumps onto Clara's lap. The air smells of spices and caramelised sugar. It teases her hair and dances across her skin, pleasantly warm even at this time of evening, rich and exquisitely soothing.

This is Dr Goel's home, his life. No wonder he was eager to get back to it when on board the ship. *Why doesn't he get in touch?* Clara had wondered, for despite telling herself otherwise, she had missed him.

Now she sees, her heart aching, that he probably did not give her a second thought until the maharani needed help. *This is why you promised yourself not to care too deeply for anyone. It hurts*, her conscience chides.

He is just a friend.

So you say.

They sit companionably until darkness steals all the fading light. Henry yawns.

'Bedtime for you, young man,' Clara sets down her glass.

'You haven't finished your drink. I'll show Henry to his room,' Mrs Goel says.

'I'm not tired,' Henry demurs but another huge yawn gives him away.

'You have a busy day tomorrow, at the maharaja's zoo. You need to be bright and alert for it.' Mrs Goel smiles, holding her hand out to Henry.

Henry who had opened his mouth to protest, closes it again and takes her extended hand.

'Nurse Knight will be along presently – her room is right next to yours,' Mrs Goel says as they walk away.

When the music of her anklets, keeping time with Henry's chatter, has faded, Clara says, 'Your wife is lovely.'

It is the truth. So why is her mouth bitter with it?

'She is, isn't she?'

Clara is looking at the mango tree, where a bird is nesting – a parrot, she imagines, the brilliant green of limes, although all she can make out is its shadowy silhouette – but she can hear the smile gilding Dr Goel's voice.

Chapter Forty-Three

Clara

Puri Bhaji

The next morning, Clara barely touches the puri bhaji, melt-in-the-mouth globes of puffed, deep fried dough served with cumin, coriander, turmeric and mustard spiced potatoes, which since she came to India has become one of her favourite breakfast dishes, or helps herself to the chilli, pepper- and lime-seasoned mango, papaya and watermelon salad, which is another. Like the maharani, she has a pain in *her* stomach. It is anxiety. Fear.

When she agreed to Dr Goel's request on behalf of the maharaja, she was excited, looking forward to the adventure, to spending time with Dr Goel and to helping the maharani. But now that it is about to happen, she is recalling how scary her encounters with the maharaja were – she was always on a knife-edge, it was like playing a game with very high stakes. She knows he doesn't like to be thwarted, it was obvious from the reactions of his staff, how they always appeared to be on tenterhooks.

She couldn't sleep the previous night, time stretching and tormenting, interminable, although the room allotted to her was luxurious and equipped with every comfort. She was imagining Dr Goel's wife in his embrace, wanting, despite desperately trying not to, those arms to steady her, those eyes to look at her with that secret glow, calm her worry: *What if I cannot help the maharani?*

Henry, she is glad to see, is his usual self, hardly able to eat but in his case due to excitement. He and Mrs Goel chatter away and Clara is glad of the distraction and feels renewed shame at that stab of jealousy the evening before when Henry asked to sit with Mrs Goel and at wanting her husband to look at Clara the way he looks at her.

I don't really. It's just worry about the maharani that is making me feel this way. He's just a friend.

If she repeats it often enough, perhaps she will believe it and all those other involuntary, unwanted, uninvited thoughts will disappear…

As they are leaving for the palace, Mrs Goel says, 'Miss Knight, a moment, please. You go ahead, Henry, with my husband.'

Dr Goel's wife takes Clara's hand in both of hers and looks into her eyes, her chocolate gaze tinted with solemnity. 'You saved my husband when no one else would and countless others during the war and the terrible epidemic after. The maharani is lucky to have you, the very best in all of India and England, assisting her. In a few hours she will be celebrating, for you will have helped her deliver her child safely.'

She places one hand upon her heart, the other still clasping Clara's: 'I know it here.' She pats her chest, the sequins on the maroon veil framing her face aglow in the morning sunshine, her eyes shining with sincerity. 'My husband has been working for the maharaja for years now and there have been times he's got things wrong. Believe me, the maharaja is not as bad as he makes out. And even if he was, he wouldn't dare do anything to a British citizen. But having said that…' She squeezes Clara's hand hard before letting go, smiling widely, '…it will not apply to you, as all will be well.'

Clara leaves Dr Goel's house with a much lighter heart, charmed and touched, despite herself, by the doctor's wife – a gem of a woman who divined Clara's worry and self-doubt and in her sincere, unobtrusive way, attempted to soothe it.

*

Henry asks to sit in front beside the driver on the way to the palace, the better to observe the animals that are sure to saunter onto the road, untroubled by approaching vehicles, taking their own sweet time to move away.

And sure enough, while they are waiting for a cowherd to usher his mooing flock across the road, a camel train ambles past and Henry is transfixed, noting the interactions between the camels and the cows, peppering the driver with a thousand questions in Hindi, each of which he has to repeat to be understood as the driver insists he speaks with an accent.

'But Mrs Goel understood me perfectly,' Henry complains – although not for long, as the need to know the answers takes precedence.

While he's so occupied, Clara turns to Dr Goel. He's next to her, close enough to touch, but she cannot take pleasure in his company, however innocent it might be – it feels wrong, given his wife's kindness and generosity. In any case, her nerves about her impending duty have briefly pushed aside her complicated feelings for him. She asks, 'How do you cope with being the maharaja's physician? Isn't it incredibly stressful?'

Dr Goel smiles. 'It was, initially. For the first few months, I was a bundle of nerves.'

A barber has set up shop beside the road, a small cloth awning held up by chopped tree trunks, an old sheet masquerading as towel to wrap around the customer, a pair of scissors and a mirror that he gives the customer to hold, the chopped hair falling conveniently into the drain beside him, which also carries vegetable peelings from the snack vendor, who dips the vegetables in a big bowl of batter and drops them into the vat of oil he has bubbling over an open fire with a hiss and a sizzle, fish entrails being chopped and scaled by fisherwomen right there by the road, fought over by a legion of skinny cats and alive with flies.

The camels and the cows navigate around all this busy bustle and there are no accidents.

'Gradually, I realised he is just a hypochondriac who likes attention and to make a fuss. As you observed on board the ship, much of the time I placate him with placebos,' Dr Goel is saying.

'But surely sometimes he believes they don't work?'

'Often,' Dr Goel says cheerfully. 'He issues all sorts of threats. The first time he did so, I was terrified, I must admit. But he asks for stronger pills – more placebos,' he winks, 'sleeps on it and the next day he is fine, more often than not. He doesn't brood and that's to his credit.'

'The maharanis?' she asks.

The camel train has passed and the cowherd has finally managed to successfully usher his cows off the road. The driver starts the car with a sigh. Henry is still bombarding him with questions.

'They consult a succession of wise women, so I'm told. When the advice of one doesn't work, another is summoned. This is the only time I've been called in, excepting that time on the ship, when thankfully, you helped. And now, once again, you're doing so.' Dr Goel smiles. Then, warmly, 'You've nothing to worry about. The maharaja knows it's a complicated birth and he is grateful for your help.'

His warmth warming her, his smile easing her worries, lifting her spirits – this man has this effect on her. Children with hollow stomachs and protruding ribs stare at her with haunted eyes in gaunt faces, grouped in front of cracked mud huts too small to contain them, let alone whole families, their mothers tending to pots billowing steam, boiling on outdoor hearths.

I've nothing to worry about. Compared to them, I'm so very lucky and blessed.

Chapter Forty-Four

Clara

Duty

'Ah, Miss Knight, looking lovelier than ever. Reconsidered my proposal, have you? I knew you'd come round,' the maharaja twinkles.

One hand surreptitiously touching her medal, Clara manages to coax her voice to sound normal, light yet firm: 'Your Majesty, I'm afraid it's still no.'

The courtiers who can understand English flinch even as they stare open-mouthed from her to the maharaja, earning nudges from the ones who don't know the language to explain what's happening.

'I'm still looking after this young man,' she goes on, indicating Henry next to her. 'He's thriving in your wonderful country and his parents are considering extending their stay here.'

'Ah, the young man who liked my zoo on board the ship. I rather think he's thriving in *your care*, Miss Knight.'

Clara exhales. She was almost sure the maharaja was joking with regards to his proposal, but it is a relief nonetheless to have it confirmed.

To Henry, the maharaja says, 'Well, young man, that small zoo on board was nothing. Wait till you see the zoo I have here.'

'Oh, Your Majesty, *can* I?' Henry can barely contain his excitement.

The maharaja graciously inclines his head: yes.

'*Thank you*, Your Majesty.' Henry beams from ear to ear.

'You're welcome. Miss Knight, are *you* happy to stay in our country for longer?'

'Oh yes, I love it here.'

'Good. So, I've time to convince you to accept my proposal then.' The maharaja winks.

The courtiers gasp, looking at Clara in amazement.

'Your Majesty, I'm honoured—'

The maharaja cuts her off. 'Miss Knight, thank you for coming to the rescue of one of my maharanis again. I have no doubt you're going to help her deliver my child safely.' He smiles sharply, snake eyes glinting, crowded teeth flashing.

He is issuing a warning, a threat via a charm offensive.

Clara clasps the St Christopher medal. *You're here to help the maharani. Your duty is to do the best you can by her, and you will.*

And when she thinks this way, she is able to breathe, subdue somewhat the panic engulfing her, smile and thank the maharaja with a steady voice.

Chapter Forty-Five

Clara

Broken Glass

A very tall, well-built woman is waiting at the end of the maze of rooms Dr Goel leads her through, Henry hurrying along in impatience and anticipation – the doctor has promised to accompany him to the zoo once they deliver Clara to the zenana.

'Are we there yet?' Henry asks as they go deeper and deeper inside, past staterooms and ballrooms, courtyards with swimming pools and others with elaborate gardens, winding staircases disappearing into turrets and towers, past paths that lead, Dr Goel says, to fortressed embankments.

Finally, 'Dr Goel, will we *ever* get to the zoo?' Henry sighs in exasperation, 'We've been walking forever and are not even at the women's section yet!'

Clara smiles despite the apprehension she can't quite keep at bay and Dr Goel is still chuckling when they reach the end of a corridor, turn the corner and are met by an amazonian woman, clad in a turmeric-yellow sari, her face caked with make-up but failing to hide the shadow of a beard and moustache.

She is grim, unsmiling, and in the glare of her censorious gaze, both Dr Goel and Clara's smiles dry up.

'This is Shalimar, she'll escort you from here,' Dr Goel says.

Ah, the infamous Shalimar who is not a fan of the doctor.

She nods at Clara, her scowl firmly in place, and with another disapproving frown at Dr Goel, she turns and starts walking, not caring to check if Clara follows.

Dr Goel casts Clara a meaningful glance before turning away, Henry waving her off a bit too enthusiastically, finally about to visit the zoo he's fantasised about. Watching his retreating back, Henry skipping beside him, Clara is bereft. She wants to join them, go with them.

You are here to help the maharani, she reminds herself and, taking a deep breath, she hurries after Shalimar, trying to keep pace with her long strides.

Shalimar leads her through even more winding corridors until they come to a gate set into high walls that are topped, Clara can see, by broken glass, the sharp, uneven edges piercing the sky, glinting forbiddingly in the blinding sunlight.

Women clad in khaki saris and matching turbans stamped with the royal insignia, sporting belts adorned with spears, cudgels and knives and carrying *guns*, patrol the walls. Three women, uniformly tall and hefty, guard the gate. They smile at Shalimar, who does not smile back, but her grim expression relaxes slightly as she converses rapidly with them.

Clara, who fancied she understood Hindi quite well, thanks to Henry's lessons, only picks up a word here and there; Shalimar is speaking too fast for her to make sense of what she is saying. The women look Clara up and down, unimpressed. One of them opens the gate just wide enough to slip inside, revealing to Clara a glimpse of immaculate lawns, replete with fountains and pools, the tinkling chime of anklets, children's laughter, glorious as applause.

Then the gate is shut. The other women go back to patrolling the high walls surrounding the gate, one on each side. The sun beats down relentlessly. Shalimar ignores Clara. She wonders whether Dr Goel and Henry have arrived at the zoo – doubtful, given the sheer scale of this palace. She hopes Henry is not disappointed by the reality of the zoo after all the build-up. She envies him Dr Goel's company and wishes the doctor was here with her. She hopes she is able to help the maharani deliver her baby safely.

Sweat trickles down her back, soaking her dress, the medal sliding gummily from her fingers. From behind the gate, sounds waft, the walls not high enough to completely shut out the musical chatter of women, the high-pitched joy of children at play.

Chapter Forty-Six

Clara

Utopia

Finally, the gate opens and the guard who went inside emerges, beckoning, unsmiling, to Clara. Shalimar, also unsmiling, nods grimly. She appears reluctant to allow Clara entry, folding her muscular arms firmly against her chest as if to stop them from holding Clara back. Clara ducks inside the gate and it shuts immediately, firmly behind her, nearly catching at her heel.

'This way, Memsahib.' A woman's voice. She speaks in Hindi but this, spoken softly and slowly, Clara understands.

The woman is small and slim, clad in a sari the celebratory ruby of joy. But the most surprising thing is that she is unveiled, her beautiful face open and smiling shyly at Clara. And then, Clara understands. The zenana is exclusively for women, even Shalimar didn't come past the gate, so there is no need for the women to shield their faces.

'Look, a visitor.' A high-pitched child's voice.

'Off with you,' the maid chuckles to the two children who have materialised before Clara, hair and clothes dusty and dishevelled, eyes glittering curiously from passionate brown faces gleaming with perspiration.

The children disregard the maid's smiling admonition, staying put, and, in a matter of moments, more appear from behind pillars and across the grounds, as if sensing her arrival via telepathy. They are all, Clara notes, around Henry's age or younger.

The maid leads her through the grounds, the children following at a discreet distance and, behind them, a posse of chattering monkeys imitating the children's every move – the children ignore the monkeys; they are too commonplace to be given attention.

And once more, Clara thinks of Henry, who, despite having seen many monkeys since they arrived in India, would nevertheless be delighted, asking questions non-stop. Her thoughts almost seamlessly move to Dr Goel, who is so patient with her charge, his eyes twinkling with amusement when chatting with Henry.

His eyes, the warmth in them. That gaze…

Enough.

The zenana is a town in itself – buildings interconnected by canopied walkways, surrounded by immaculate lawns and elaborate gardens, palm trees, rose arbours, gurgling fountains and twinkling pools – a utopia within the maharaja's palace of wonders.

Women flit about in kaleidoscopic saris like exotic birds, no veils, their hair gleaming in glorious ebony plaits. Their chatter is as gentle and soothing as the burbling waters of the various fountains dotted about the courtyards separating the regal and splendiferous multistorey, turreted buildings.

'Each of these belongs to a maharani,' the maid says. 'I am taking you to Maharani Usha's palace. We're all hoping you can help her – she's in terrible pain.'

'Ah,' Clara says, and thinks, *I hope so too*, clutching her medal.

'That's the school for princesses over seven.' The maid points to a sprawling building in a less ostentatious, more functional style than the extravagant palaces housing the maharanis, each one more flamboyant than the last. 'When the princes turn seven, they are sent away to boarding school.'

They pass another building, from which wafts the heady fragrance of incense; the glimmer of a pool, the sombre brass notes of bells, the barest glimpse of a pedestal choked with marigold and jasmine garlands.

'The temple,' the maid says. 'There's no priest as they're all men.'

Finally, after walking past several buildings, attracting curious glances, women stopping what they're doing to look at Clara, they arrive at a domed, pillared building grander than all the others.

'Maharani Usha is the maharaja's current favourite, so she has the biggest residence,' the maid says, a hint of pride in her voice.

The interior of Maharani Usha's palace is just as sumptuous and richly furnished, spilling with antiques and treasures, as the main palace. The maid accompanying Clara stops at an elaborate, carved wooden door and knocks. The door is opened by an older maid with a severe face.

'This is the Nurse Memsahib who has come to help…' The words of the kind maid who has led Clara here wilt away as the other maid brings a finger to her lips.

'Shhh… quiet. The maharani needs peace,' the woman hisses. She looks Clara over and apparently finds her wanting, for her lips disappear as she nods curtly and wordlessly turns round and sweeps into the room, obviously expecting Clara to follow.

Chapter Forty-Seven

Clara

Fury

The queen is in a bedchamber the size of the entire men's ward at the hospital in England. She is moaning as she clutches her stomach. Maids are tending to her, one holding her hand, one kneeling beside her. Another hovers with a pile of towels. The maid who brought Clara bows before the maharani and announces demurely, 'Your Majesty, the Nurse Memsahib is here.'

Maharani Usha turns towards Clara. As with the other maharani aboard the ship, Clara is surprised at how young she is – although by now she should know better. She pushes down the sharp pulse of fury at the maharaja – now is not the place nor the time. The maharani is sweating profusely and a maid gently wipes her face while another feeds her sips of a concoction smelling of roses. The girl's face is flushed, eyes exhausted and awash with pain, red from burst blood vessels and swollen from tears. She looks worn out with agony.

Clara bows. 'I'm Clara Knight, Your Majesty,' she says in Hindi. 'I'm an experienced nurse and I've come to help.'

Now that she is here, all Clara's fears disappear, her worry and self-doubt feeling indulgent and shallow in the face of this girl's intense agony. She only wants to make her better and she *will*.

'My baby's coming,' the maharani says, a world of pain in her voice.

'Can I feel?' Clara asks, rubbing her hands together to warm them, even as she thinks of Dr Goel trying to help the maharani via Shalimar and the maids.

The maharani shuts her eyes, tears leaking from under closed lids. 'It hurts. The pain was coming in waves, but now it is more or less constant.' Her voice small and cowed.

She's just a child. Clara aches for her.

Dr Goel was right, she thinks, as she gently probes the maharani's womb, her respect for the doctor, diagnosing this without being able to examine the girl, increasing. *The infant is in breech position and the labour must have started yesterday as he surmised, for she is about ready to deliver.*

'Is my baby okay?' the maharani breathes.

'It is, but it is coming feet first. So, when I tell you to push, you do so, alright?'

The maharani nods. Then, softly, 'Will we die like the wise women said?'

Not if I've anything to do with it.

Before Clara can reassure her out loud, the maharani says, urgently, 'Please save my child, promise me.'

'Your Majesty,' Clara is tender but firm, 'you will experience pain even worse than you're doing now. But you will not die. And neither will your child.' *I won't let it happen.*

The maharani manages a small smile that is more a grimace from the pain. But Clara can see the relief in her eyes. Clara nods at the women grouped deferentially around the maharani, to indicate that the child is coming. The maharani moans as a contraction takes hold.

And Clara gently but firmly guides the maharani through the delivery, her whole being concentrated on helping this child-woman give birth safely, all doubts, worries, conflicted feelings cast aside.

Chapter Forty-Eight

Clara

Royal

Once Clara has helped deliver the newest royal offspring, his mother exhausted but happy, the chamber is suddenly busy with bustling, purposeful women. And then she is outside the palace, blinking in the liquid gold sunshine, which is even more potent now that the sun is higher up the sky, and the maid who conveyed her here is beside her, bashful, admiring.

'Maharani Maya Devi, whom you helped on the ship, would like an audience with you,' she says.

Clara smiles at her – she'd like to find Henry and Dr Goel, but knowing her charge, he will most likely want more time at the zoo and would prefer it if Clara took her time in the zenana. She can hear him in her head, 'Don't hurry on my account, Nurse Knight.'

She smiles at the maid. 'Would you take me there?'

The maid beams.

The maharani, who is lounging on a divan adorned with velvet throws, stands when Clara is announced, steps forward and takes her hand, to the astonishment of her maids. She smells of spiced sandalwood.

She is just as beautiful as ever, but, in the months since Clara saw her last, bitterness has settled at the corners of her mouth, pulling her lips down, the innocence quite gone. She smiles but even the smile lacks sparkle; it doesn't quite touch her eyes.

'Welcome to my abode,' she says in English.

'It is my pleasure. Thank you for inviting me, Your Majesty,' Clara replies in Hindi.

'You've learned our language!' The maharani offers another weak smile. 'And I've been practising yours, but learning on one's own is not the same as conversing with someone else. I'll speak in English with you, if you don't mind.'

'Not at all. And your English is very good.'

Again, that wan smile. 'None of the maids speak it, so it affords privacy. This is why I've been determined to become fluent in it.' Her mouth pulling down further and her eyes flashing with a secret sorrow.

What happened to you? Clara wonders, thinking back to that young innocent on board the ship. Out loud, she reassures, 'You are very fluent.'

'Thank you. The pleasure of your visit is all mine. You truly are a miracle worker. You cured me and now you've thwarted the wise women's prophecies and saved Maharani Usha and her son's life.' She leans in close to Clara, whispers, her breath honey-sweet. 'The rest of us think her distress about the prophecies was exaggerated, a cry for attention, a ploy to see her mother – she has been whining for her since she arrived at the zenana. As if that will work with the maharaja! The rest of us were just as young when we first arrived and have learned to live with—'

A kittenish cry interrupts her and in two graceful strides she's at the divan, ahead of a maid, who arrives breathless and whom the maharani waves away irritably. Beside the divan, Clara now sees, is an elaborate bejewelled cot, suspended from the rafters with flowing silk ties. The maharani gently rocks the crib and the mewling settles. Clara is transfixed by the tenderness on the maharani's face, the pique wiped out.

'Miss Knight, let me introduce you to my son, Hari.' Even her voice is softer.

'By rights he should be in the nursery,' she says as Clara coos over the babe, swaddled in shimmering cloth. 'But I can't bear to let him out of my sight. The maids don't approve; I know they go bearing tales to the king.'

'They wouldn't!' Now Clara understands why she's speaking in English.

'I know what you're thinking. I'm *not* crazy – they are in the maharaja's employ. He has power not only over them but their entire families, so they are loyal to him first, always. They're all his spies.'

'But why would he...?'

'For my husband his reputation, his standing among the other maharajas, is everything. A maharani is a status symbol and she should not lower herself to look after her own child when there are maids employed for that very task. What would the other maharajas say if they heard? And everybody knows maids talk – the news of misbehaving, out-of-control maharanis would spread to all the kingdoms in a blink.' Her face scrunches up like a fruit sucked clean of juice. 'How do you suppose I heard about the maharaja's latest offspring even before you, who had delivered him, made your way here?'

'I was wondering about that.' Clara smiles.

The maharani returns Clara's smile but it is so effortful that it resembles a scowl. 'Ah, but I'm forgetting my manners. Please, sit.'

As soon as Clara does, on the chaise longue opposite the maharani, so soft that she sinks into its silky velvet caress, maids arrive with chiming anklets and singing bangles, bearing food.

Honeyed cashew nuts and salted pistachios, dates and papaya, sweetmeats sticky with sugar, perfumed with rosewater and dripping syrup, spicy fried snacks, platter after platter.

The aroma of spices and sugar makes Clara's senses tingle and her stomach advertise how hungry she is with an embarrassing growl – she couldn't eat breakfast earlier, for nerves.

'Help yourself, please,' the maharani says, waving her hand at the feast, the jewels on her person winking and dazzling. 'I'm sorry, I won't join you. News of the arrival of the maharaja's twenty-third child has ruined my appetite.'

Clara is taken aback by the extent of this girl's acerbity but it doesn't stop her enjoying the food – hot and sweet and delicious – washed down with fresh mango juice.

Through it all, the little prince sleeps, the maharani casting glances laced with an almost painful love at the baby every so often. Once they've served the food, the maharani dismisses the maids. They appear shocked.

'All of us?' the oldest one asks.

'Yes.'

'The baby…'

'Will be fine. He's asleep.'

'If you want us—'

'I will call.' She is sharp.

Once they have left, their anklets and tinkling bangles fading out of earshot, the maharani seems to relax, the bitterness leaving her face, the lines that have made her look older than her tender years easing. 'I'll have to bribe them to stop them running to the king – I won't have money left to send to my parents this month,' she sighs. 'But it's worth it for the brief freedom.' She stretches her legs luxuriantly, one hand gently rocking her son's cot. 'Even if they don't understand what I'm telling you, they'll watch and judge my every action. I can't completely let go when they're around.' She gestures at Clara's plate. 'Take some more, go on.' Then, her voice becoming darker, venomous: 'Usha Devi. She's the current favourite because she's *young*.'

Clara can't help saying, 'But you're only, what, a year older?'

'That makes *all* the difference.' The maharani smirks. 'But she won't lord it over us for much longer. He'll get an even younger one who'll be the new favourite.' And, correctly reading Clara's expression, 'I know what you're thinking and you're not wrong. Petty jealousies and squabbles are all we have to resort to.' She sighs deeply. Then, once again her voice changing, 'Tell me about you. Your life. How you came to be here.'

She looks so young. She *is* young. She appears starved of information, so eager. And so Clara obliges.

Maharani Maya listens avidly. 'The adventures you've had,' she whispers.

And Clara thinks, touching her medal, *I've had some knocks, but life has turned out well.*

'Sometimes, when we walk close to the zenana wall, we can hear the eunuchs talking outside – that's the closest to male voices we hear, apart from the maharaja of course. You have such freedom. No covering your face. No hiding from men. No restrictions.' The awe in her voice.

And Clara, for the first time, appreciates how much she has. She can go where she wants, do what she wants. She has *choice*. If she decides to leave Henry and return to England she can.

I've forged my own path. I am independent, free, practising a profession I love; I answer to no one but myself, not even the king, whom I've spurned.

'How is the doctor?' Here, the maharani is wistful.

The doctor... The way he looks at his wife; the ache it engenders within her... *I have everything except—*

Stop.

'He's keeping my charge, Henry, company at the maharaja's zoo.'

'We too are like animals, the maharaja's pets, imprisoned in a gilded cage. We don't want for anything except freedom.' The maharani's voice drooping with ache. 'My parents were thrilled when I caught the king's eye, when he picked me. We weren't one of the best families, not the noblest and definitely not the richest. But my beauty and youth – well, the king noticed. Their daughter a maharani! They didn't realise and neither did I until it was too late…' The maharani swallows. 'I haven't seen them since I married. I have seen no male face except, once in a blue moon, the maharaja, and little boys under seven. I…' She swallows. 'I miss so much. Walking in my village. Listening to men talk. The rumble of their laughter. My father's snores, the crags and planes of his face. My mother's touch…' She takes a breath. 'When my son was born, I wanted so much to show him to my parents. I wanted my mother. I…'

Clara is moved to reach across, touch the maharani's hand. The maharani looks at Clara's hand in hers, squeezes it. 'I miss this, the simple touch of understanding. I can't have this with the maids. I… I'm *jealous* of them. They get to go home. They get to live a life where they don't have to give their son up when he is seven, like I will have to. They get to keep their husband and not share him. They get to walk, talk, live with and beside men, not in a village of women where each is isolated in a palace, sequestered by maids who are reporting to the king so she can't, won't step out of line…'

'What would the king do?'

'Oh,' the maharani's hand goes to her heart, her eyes wide and sequinned with tears. 'Send me away. Send me back in disgrace. My parents would die, the ignominy would kill them. They are so proud now, even if missing me and longing to see me and their grandson. So, you see, I'm trapped. I don't want to stay but I can't leave.' She swipes at her eyes angrily. 'I thought I knew what I'd signed up for when I married the king but I didn't. I didn't…' The maharani's gaze far away.

I have so much. Freedom. Choice. Independence. A job I love. My health. I should count my blessings and yet…

'I miss the girl I used to be,' the maharani is saying, as she gently rocks her son. 'She loved brown rice with pickle spicy enough to make her eyes water, trees with hidey-holes, velvet moss, walking beside the riverbank in her village and finding pebbles washed smooth by water and time. She laughed without restraint, danced when no one was watching. I cannot find her. She is lost, gone forever.' The maharani sniffs. 'I miss the life I had, that I took for granted. I miss my parents. I miss freedom. I am even jealous of the birds that fly over the palace. But mind you, they're all females – male birds aren't allowed,' she jokes, wryly, and smiles.

It is the saddest thing Clara has ever seen.

Chapter Forty-Nine

Clara

Exasperated

On their way home from the palace, Henry chatters about the animals he saw and how much he would like to return so he can make a study of the zoo.

When he brings this up, Clara sneaks a glance at Dr Goel, who insisted on accompanying them back, to her secret delight: 'Just to make sure you get home safely.' *Did this mean he wanted to spend more time with her?*

Stop.

'Well,' Dr Goel beams at Henry and Clara in turn, 'you are in luck then. Miss Knight, the maharaja was very pleased with you, as is to be expected, and would like you to visit the maharanis to see to any health issues they might have, once every two weeks, if you are willing? He's happy for Henry to accompany you and visit the zoo while you're at the zenana.'

'Of course,' Clara says. *I'm more than willing as this way, I'll get to see you on a regular basis.* Even as her heart rejoices, her mind wants to know, *Do you want me to, Dr Goel?*

'Capital!' Henry enthuses, going on to detail the sections of the zoo he'd like to study further on subsequent visits.

Clara smiles and nods as Henry talks, but she's distracted, wondering if the prospect of seeing Dr Goel every fortnight is a good thing or not. She is constantly on tenterhooks while with him, pain and joy, happiness and upset. The feelings he engenders within her give a lie to her constant reassurances to herself that he's just a friend, rendering the words empty, without substance.

Henry bursts out, 'Nurse Knight, you're not paying attention!' Hands on his hips, lips puckered in a frown. He sounds so like an exasperated old woman. She wants to laugh, but his expressive eyes are sparkling with the shine of tears.

'I'm not, I'm sorry,' she admits. She gathers him in her arms. 'I'm tired but it's no excuse. I was very nervous about helping the maharani and now it is catching up with me.'

The dry, red-dust-painted countryside rushes past outside their window. For once the road is clear, unoccupied by monkeys or dogs, goats, cows or undulating pythons, and the driver is taking advantage, going at full speed. The afternoon is gently tipping into evening, burnished buttery gold, perfumed with roses and dust.

Eventually, wiped out from his adventure, Henry falls asleep, his downy head nestling against Clara's shoulder. Looking at his beautiful innocence, her thoughts return, as they have been doing, to the little boy she helped birth. One lesson the zenana has taught Clara – she is lucky. Several times luckier than the maharanis. She might have lost her family, but she has her freedom. Sometimes at night she is lonely. But not often. And it is but a small price to pay for her independence. She has a job she loves. And the St Christopher medal for protection. She touches it, her talisman, the medal that, despite her now being the owner of some of the maharaja's personal jewels – reward for helping bring his latest offspring and heir safely into the world – means more to her than them. This medal, which rested against her mother's chest.

Clara turns to Dr Goel. 'How do you manage to serve the maharaja, knowing he's…?' She struggles to find the words. 'The maharanis, they're *barely* women.' She shudders. 'At twenty-four, I'm old for him. He acquires these young girls who should be enjoying their childhood, only to keep them within walls, in luxurious surrounds yes, but confined all the same, imprisoned with no male presence, none above the age of seven. Even his animals have more freedom…' She swallows down bitter bile, blistering with fury.

'Ah, that's exactly what Rathi says.'

His wife's name. Respect and love and awe and admiration all wrapped up in that one word. It makes her ache.

It has been a strange day. It has made her question some things, see others in a new light. And now, hearing Dr Goel say his wife's name in that particular wistful, tender tone that encompasses so much, she wonders if anyone will ever say her name that way.

If she's honest – and she hasn't been, even with herself; *especially* not with herself – she doesn't want just anyone to say her name that way. She wants *him* to.

'The maharaja is an enigma,' Dr Goel is saying. 'He's a good *king*, generous and fair, and yet he has a penchant for acquiring wives—'

'Girls, you mean.' Her voice sounds bitter. The sun is setting, the sky on fire, a kaleidoscope of orange and magenta and dusky raisin like a blushing bride. Birds fly home, inky slashes upon a multichrome canvas, the evening flavoured with jasmine and waning day. 'To add to his collection and keep under lock and key.'

'Yes, but you see, he is indiscriminate about whom he picks. He does not only choose from the best, most noble houses, so he does these girls' families a favour. He transforms their lives.'

'But the girls…'

'They get to live in luxury.'

'At the price of their freedom.'

'You're just like my wife, you think alike.' He turns to smile at her and again the depth of love in his voice at the mention of Rathi blows her away at the same time as igniting pain.

'We think right for we are discerning, intelligent, questioning, caring women,' she says.

He lifts his head to the coral heavens, the setting sun haloing his hair rose gold, and laughs, silvery bubbles popping, a shimmering starry constellation of celebration. 'You are.'

She is aglow, blooming from the heat of his smile.

Then, looking at her shrewdly, 'You mentioned meeting with Maharani Maya and I sense it upset you. Do you want to talk about it?'

Again, as when he asked about the significance her medal held for her – the only one to have noticed – she is touched and blown away by his perceptiveness. As Clara recounts her encounter with Maharani Maya, Dr Goel's eyes shine with empathy.

When she has finished, they lapse into companionable silence. After a bit, he says, 'I've a suggestion to make. I've long been thinking of opening a clinic in town for the poorer patients who cannot afford or are suspicious of English medicine and rely on the prophecies and potions of wise men and gurus. The only thing holding me back is my schedule with the maharaja – he's very demanding and I can't commit the time. But if you were to run it…'

'Me?'

'I can't think of anyone better or more competent.' The sincere warmth in his voice sparking a flame in her heart. Then, 'Will you consider staying every alternate week with Rathi and myself, and we can run the clinic together? That way, you can be nurse to Henry one week and during the other week, stay with us and help run the clinic. Henry can come up at the weekend and visit the zoo while you attend to the maharanis. What do you say?'

To spend the week with him, one week in two… Already she is feeling bereft at the impending parting from him. But if she had a week to look forward to, working with him, staying at his house… It would be torture, seeing him with his wife. But, spending that time with him…

'I'll ask the maharaja if I can do half-days during those weeks, and seeing as I'll be utilising that time to help his subjects, I can't see him objecting. As I said, he's a good *king*.' Dr Goel is looking anxiously at her. 'You don't have to agree, it's just a suggestion.'

She has missed nursing. But this decision, the decision she has already made, has nothing to do with nursing. It is everything to do with the person who is asking. 'It is a glorious idea and I'm all for it. Of course I'll have to run it by Captain and Mrs Adams first.'

He smiles and it is a flower blossoming. It is happiness and joy and every good thing. It is friendship. That is all. That is enough.

Part Thirteen

India

Another Chance

Chapter Fifty

Indira

1995, All in a Day's Work

Indira and her mother sit side by side in the cramped hospital waiting room sweating desperation, tasting of anguish, as they wait on news of Baba.

'I told him he needed to exercise.' Her mother worries her sari pallu, tear tracks drying on her face, eyes swollen and red. 'But he said navigating his moped through the rush-hour traffic twice a day was exercise enough.'

Indira repeats, for the millionth time, with more conviction than she feels – the longer they wait, the more her confidence wavers – 'He's going to be fine. And when he comes home, we'll put him on a strict diet.'

She says 'we' and she means it.

It is a novel experience, sitting with her mother, offering comfort. These few hours in these terrifying circumstances, she's felt closer to her mother than she has all her life. She will be more involved in her parents' lives and that of her son and husband, she resolves over and over as she keeps vigil, as her thoughts alternate between panic and fear, as the hours drag with no news.

Every time a weary doctor comes into the room, suffused with the collective anxieties of a hundred relatives, taut and high-strung with nerves, a hush descends, threaded with tremulous hope as each person studies the doctor's face, praying it is their name that is called, their relative who is out of the woods, even as they try to find some indication of a positive outcome in the poor man's exhausted features.

There has been laughter and cheering and there have been desolate, hopeless wails – doctors delivering both good news and bad with the same empathic inevitability. Lives saved and lives lost, all in a day's work.

How do they do it? Indira thought her job was hard – it is nothing, *nothing*, compared to what doctors face daily, playing God, human lives dependent upon their skill. Indira shudders with guilty relief, even as she marvels at this renewed evidence of the fickleness of life, the shadow of death in every breath, each time the room resounds with mournful, unconstrained keening as another family receives the worst possible news.

Indira and her mother spared. For now.

But Baba is *still* in surgery. Does that herald good news, or bad? Does it mean he has a chance? Or that his doctors are trying one option after another to save him, desperate, on the verge of giving up? It terrifies Indira to think her father might die without her having told him, shown him, how much he means to her. Without her having said, 'I love you.'

Her last phone call with her father, over a month ago, had ended in argument, as always. 'I'm thinking of retiring when I turn sixty, Indu,' he'd said.

'Baba! How can you even think of retiring early? You'll lose all sense of purpose!'

'But there's so much I want to do. Potter in the garden, teach myself Mandarin or Russian, take your mother travelling – she's always wanted to go on a pilgrimage of temples in India…'

'Those are *hobbies*. They won't take up *all* your time. You can do them now, after work or during the holidays. You surely don't need to retire *early*.' She recoiled at the thought of all that wasted time. She couldn't quite disguise her disgust.

He sounded upset when he said, 'When you get older, Indu, you realise you don't have much time left and then you want to make the most of it—'

'Baba, you're not even sixty. You have at least a third of your life left – you'll be bored in two days, at most two weeks, doing the activities you described; what will you do with the rest of your time?' she'd snapped.

'If you visited with Arun more, we'd spend time with our grandchild. And I really think you need to get your priorities right. *You'd* benefit from spending more time with your fam—'

'I have to go.' *Unlike you, I don't have time to waste*, she nearly said. That was her last conversation with her father.

She has been smug, thinking she has all the time in the world to repair relationships that have been the casualty of her focus on work.

Is it already too late? She bargains with the heavens again. *Please let me have another chance with Baba. I'll never take him, any of my loved ones, for granted again.*

Part Fourteen

India

Conviction

Chapter Fifty-One

Clara

1928, Resolve

'Is something the matter, Rathi?' They've long since dropped the formal titles. Anand had asked Clara to address them by their given names the first week she stayed at theirs. After their first few meetings, Rathi also stopped covering her head with her veil in Clara's presence.

'You're my friend, you work with my husband. You're family now,' she'd said. Her words stabbed Clara's treacherous heart and she resolved, for the millionth time, to stop wanting Rathi's husband, a resolve that lasted until Anand appeared, handing Clara a drink and smiling warmly at her.

They are in the jasmine and rose arbour in Anand and Rathi's house, relaxing after a delicious supper. Rathi, over the course of Clara's visits here these past two years, has become a close friend. She is kind, caring, intelligent, understanding. Clara can't help liking her – her impression when she first met her, of a beautiful, charming, *good* woman, the right companion for Anand, has solidified into conviction.

It is sheer torture given her feelings for Anand, which she keeps tightly reined in, to see him with his wife, their every interaction laced with meaning and understanding that comes from being perfectly matched, loving and *in love with* the other.

A part of her had hoped that perhaps working with Anand at close quarters would take the shine off her crush and it would fade away. Instead it has intensified and although she fights it, in the deepest, most secret part of her she knows it is much more.

Which is why sitting here with his wife, the evening breeze fragrant as it whispers heady confidences, the fountain gurgling merrily, is bittersweet agony.

Anand has excused himself to write a couple of letters. Henry is asleep. Henry's parents did not return to England after their initial year, having, like Henry and Clara, fallen in love with India. Henry was thriving; the heat suited him and his health was no longer a worry. His mother did not want to send him away to school and he didn't want to go either, so he is being tutored at home.

When Clara put to them Anand's suggestion of her working at his clinic in town, they were all for it. 'It's a capital idea, Miss Knight,' Captain Adams said. 'I see enough of the poor suffering for lack of proper medical care. And we are quite selfish to keep you to ourselves when your expertise could benefit others, as it has our boy.'

Henry was initially upset that she'd be away every other week, but when she assured him that he could visit at the weekend so they could travel to the palace together – Mrs Adams was agreeable now Henry had already been and returned safely, bursting with news – he was all for it.

'Not that I wouldn't rather you stayed with me, Nurse Knight. But like Father said, I understand that I've to be the bigger person.'

And as was often the case when this precocious, delightful boy solemnly made a pronouncement, Clara and Mrs Adams hid their smiles behind their palms while his father coughed to disguise his mirth.

Clara's days are packed, no two the same. During the week when she's at the Adamses', she runs her own clinic – Anand's idea for his clinic spurred her to help those in need in the village down the hill from the Adamses' residence. With Captain and

Mrs Adams's blessing, she has established a little surgery in the outhouse attached to the vast house, which was lying empty and unused, given over to cobwebs; Henry had carefully moved all the spiders to his terrarium.

Initially the villagers were hesitant, suspicious of this white woman with her English medicine, her scalpels instead of potions. But then Clara came upon a maid sobbing into the china she was supposed to be dusting because her cousin had died of fever.

'She must have angered the gods and incurred their wrath.' The maid sniffed, wiping her nose with her sari pallu. 'Now her younger brother is ill too. It doesn't look like he'll make it either.'

'Can you take me to him?' Clara asked.

She had visited the family in their one-room hut, gathered around the boy, who was wrapped up in saris, nearly comatose and so hot she burned when she touched him. It had taken all the expertise she had picked up in her years of nursing but after a tense couple of days, the boy turned a corner.

Following this, there was no stopping the villagers, when ill, coming to the clinic to be looked at by the *Jadoo* – miracle – Memsahib.

The arrangement has worked well – *too* well perhaps, Clara's feelings perpetually on a rollercoaster of ecstasy and misery.

The week that she works with Anand – which she looks forward to, counting down the hours until she sees him again, no matter how busy she makes sure she is, no matter how much she tells herself: *This is madness; he'll never be yours, you're setting yourself up for heartbreak* – Clara leaves the clinic at the Adamses' in charge of some village girls she has trained up. They are quick, bright and eager to learn, like she herself was when she first started at the hospital in her aunt's village.

The girls are now able young nurses and compete with each other to run the clinic in Clara's absence – in fact, it's got so bad that Clara has to draw up a rota – and a few of them have gone on to make nursing their career. Mentoring these skilled young women fulfils Clara in a way her unrequited feelings for Anand never do.

During her week at Anand and Rathi's, after supper – always a feast – Rathi and Clara chat late into the night, like now, Anand joining them after catching up on work, sitting beside his wife, holding her hand, playing with her hair. Clara's heart aches at this casual intimacy that she yearns for, but will never have.

She watches them together, each reading the other's mind before they've spoken, a look conveying an entire conversation, feeling left out. Wanting inside that circle, those arms. Wanting that free, easy affection. Wanting *him*. It is her fate to desire a man who loves someone else. To long for someone who will never be hers.

At the clinic they run together she watches his hands deftly clean wounds, tenderly explore for the source of inflammations, skilfully slice through human flesh, gently administer pain relief, and she imagines how they would feel on her skin.

Later, in her room at their house, Clara torments herself with images of those hands on his wife. And her medal is no comfort during those hot, tropical, sensual nights. She throws open the window to the susurrating breeze, pregnant with shadows. Its scented embrace is heady with night, jasmine and frangipani, whispering soothing sweet nothings as it kisses her fevered cheeks, offering little solace.

She had considered stopping helping at the clinic several times, when her feelings were in danger of overwhelming her, when she worried she hadn't been discreet, hadn't looked away from her study of him quickly enough and she was afraid Rathi had noticed. (One of her secret joys: she commits Anand's every expression – when he's reading a book, writing a letter, when he's otherwise occupied – to memory to unfurl later when she's alone.)

The last time she decided she couldn't continue working with him was the previous fortnight. She had helped him through a particularly tricky amputation. She had held steady but afterwards, she was sick, sorrow for the farmer whose family would now struggle to put food on the table overwhelming her. Anand had heard her heaving and held her.

Exquisite torture. Wanting to sink into his arms, wanting him to hold her like this, always, forever, but not *right* now when she was at her worst. She was bereft when she was done and he withdrew his arms, releasing her from his embrace.

'You're the most amazing person I know. You care with all your heart. You have such empathy yet in there you didn't flinch once.'

He reached up to her face and she thought…

She thought.

She almost leaned into him. But he was just brushing away a fleck from her cheek. A kindness, that's all. His touch, oh so tender. It was torment. Beautiful agony. She cannot leave and should not stay.

Now, 'You've not been yourself today,' Clara says gently to Rathi, even as her heart screams warning. Has Rathi guessed at Clara's feelings for her husband? Is that why she has been so down this evening? Clara has tried to hide her feelings, but perhaps not hard enough?

When she noted her friend's upset, she'd lost her appetite, even though the meal included her favourites – spinach with paneer, roasted aubergines in a tangy tamarind sauce, dum biryani. Anand didn't appear to pick up on his wife's disquiet. Clara had dithered and agonised and finally decided to ask her friend, have whatever was bothering her out in the open.

Her mouth is bitter with fear and angst, at odds with the cool, dusk-flavoured, shadow-speckled breeze flirting with their cheeks as it strokes and caresses, making tendrils of hair dance to its coy tunes.

'I… it's hard to watch Henry with Anand.'

'Oh?' Clara is taken aback even as sweet relief ambushes her. Her foul secret is safe yet. But what Rathi is saying doesn't make sense. Rathi loves Henry, she knows, and she'd always thought her friend liked Anand's easy-going relationship with her charge.

'I… I know he'd like a child. But I… we've tried…' Rathi swallows, trying to rein in her obvious, overwhelming emotion.

The relief Clara was experiencing is replaced by hot bilious jealousy, her attempts to swat away the thought of Anand with Rathi, trying for a child, failing miserably. She tries to concentrate on her friend's distress even as a tiny, horrible part of her is relieved that a child, Anand and Rathi's child, irrevocable proof and culmination of their love, is not forthcoming.

I'm a terrible, terrible friend.

Guilt acrid in her mouth, tainting her cheeks the scarlet of sin even as she takes Rathi's hand in hers.

'I'm an only child, born after several miscarriages when my mother was almost too old. I hope I don't have to wait that long…' There's such pain in Rathi's voice, a sadness her bubbly friend has never hinted at before.

Clara pushes away all thoughts of Anand and her own tormented feelings, concentrating instead on this wonderful woman, who cares so genuinely and loves so generously.

'And the king with his wives and procession of children, it must be so hard for Anand,' Rathi continues.

'He's happy with you.' It is the truth. It hurts Clara to say it and in that secret, selfish part of her that houses her deepest desires, her worst thoughts, she has wished otherwise. She thinks of his voice when he says his wife's name, that particular blend of love and pride and admiration and affection that makes her heart long for him to say her own name that way.

'I know,' Rathi says, 'but I'd like to give him a child. *I* want his child. It would complete us.'

Clara will not allow the thought that is pushing through: *I want what you have. I want him to be mine. I want to say his name with that same casual possessiveness.*

'Have you been to a specialist?'

'Several. They say it will happen.'

'Then it will,' Clara says, squeezing her friend's hand, even as her heart protests, *If he has a child with Rathi, he'll never be mine.*

He will never be yours full stop. He is hers. The scent of jasmine and ache, yearning.

'I'm sorry,' Rathi says smiling wanly, 'usually I can shake it off, but I was pregnant, you see…'

She was pregnant. Carrying Anand's child. Was it conceived when Clara was in this house, sleeping in a room across the courtyard from theirs, the windows open to the hot, tropical, perfumed night?

'This one hung on longer than the others.'

There were others. Anand's babies…

'I lost it just last week. Usually I can rouse myself but this time, it's been hard…' Rathi's eyes sparkling.

'What are you two talking so seriously about?' Anand is behind them, his entrance saving Clara from replying while at the same time causing her heart to lift, to sing, even as her mind chastises, chides, scolds.

'Here you go, *jaan,*' Anand says, handing Rathi her drink.

Jaan. My love. A pang of pure pain cuts Clara's heart, replaced by utter joy as Anand fixes her with his sparkling caramel-gold gaze as he hands her a glass of the salty-sweet lime sherbet she loves. Their fingers touch briefly, her body thrilling at the contact, even as she breathes in his scent of sandalwood and ginger. Familiar. Heady. Cherished.

Stop. His wife is mourning the loss of his child, looking to you, her friend, for comfort and you – you're fantasising about her husband. What sort of a friend are you?

Rathi bends down as if picking something up and Clara watches her discreetly swipe at her eyes with her sari pallu. Then she turns to her husband and smiles, in the rose-tinted dusk, her face in shadow.

Chapter Fifty-Two

Clara

1929, No Fool

But Anand, Clara can see, is no fool.

'What's the matter?' she asks.

He's been upset and distracted all day and had disappeared during their afternoon session at the clinic. Now he's propped against the wall of the clinic, looking at nothing, appearing dejected.

'It's Rathi,' he says.

His wife's name trips on a sigh, a tender pang that ignites fiery pain in Clara's heart. How she wishes she didn't care for this man, that she was spared the agony and complications of love, like she had so naively vowed to before she met him.

I will be better off on my own, she'd told herself, containing her family within her heart and sealing it.

She should have guarded it harder, secured it against toffee eyes and a chocolate voice bestowing honeyed compliments adorned with gilded smiles, she should have made it a fortress like the walls of the zenana, topped with shards of broken glass to repel intruders brave enough to weather the amazons at the gate and scale the walls.

'She wants a child desperately,' Anand is saying. 'I've told her repeatedly that I'm happy without. That she is more than enough.'

How much pain can her heart take? It pulls her in directions she doesn't want to go. It *hurts*.

'We...'

And again, her heart lifts. Hope.

'Rathi and I,' he says and her heart falls.

Serves you right. When will you learn? 'We' will always mean Rathi and Anand. They are *married.*

When Anand gazes at Rathi – who's becoming increasingly melancholy; now her smiles are brittle, riddled with cracks, crumpling at a moment's notice – as if he wants to take her in his arms and kiss her better, Clara is angry at her friend. *Rathi!* she wants to yell. *You have what I want. If I had him, I'd cherish him. If I had him, he'd be enough.*

'This yearning of Rathi's for a child that she thinks I want is ruining our marriage.'

Clara resolutely dumbs down the thrill of hope she once again cannot help experiencing. Romantic love brings nothing but pain, she is learning. Even happy couples are not immune. Her own parents loved each other and yet their years together wrought crushed hopes, broken dreams that pushed them apart before war destroyed them altogether.

And now, Anand and Rathi...

Perhaps Clara is happier this way, desiring – she still will not label what she feels for Anand as love, even to herself – from afar. If she and Anand were together – ah, her heart sighs, if only – perhaps they would become disillusioned with each other too.

Never.

'She insists on trying and each lost child breaks something within her. She thinks because her mother had many miscarriages before she was born, it will happen. But at what cost? I'm losing her.'

The ache in his voice sparks a reciprocal one in hers.

'I can't bear to see her in pain. It hurts.'

And I hurt when you hurt for her.

'Will you talk to her?' He rubs his face with his hand, the gesture so weary.

She wants to take him in her arms, kiss his worry away. But he doesn't want it from her. He doesn't want her.

'Will you tell her I care only for her? I would be happy to have her child, but I want her.'

Every word a stab. *This is why I didn't want to care.*

'Will you, Clara?'

And this is why I should go away, back to England.

He is looking at her, pain and plea in those golden eyes whose every expression she's studied, every flicker she knows.

She cannot deny him anything.

Even this.

'I will.'

'You are a good friend.'

His smile, those eyes.

I will never be more than that.

Chapter Fifty-Three

Clara

1933, Storm

'She's just, we're so far apart now. She's retreated into herself. I cannot reach her,' Anand says, his voice the hollow gold of wind whistling through reeds.

Hard though it is, Clara has kept her promise to Anand and tried talking to Rathi often in the past four years. 'Rathi, you're losing yourself,' she's warned. And, 'Anand would rather have *you*.' Knowing it to be true even though she wishes with all her heart it wasn't. But...

'Once I have a child, I'll become myself again,' Rathi insists, eyes shining.

The child hasn't materialised and Rathi is a shell of the vibrant woman Clara first met.

Clara and Anand are at the clinic, finishing up for the day, later than usual. A patient had come in just as they were closing, in terrible pain, so they hadn't the heart to ask her to return the following day. It is one of those evenings when thunder crackles and the air sizzles with the impending storm, lightning splitting the sky and shredding the descending darkness with a silver scythe.

'I'll speak to her,' Clara says now, knowing it's what Anand wants.

He looks at her. In the shadows, his eyes glint, chocolate with scoops of melting caramel.

She knows his every expression. But this… There's something there that wasn't before. Warmth, friendship and—

'You're so good, Clara. Kind and caring and such a good friend. I…'

Is she imagining the tenderness in his voice, that tone, the cadence of which was once reserved for his wife?

He takes her hand. It is a jolt, as always.

'Thank you,' he says.

The air vibrates with the imminent gale, electric.

His touch lingers.

Despite herself, she leans closer. His smell, ginger and sandalwood. He is a whisper of a breath away. She looks into his eyes. There's definitely something there.

Thunder bellows warning and she jumps, thinking of Rathi, her kindness, her trust, her pain at the miscarriages she suffers, her heart breaking more with every one. And even though Clara wants nothing more than this, whatever it is, to continue, she pulls away, just as the storm breaks, a raging monsoon.

The next evening, when they're finishing at the clinic, he says, 'Will you sit with me?'

Her heart lifts, especially given what nearly happened the previous evening – she had not slept all night as the monsoon roused the trees into passionate frenzy outside her open window, depositing warm wet kisses upon her body, imagining what would have happened if she had given in to the charged moment when his hand lingered on hers and he looked a question at her, if she had followed it to its conclusion instead of pulling her hand away. Across the courtyard the man tormenting her with unrelinquished fantasies had slept peacefully, she'd imagined, in his wife's embrace.

'Please?'

Is she imagining the affection in his voice, reading her own feelings into his expression, laced with tenderness?

No.

Those eyes. That soft, caramel-gold gaze, gentleness and something else she's noticed since the previous evening.

'Just for a bit.'

Oh, how she wants to sit here listening to his gilded voice, thrilling at the underlying current of tension she is sure he is experiencing too. It makes her abrupt as she says, 'Your wife is waiting.'

Your wife. Hating the casual possession inherent in the words. The possession she will never be party to.

'Rathi, she…' Bitterness pulsing with upset in his voice.

'She loves you.' It hurts but she must say it, reminding herself as much as him.

I love you.

'Yes.'

'You love her.'

'Yes.'

She turns away.

'Clara.'

She has yearned for him to say her name in this way. Dreamed of it. She cannot resist looking at him.

'You are amazing, so talented, kind, clever. You are perfect.' His gaze mellow in the shadow-stippled dark.

She blushes, once again turning her face away, even as she hugs his words close. Does he know what he is doing to her? Can't he see how torn she is? How much it is taking not to throw caution, her feelings for his wife, to the wind and throw herself into his arms?

'Why haven't you found anyone?' he's asking.

Because I love you. There. She has admitted it to herself for the second time in as many minutes.

'I made up my mind long ago that my family was enough,' she says.

'But don't you get lonely?'

If only you knew.

'I have my medal. My memories of my family.'

'I admire you, Clara.'

She stands very still. It is agony, what he is doing.

'You're so self-contained. You lost your family in the most horrific circumstances yet you're so giving, capable of so much love. You care for everyone. You—'

'Anand.' It is warning and it is yearning. Longing and ache.

'Is it possible to love two people at once, do you think?'

Is he saying what she thinks he is?

'Anand, you love Rathi,' she says firmly, although inside she is shaking, aching, torn. If she has read him right, she could have what she has been dreaming of for so long…

She will not regret it.

But he will.

And so she adds, 'You're going through a tough time now. It will pass. All marriages go through their ups and downs. Don't do or say anything you might regret.'

It breaks her to say it. But she must. For Rathi's sake. And her own. For she knows that Anand, while he might admire her, loves Rathi. He is missing Rathi as she once was, the woman he married, bubbly and positive and not worn down by distress and yearning and loss. He will regret being with Clara afterwards and she won't be able to bear it. Although this pain right now feels unendurable.

'I admired you before but I do so even more now.'

He admires her. He does not love her. Not the way she wants him to. The way he loves his wife. It takes all the strength left in her to say, in a brusque voice that masks the salty gush flooding her mouth, 'Let's go, Anand. Rathi is waiting.'

Chapter Fifty-Four

Clara

1934, Too Much

When Anand pops his head round the door of the clinic, wearing an expression Clara has never seen before, she knows something's wrong. 'Clara...' His voice. Despair and upset.

It is the first day of her week at the clinic with Anand and as usual she'd come straight here, opened up and was waiting for him to join her after his duties at the palace. Later, they'd head home to Rathi together.

Rathi... Clara hasn't seen her friend since her stay the previous fortnight. Did she give something away then? Has Rathi discovered Clara's feelings for Anand?

Her heart thuds painfully against her ribcage. 'Is it Rathi?'

'No... well, yes, but it's not that...' His voice tremulous, unlike any other time she's heard it. Unsteady.

'Anand, you're not making any sense. What's the matter?'

'The maharaja... He's asked me to tell you you're not welcome at the palace and you're not to tend to his maharanis any longer.'

She is surprised. 'But why?'

'Your friend...'

'Maharani Maya.' Over the years, Maharani Maya has become a special friend to Clara. 'You're my lifeline,' she says during their heart-to-hearts. 'You see *me*, not my facade.'

'The maharani, yes.' He is defeated.

'What happened?'

'The maharaja sent their son, Prince Hari, away to school in England.'

'And…' Now her voice is trembling as she fears the worst.

'Ah, Clara…'

'*Tell me,*' she says fiercely.

'She hanged herself.'

Clara shuts her eyes, sways on her feet.

'The maharaja thinks as nurse to the zenana you should have picked up on the maharani's mental state. I tried to tell him…'

But Clara is not listening, her heart overwhelmed by remorse, choked with upset. 'I cannot live without my boy. If he goes away, I will die,' her friend had said the last time Clara visited, as they watched Hari run around the room. Clara hadn't realised she meant it literally.

Pain branding her heart, she clutches her St Christopher medal with all her might as she mourns the lonely, sad woman suffocating in the zenana until her one source of joy and love was snatched from her and she couldn't take any more. The beautiful bird who was trapped in a gilded cage. *Maya has found the only way out she could…*

The sky is peach gold daubed with crimson, silhouetted with navy fans of birds flying to their palm, banyan and mango tree homes to roost. The fragrant, memory-scented air tastes hauntingly sweet, of candied fruit and happier times and abrupt endings, flavoured with loss.

'Let's go home. I need a drink and I'm sure you do too after this awful news,' Anand is saying. 'Rathi is not home, she's visiting her mother.'

And it is the way he says it, the hint of desolation and something darker, that jolts Clara out of her sorrow.

'What's the matter? Is everything alright…?'

'We'll talk about Rathi at home,' he says, and there is such pain in his voice.

His voice has always been nuanced when he says his wife's name. During the first years of Clara's acquaintance with him, she had heard pride resonate alongside love, awe, disbelief that Rathi was his, admiration and respect all mingled together. Later, sadness, hurt, confusion. Now, together with all those emotions, an added layer of pain, ache.

They sit in the arbour, creamy jasmine and blood-red roses spattered with shadows, nursing their drinks and their separate sorrows.

'Rathi had another miscarriage and she wouldn't get out of bed,' he says.

'When was this?'

'Just after your last visit.'

A fortnight ago. *Oh, Rathi.*

Anand is saying, 'She must have written to her mother, for she came and took her away. I... I don't know if she's coming back.' The despair in his voice. It is his heart scraped inside out. Like she is feeling.

'Anand, she *loves* you. Of course she's coming back.' *I wish it wasn't true but it is.*

'You didn't see her after the miscarriage. She's a shell. Nothing left. No emotion. She said losing this last child took everything from her.'

'She just needs to heal. She'll come back,' Clara repeats.

'I don't think so.' He sighs.

A secret part of Clara that she has resolutely suppressed has hoped for this. But the desolation in Anand's voice, the utter defeat, is heartbreaking and drives home the truth she already knows. Her love's heart belongs to one friend, while her other...

Maya... The pain ambushes, overwhelms.

A peacock cries mournfully somewhere behind them and all of a sudden it's too much.

The cloying scent of roses, images flooding her mind, of one friend dead, another drained from losing her unborn children, yet another beside her, her love, hurting from missing his wife. It's too much.

She doesn't realise she is weeping in the jasmine-flavoured, rose-gold dusk until Anand says, his voice tender, 'Ah, Clara, don't cry.'

She sniffs, rubs a hand across her face, sprays her drink all over the rose bushes. And that is the last straw. She cannot contain it. She sobs and sobs.

She does not know if she is crying for Maya, or her little boy on his way to England unaware of his mother's death, or for Rathi, her desperate and painful longing for a child destroying the gregarious, happy person she was, or for herself and her ill-fated love of a man who does not love her the way she wants him to, the way she loves him.

And suddenly, as if she has wished it into being, Anand's arms are around her and she is leaning into his embrace, his scent of ginger and sandalwood, the solid, reassuring feel of him. Then she is tasting his whisky, sunset gold on his lips, flavoured salty with tears.

Somewhere among the fruit trees in the courtyard, an owl hoots, mournful and startling, sounding very much like a warning.

She has waited and yearned for this moment. Longed for it and dreamed of it. And although she knows she must pull away, she allows herself to drink, for a moment, deeply of this heady, desperately longed for masculine nectar, so alien and yet so potent, thrillingly delicious. It is wrong and yet it feels so completely right.

She is thirty-two years old and she has never been embraced like this. She has fantasised about this man's arms, of being held like this, by him, her deepest, most clandestine desires made real...

She should stop this, she knows. But she forgets all the reasons why. For it is everything she dreamed of. It is more than she imagined.

For the first time since she lost her mother during the air raid all those years ago, she feels complete. The moment stretches, elastic, addictive, and then he is pulling her closer and she thinks, just a little longer, and her body is fitting into his, so perfectly and then...

And then it is too late to pull away. It is too late.

Part Fifteen

India

Realisation

Chapter Fifty-Five

Indira

1995, Mango Pickle

Around Indira and her mother in the hospital waiting room, families share meals from tiffin boxes, the doughy heat of chapatis, vinegary tang of onion, piquant spiciness of dum aloo, the mustard-tempered pungency of mango pickle. When the anxiety gets too much, they hug each other and cry, tired faces lined with worry, drooping mouths.

A man throws his mat down on the floor in one corner of the room, kneels and calls to Allah, arms raised in passionate plea to the heavens. In another corner, a woman chants the rosary. Children run and laugh, chatter and whine. Mothers wilt under the strain of coming up with answers to questions they'd very much like to know the answer to themselves: 'Where's Baba? Is he alright?' Smiles pasted on, saris dishevelled, they feed their children, hoping boondi laddoos and pistachio barfis will distract them, or if that fails, at least keep them quiet for a blessed minute or two.

'Did you just suggest putting your baba on a diet?' Indira's mother asks.

'Yes, when Baba comes home, we'll make sure he eats the right things, draw up a diet plan.'

'Your father, diet!' Her mother offers her a wan smile. 'He loves his food. He'd rather die.'

At the realisation of what she's said, her eyes go wide and startled. She claps her hand to her mouth, tears silently pooling on her cheeks.

Indira reaches across, pats her mother's arm. She smells of anguish, sandalwood talcum powder and sweat-laced panic. She feels so small, a tiny bird, trapped in fear and upset.

When Indira arrived, her mother, after relaying that Baba was in surgery, and asking after Karan and Arun, had queried, 'What about your job?'

'They can manage without me a few days.' Indira had spoken in passionate haste, but even as she uttered the words, she'd thought, *Yes, they* can *manage without me.* It was a revelation. She had sacked directors who were getting by doing the bare minimum of work because they thought they were indispensable – she had proved no one was.

But she is realising now that she had thought this didn't apply to *her*. She thought as CEO, she *had* to be there. That the company wouldn't run without her. And perhaps it wouldn't the way *she* wanted, but they'd get by. Silly really, how such a simple realisation needed her father on his deathbed – *no, please, no* – to register.

Part Sixteen

India

Culmination

Chapter Fifty-Six

Clara

1934, Impulse

When Clara is two weeks late, she begins to suspect. When she wakes up nauseous, unable to keep food down, and certain scents, especially those part and parcel of her nursing life, trigger queasiness, she understands that her body is changing. *Has* changed. That it is harbouring new life. One mad evening of giving in to impulse, pushing the voice of sense away, and it has spawned a miracle.

She has not been in touch with Anand since that fateful evening.

Afterwards, he had not looked at her, just wordlessly left her, and she was bereft – cold, lonely, heartbroken, as devastated as she'd felt fulfilled just moments before.

In the morning he still wouldn't look at her. And that made her lonelier than ever.

Dawn kissed the edges of darkness, night dancing away on stealthy tiptoes, streaks of buttery gold heralding the morning following the best and the worst day of her life, the culmination of her dreams and also their irrevocable end, leaving her broken, heart heavy with loss, the implications of what they had done weighing her down.

One friend, Maya, gone. The other, Rathi, betrayed.

And Anand?

He had wordlessly walked away from her, averting his eyes.

Was it that bad, Anand?

By allowing her feelings, that she had suppressed for so long, to get the better of her, had she lost him too, while betraying his wife, the one friend she had left?

She wanted to lie down on the red earth of this country she loved and sob, even as her conscience berated her, *This is why you should have stayed away from love. This is why you promised yourself not to care. Caring hurts. Love brings nothing but heartbreak.*

I love you, she thought. *But you have never loved me.*

She had always known it, but a stubborn part of her had persisted in hoping he reciprocated her feelings in some small way. She had hoped that when their lips met, their bodies merged, their hearts would become one, their souls would commune, a man and a woman from opposite ends of the world joined in a love as forbidden as it was sweet, as beautiful as it was desperate, as wanton as it was poetic, and he would see how right they were together.

She had fantasised that afterwards he would whisper, in a husky voice, 'I love you.' And, 'I always will,' he would promise before loving her again.

She would fall asleep to his rich chocolate voice quoting sonnets of adoration in her ear.

But he would not meet her eye. Not when she came downstairs and he was waiting beside the carriage he had arranged – he wouldn't even accompany her back. He did not want to spend another moment in her company.

He held the door of the carriage for her, without touching her – he usually handed her in. Every action a hammer to her already shattered heart, devastating it even more. *Last night you kissed every inch of me. Now I am a pariah?*

She sat upright in the carriage and looked straight ahead, giving nothing away. If he would not deign to look at her after their intimacy the previous night, he did not deserve to know how much his callousness was destroying her.

Then he leaned in, so close she could feel his hot breath caressing her cheek, recalling the taste of his kisses, his scent enveloping her. She turned to him, her lips a whisper away from his.

But he was looking, not at her, but at a point above her head. 'I'm sorry. It was a mistake.'

A mistake. While for her, it was everything. A culmination of the love she had harboured for him for what felt like forever. She had thought the pain of unrequited love was bad. She had thought her heart was breaking when he left after they were together without a backward glance, when he refused to look at her just now.

But this… so much worse.

'We'll not speak of it again. We can shut the clinic for a bit, you're grieving for Maharani Maya and I… Rathi…' His wife's name agony on his lips, bitter with the betrayal he had wrought on her with her best friend.

She nodded, looking straight ahead at the horizon, white bright, which blurred and blazed before her eyes. She understood that he had leaned in close, not for some last vestige of intimacy as she had desperately hoped, but so the groom would not hear what he said.

'Goodbye, Clara,' he said, and there was a horrible finality to it. But… his voice wavered ever so slightly as he said her name, as he stood back from the carriage.

She was tempted to look at him then, but, although her heart was crushed, her pride was not and would not allow it.

'Goodbye, Anand,' she said, equally formally, giving no indication of the desolation ruining her, looking ahead at the uncompromising horizon and a future without him in it, even as the groom clicked to the horses and the carriage took her away from the house that had been a second home to her in India and where she had spent some of the happiest days of her life.

*

She has not heard from Anand since. She assumes he has temporarily shut the clinic they ran together, like he said he would. It has taken all of her effort and willpower to keep on going as normal, to get out of bed and face each sunny day when within her it is the darkest night, stretching endless without hope, her heart shattered, love disillusioned, when all she wants to do is lie in bed and sob.

But Clara will not give in to the depression that threatens to sink her. She will not let the darkness win. And so she pulls herself out of bed each morning, pastes a smile on her face and goes about her day, despite the magic having gone out of it, despite thinking everything pointless, despite being unable to find comfort and solace in the caring and giving that is her profession. She nurses by rote, smiles by rote, eats by rote, lives by rote.

If I pretend long enough, it will become my reality. If I pretend long enough to be happy, to be myself, perhaps I will find myself again.

She cannot imagine ever being happy again.

He is not worth it. He was never worthy of your love. You are young yet. You have a long life ahead of you. Don't let him destroy it.

And so she goes on, although everything feels bland, stripped of colour, of happiness, of life. She misses Maya and grieves for her. She misses her chats with Rathi, dusk thick and pressing, fragranced with jasmine, fraught with intrigue, shadows dancing upon the foliage, the air that caressed their faces perfumed with secrets.

And, most of all and despite everything, she misses Anand – the man she has loved for so long – his reassuring presence beside her at the palace. His understanding. Their chats while working at the clinic. His kindness before and his passion during that beautiful night.

But what they did has tainted everything that came before, their friendship now stained the scarlet of sin. What they did was wrong on so many levels – he is married. He loves his wife. *She* loves his wife. And yet, at the time, to her at least, it felt so right.

She had hoped he harboured some feeling for her. After all, there was that time he had asked her if it was possible to love two people at once…

Then, she had sensibly rebuffed him, and in this way preserved their friendship. But that fateful evening, she was grieving Maya. She was low. She did not have the strength to reject what she had for so long longed for.

And now. She strokes her stomach in bemused awe. Now she has compounded her treacherous betrayal of one of the two friends she has left since Maya died by creating a child with her husband, her other friend, the child Rathi desperately wants to give him. A child!

Something she never dared imagine, having resigned herself to a life of loving Anand from afar. Rathi must *never* know. Clara needs to make some decisions before it is too late. She has lived her life on her own terms thus far. She will continue to do so. Anand came into her life out of the blue and entirely by mistake one foggy winter's morning a world away and changed it. He arrived again on the ship on her way to a new life and altered its direction. Now once again, his presence in her life has left a legacy.

At her lowest point, hope in the form of a miracle. Something to look forward to, when she felt she didn't have the energy to go on. A new *life* to look forward to, growing within her! Something of the man she has loved for so long living on in her.

She strokes her stomach as around her the morning comes alive with sound, a bright sunny yellow dawn in India heralded by the call of peacocks, the crowing of roosters and the cackle of crows, the scent of night jasmine chased away by the potency of roasting spices as the dew is by the dazzling glow of day, the tinkle of maids' anklets and their gossipy giggles, the breeze pleasantly cool but carrying the dust- and grit-flavoured, burnt orange promise of heat.

For the first time since Anand's rejection, she looks forward to the new day, a future without her love, but with a brand new life, of him, of her, growing within her.

'Hello, you,' she whispers, one hand caressing her stomach, the other clutching her medal. 'My glorious, unexpected but very welcome Indian miracle.'

Chapter Fifty-Seven

Clara

Blameless

Now, Clara must decide what's best for her child.

Anand had worried that Rathi might not be returning to him. If his marriage is over, despite how badly he treated Clara after sleeping with her, she will put her pride aside, do the best by her child and tell him. Then he can choose. But even if Rathi has left him, how will she feel when she finds out Anand has had a child, the child she desperately wants, with Clara, whom she so warmly welcomed into her home, generously offering friendship, love? Rathi will be devastated and Clara cannot bear it. For in all this Rathi is blameless.

Oh, what a bind this is.

The days pass, and Clara, knowing she doesn't have the luxury of time to indulge her dilemma, that this baby is arriving in less than nine months and she needs to set things in motion, writes to Anand and Rathi. A cheery letter full of news, her intention to discover if Rathi is back with Anand or still at her mother's, and the state of their marriage.

Dearest Anand and Rathi,

How are you both? Henry and I miss seeing you. But I'm grieving Maharani Maya every day and decided to take a break from travelling up there and from the clinic for a while.

Henry has been so kind, trying to cheer me up when I appear sad by thrusting animals at me – 'They are calming, Nurse Knight.' I just wish his 'calming' animals of choice weren't mongooses, which I cannot take to, or chameleons, lizards and centipedes – I did draw the line at snakes.

Although disappointed about and missing his fortnightly visits to the maharaja's zoo, Henry is philosophical: 'I learned all I had to and I've taken notes. And who knows, if we ask nicely, he might allow us back.'

Meanwhile, he is keeping busy with his lessons and his own zoo, which keeps growing.

With all my love,
Clara

It is Rathi who replies and with that, Clara has her answer.

Dearest Clara,

I have missed you so much. I am so sorry I wasn't there that evening when you found out about Maharani Maya. I'm sure Anand tried to comfort you, in his way. But I wish I'd been there for you that evening all the same.

Anand said he told you I went to my mother's. I don't think he told you the whole truth. I… I am struggling, Clara. Each time I miscarry, it's… Oh, I can't describe it except to say it gets harder to find the will to go on, to smile, to live, to love. I do love Anand more than life itself and yet, after my last miscarriage, I couldn't bear to be around him. I couldn't bear it.

Going to my mother helped – I needed to grieve for all the babies I lost without carrying all the emotions Anand engendered, without experiencing sadness and guilt and sorrow for his grief, without feeling I had to comfort him. I just needed that time away.

I have returned determined to try again. Clara, I will give my husband the child he desires. The child I desperately want. And if I cannot, we will adopt. We will be a family, I have decided, one way or another.

Come to visit, Clara, and we will talk about this and all that's going on with you. You don't need an excuse, you are always welcome.

With love,
Rathi

Clara puts the letter down and gently, tenderly, pats her stomach, Rathi's words resounding in her head. Telling Anand about his child is out of the question. *I will need to make some difficult decisions. But I have survived worse. And, my child with me, I can and will face anything.*

Now she understands why Maya gave up when her son was sent to England. This fierce, possessive, protective maternal love is one of a kind. Clara cannot imagine losing this child. How must Rathi feel to experience this love, bond with the budding babe and then lose it?

What have I done?

*

Everything will change, my love, she whispers to her child, *but I will make sure you are protected, looked after, loved.* Her mother and brother wanted to come to India, their fantasies fed by Father's stories, and Father always meant to return to the magical land of his childhood. None of them got to do so. But *she* has. Clara has achieved more than she imagined; she has travelled to India, met and been propositioned by a maharaja, become friends with, loved and lost a maharani.

She has loved and cared and laughed and cried. She has healed, saved many lives, helping run Anand's clinic and starting her own, changing the mindset of villagers suspicious of English medicine, inspiring young girls to become nurses. She has made and betrayed friends, and created a baby.

She has had a splendid and devastating time, more wonderful and painful and magical than her wildest imaginings. Now it is time to go back to England. Carve out a new life for herself and her miracle child, snatched from fate, conceived during an enchanted night stolen from time. But before she does so, she will have to endure seeing Anand and Rathi one more time, for she cannot leave without saying goodbye.

Chapter Fifty-Eight

Clara

Radiant

Rathi is glowing, dazzling, radiant. Even her obvious distress at Clara's leaving cannot camouflage her bloom. She beams at Anand when she looks at him, in the way she used to when Clara first met her.

Anand. It is torture to be in such close proximity to him.

Seeing him brought all her desire, her love for him, which she has managed to push away, hurt by his rejection, flooding back. His features that she has learned by heart, that profile that she traced with her lips that night, his hands, his lips on every part of her body…

She had known it would be hard facing the father of her child and his wife whom they had betrayed but this is excruciating, sheer torment. It is taking all of her willpower to treat Anand normally. He has avoided looking at Clara directly. He is stilted with her, formal, distant. And that helps to contain her emotion, although she worries she is not being friendly enough, a little too cold in response to his aloofness. But Rathi, her sweet, loving, wholesome, trusting friend, is oblivious.

'Clara, can't we convince you to stay?' Rathi says.

What about you, Anand? Won't you ask me to stay?

They are in the courtyard, in the shade of the palm trees, the gloaming fragrant around them, enveloping with its sweet embrace, the peacocks coming up to them as night steals light from evening. The brash heat has faded along with the day, dusk mellow and tasting of wistfulness, whisper-soft with settling dust. Mosquitoes drone and flies circulate, but are kept at bay by the citronella candles, which cast golden streaks upon their faces.

I wish I could stay.

'I'm sorry about what happened to Maharani Maya Devi. As for that maharaja, I don't know how Anand can bear to work for him.'

Anand shrugs, turning away, saying tightly, 'Just remembered I'm running low on the headache pills the maharaja favours. I'd better sort that out now before I forget again.'

You won't spend time with me even on my last evening here, given all our history, our years of friendship?

But she breathes easier once it's just her and Rathi, even as she feels his absence keenly.

Her friend is saying, 'I understand that you must feel at a loose end with Henry almost grown, but must you go back to England?'

Clara closes her eyes at the mention of Henry. It was absolutely heartbreaking saying goodbye to that child whom she loves so dearly. He had wanted to come with her, see her off to the ship, but she wouldn't have been able to bear it and so she dissuaded him. He had maintained a brave face when he waved her off, but his lower lip trembled and she had watched through the haze of red dust blurred by her tears until he was just a fading dot.

She feels Rathi's hand pressing something into hers. A handkerchief. It is only then that she notices she is crying, that the handkerchief, even before it has reached her face, is soggy from the tears dripping onto her fist. She is clenching it tight with one hand, the other clasping her medal. She sniffs, blows her nose.

'Thank you,' she says when she can speak, offering Rathi a watery smile.

Anand returns and they sit, as they have over the years, watching the crows and parrots fly home to roost in the trees above them, fronds gently waving, jasmine-scented shadows dancing upon the softly bubbling water of the fountain, shimmering navy in the glow of twilight.

I haven't even left yet and I miss, already, this beautiful country and the people who've claimed my heart.

'You've always been such a hard-working trailblazer. Anand sings your praises, don't you, love?' Rathi smiles fondly at her husband.

He mumbles about getting drinks, escapes indoors once more.

'He's been preoccupied, poor love. That maharaja is giving him hell. Since the maharani— I'm so sorry, I've been thoughtless again...' She is distressed, clapping a hand over her mouth.

'It's alright, Rathi, do go on,' Clara reassures her.

Talking about the maharaja is a respite from her conflicted emotions. She loves Anand, still, whereas he can't stand to be around her. And yet all she can think is, *how can I bear to live without you? When I was at the Adamses', at least I had the prospect of seeing you every other week to look forward to.* Discreetly, so Rathi won't notice, she pats her stomach. *I will bear it. For you, my babe. And for this good, kind woman beside me.*

Rathi reaches across, squeezes Clara's hand, still appearing anxious. 'The maharaja has been in a terrible mood – he feels the other maharajas are laughing at him, one of his maharanis so fed up with him that she would take her life. He's taking it out on all those working for him. Anand has been rushed off his feet – he's not been able to reopen the clinic you used to run together...' Rathi takes a breath. 'Clara, I'm sorry I wasn't here that day. It was a difficult time. The worst... Oh sorry, look at me, selfish. You were going through a tough time too.'

'Rathi, we were both grieving, you for your child and me for the maharani.'

Rathi smiles gratefully, squeezing Clara's hand again. 'I needed a break. I talked things through with Ma. It helped. And Anand, he's changed too. I think my going to Ma was a wake-up call for both of us. He's been so loving. It's like the early days of our marriage.' She beams.

Guilt, Clara thinks. Unconsciously her hand snakes to her stomach. She pushes it back to her side. She cannot give herself away.

'And Clara,' Rathi whispers and she glows even more, 'I'm pregnant.'

Oh.

Anand creating a child with her, and one with Rathi. One sanctioned, the other secret. Two siblings who will never know each other...

'That's wonderful.' She injects joy into her voice. Forces it to sound as cheery as possible, even as her hand once again rests upon her stomach, as her throat floods with brine.

'I hope this one hangs on.'

'It will,' Clara promises, thinking, *I'm doing the right thing.*

'Stay. Be my child's favourite aunt.'

Rathi, if you knew what I'd done, the secret I'm hiding, you wouldn't ask. 'I wish I could...'

'I understand. You're destined for great things. Now that the clinic you established is being run by the young nurses you trained, you're going where your experience and expertise is needed more.'

'I...'

'Anand says you'll save more lives, like you saved his.' Rathi is earnest.

Do you want me to go so badly, Anand? Clara asks the father of her child in her head.

'Although, selfishly, I want you to stay. If you miss us all too much,' Rathi's eyes glitter with a sheen of tears, 'you'll come back, won't you?'

Anand joins them at that moment. He is handing Clara a glass of wine when Rathi says, 'You'll always have a home here with us.'

His hand jerks. Some of the wine spills.

Am I welcome, Anand?

He hands his wife her glass of mango juice and smiles tenderly at her. There's Clara's answer. She sets down her wine, untouched. *I can't drink this, I'm carrying your child.*

Rathi takes a long gulp of juice, draining half the glass. She is sporting a moustache of bright yellow when she says, 'Ah, I needed that. Clara, since I cannot convince you to stay, promise me you'll write and tell me all your news.'

'I'll write so much, you'll be sick of my letters.'

'Never. I'll miss you, Clara. So very much.'

'I will too,' Clara says.

What about you, Anand?

'You're such a good friend to us.' Rathi's gaze ornamented with tears.

Anand drains his glass in one quick drag and turns away.

Part Seventeen

India

Declaration

Chapter Fifty-Nine

Indira

1995, Phone Booth

As the shadows lengthen and the lights come on, the children fall asleep on saris their mothers have laid upon the dust-tracked floor while they doze on the hard-backed chairs. Indira, never one for sitting still, jumps up. 'I'll call Karan, see how Arun is doing, and after I'll get us some food.'

'I can't ea—'

Indira cuts short her mother's protest. 'You must.'

The queue for the phone booth is long. As she waits, breathing in the body odour, desperation and weariness of others in the queue, the pungent tang of sambar mingling with the heady nuttiness of roasting coconut wafting from the canteen, she seethes, *How can this huge hospital have so few phone booths, for God's sake?* Now, if she was in charge...

'But you are not.' Karan's voice in her head.

Karan. A stab of pain as she ruminates upon the distance that has crept between them while she was not paying attention. How to bridge the gap?

She loves him, just as much as when they met; in fact, more so, for he has proved to be just as good a father as he is husband. And not too long ago, she'd have said without hesitation that he loved her too.

But now... she doesn't know.

When they first met, they used to talk for hours about everything under the sun, Karan actively courting her opinions.

Now if he does initiate conversation, it's to do with their son. She, of course, has been too busy to think of anything other than work. She can't remember the last time they laughed together, wholeheartedly, unrestrainedly. She can't remember the last time they kissed, hugged, made love. *I need to mend our relationship before it is too late.*

But how? Is it too late already? *Is he only staying with me for Arun's sake?* Please, no. But he's coming here, with Arun. *Is he only coming for Baba's sake? Or for mine too?*

I've been so closed off, only ever focused on work to the exclusion of everything else. And when I walked out in the middle of the most sacred thing at work – the directors' board meeting – I realised that I could just leave and the company would still function without me. And although I should have known this before, it is liberating knowing that I'm not indispensable.

Indira had thought she'd feel fulfilled once she achieved the goal she'd set herself when she applied for the role of school president and a boy in her class told her she wouldn't win.

'Why?' she'd asked.

'Because you are only a girl,' he sneered.

Everyone agreed that her campaign was the best the school had seen, that she was the best candidate, that her speech was rousing.

She didn't win.

'Told you,' the boy mocked.

I'll show you, she thought. And she had. The next year she stood again and she won, the first girl to do so.

After that there was a heady series of firsts, culminating when she reached the top of the career ladder, became CEO.

She thought she'd feel content, satisfied, now she'd achieved her ultimate ambition. But she found she felt no different; if anything, she was even more driven – having to maintain the position, work to keep it, prove herself worthy, required full-time, untiring effort.

She had neglected her parents, her husband, her son as she worked to climb to the top, thinking that once there she'd have all the time in the world. She'd thought wrong. Reaching the top was the easy part. The harder one was staying there. Is it too late now to mend bridges with her father? *Please, let my baba be alright.*

And Karan? She crosses her fingers even as she prays, *please.* She has called upon God more today than all the other days of her life put together. *Please.*

'Ma'am, are you going to take your turn or not?' the man behind her asks impatiently and she realises that the phone booth is empty and she's first in the queue. Inside the booth, it smells of worry and fear. She risks leaving the door slightly open – let them hear her private conversation if they wish – as she slots in the coins and dials.

The telephone is dirty and stained grimy yellow, as is the booth, cramped and graffitied, the glass opaque with dust and grease accumulated over the years and never cleaned. And then she forgets her revulsion, for Karan's voice, familiar, beloved, is asking, 'How is your baba?'

'Still in surgery.'

'Oh.'

A pause.

Indira waits. For a profession of love. For questions. For caring. For something. Anything. She wants to break this new, strange, increasingly uncomfortable silence between them but she is at a loss as to how. In their relationship, it has always been Karan who has done the talking, the chasing, the declarations of love. She has taken it for granted, taken him for granted; to be honest, she hadn't even noticed how much he does, how much of himself he puts into their relationship, until now. Now that he is no longer doing so.

Before, Karan would have asked a thousand questions; he would have told her to chase up the doctors after listening to her grumble about how this hospital was a joke, how they expected you to sit and wait for news for hours when your father had just had a massive heart attack.

Selfishly, even knowing their relationship is no longer what it was, and that it is almost entirely her fault for having let it get to this point, she had hoped, when she picked up the phone, that she could rant to him like she had countless times before when things got too much at work, and that he would listen, as always, patiently and loyally, one hundred per cent on her side. She would vent to him in a way she couldn't with her mother, not wanting to worry and upset her further, and instead squashing her own worries along with the proactive side of her, knowing her mother hated scenes, that she, like most, thought doctors right up there with gods – and to be fair, they were in that unenviable position of trying to save lives and if they saved Baba's, she'd be in her mother's camp. Ma trusted the doctors knew best, and worried that if her daughter argued with them they might not do their utmost by her husband.

'They're bound by the Hippocratic Oath. Do no harm.'

'Oh, but they're human, Indu. They're tired and stressed and have been dealing with critically ill patients all day and probably all the previous night too. If you annoy them, they might take it out on Baba.'

Her rule-abiding, meek mother twisting the abused pallu of her sari, pleading with Indira, and so she had submitted to sitting passively beside her when what she really wanted to do was create a stink until someone told them *something*.

Now, Indira realises that, despite everything, she had been hoping Karan would be on the same wavelength as her, like in the past – there when she needed him, picking up what she was not saying and managing to say exactly the right thing to make her feel better. With him, she has always felt understood. Known. Seen. Loved.

But now, 'Oh' is all he says. Then, 'Arun is fine but as planned, they want him to stay overnight just to make sure everything is okay and to monitor him, since he had a general anaesthetic. Once they give him the all-clear, we'll come there. Indu, are you and your ma okay?' His voice soft, kind.

She almost breaks down then. Almost. But sense quickly takes control, knocking back hysteria. She does not want to alarm Karan, not when he is with their groggy little boy. And it's not *just* that.

Indira had been hoping that when she heard Karan's voice, it would chase away the doubts she's been having. She'd understand that she'd been creating a problem that wasn't there. But now she sees that she has not been imagining their distance, it is there. It is real.

He doesn't know what to say, how to talk to her any more. Karan asked how she and her mother were in the same sentence. No separate assurances and questions for her. No professions of love, of care. Nothing. Worse than nothing – unpleasant pauses that neither can fill.

She wants to sob loudly and messily.

But…

Indira, who used to know exactly how Karan would behave in any situation, who could be completely herself with him, now doesn't know what he would say if she were to let go. What if he did not console her, but instead briskly told her to pull herself together?

And again, she is ambushed by pain, by the realisation, no less hurtful for being repeated, that somewhere along the way they have lost each other, their familiarity with the other, that they have become strangers. And so she swallows down her emotion and says, brightly, 'We're okay. I know Baba will be fine.'

'He will,' Karan says, quiet reassurance.

'Tell Arun his mama sends love.'

'I will.'

She waits.

'Take care, Indu. We'll be there soon.'

No 'I love you,' like there would have been, once.

She blinks back tears angrily as she walks to the canteen to get something for her mother to eat – she is not a person who cries because a man did not tell her he loves her.

But this is not any man – this is her husband, the love of her life. *You could have told him.* She wanted to. But the declaration had stuck in her throat, choked by the lump of salty hurt.

Part Eighteen

England

Another Life

Chapter Sixty

Clara

1935, Promise

Clara is in the communal garden, listening to the starlings chatter among the branches of the horse chestnut trees above. The grass sparkles and waves in the nippy, ice-edged breeze like a green river, and a pair of magpies hunt for treasure while a robin contemplates them from a safe distance.

Sounds filter in from the road behind her block of flats – horses neighing, the clip-clop of their hooves, a bicycle bell, the newspaper boy calling out the day's headlines in a young voice yet to break. Smells of cooking, boiling potatoes, cabbage and grilling meat. In one of the flats, a baby cries, plaintive.

Clara strokes her own bump and talks to her child. *You'll be here soon. I understand now why people take risks, in love, for love. Equally I can see how life and love can rub the shine off you, if you let them.*

Now I understand Aunt Helen, a poetry-loving romantic, but life stole the romance and the poetry from her. My own mother who dreamed of travelling to exotic, mysterious India, fed by my father's dreams, and yet what she got was a small dwelling in a slice of this vast city.

I loved, even knowing it was hopeless. And from it, I have you. My bright light of hope.

Anand came into my life when I was an orphan, making me believe in myself as I nursed him back to life. I met him serendipitously on my way to India. And he became my destiny. Now I know that his presence in my life was to give me you. Like spring unfurling new buds, I have finally something to look forward to.

I have hope. Promise. Anticipation. Someone of my very own, the seed of my love, to love. I will do my very best by you.

In her stomach, her child bicycles minuscule limbs, as if understanding her every word.

She is in London, in her patch of shared garden, grass pure emerald untouched by dust, weak sun that does not sear but instead gently warms, timid gold plagued by clouds threatening rain. But her gaze is far away, in another country, white-hot sun, red-dusted streets, warm people, a man she loves – still – his wife whom she also loves, who writes regularly, who lost the child she was carrying when Clara left, the child who would have been Clara's babe's half-brother or sister, the child Rathi has been longing for.

I am so sorry, Clara wrote. And she was. Even as she felt guilt that her own babe was thriving.

Rathi's letters are sprinkled with references to Anand. They hurt, they stab and yet she devours news of him hungrily. Pictures him, his every beloved feature that she knows by heart. Her traitorous heart that will not see sense, even now longing for him. She is raging at him and yet still she cares for him, despite everything, and she is angry with herself for this. When will her heart stop loving him?

Rathi's letter: *He has pleaded with me to stop trying. But I keep thinking, what if the next one is the one meant to live?*

Her friend's pain, transcending distance, seeping from words that have travelled across oceans. Clara wishes she was there, sitting beside her friend in the jasmine arbour, fountain gurgling mellow melodies, comforting her, the man they both love looking at his wife with pain-drenched love, oblivious to Clara's longing.

'It was a mistake.' His words resonating in her head, even as she strokes her bump. *You are anything but. For me you are everything.*

This is the first time since Clara's bump began to show that it's been warm enough for her to sit in the communal garden. A child waddles onto the grass, unsteady on its chubby legs, towards the pigeon that is pecking at the grass, the magpies having given up on treasure. The pigeon flusters away as the child approaches, weaving like a little drunk. The child watches the pigeon fly, his face consumed by wonder, and then he gathers his hands together and claps, even as he throws his head up to the heavens, following the flight of the bird, his laughter like iridescent bubbles bursting. Clara laughs in response. The child startles, looking at her, his face scrunching up preparatory to crying.

'Hello, little one,' Clara coos.

'Don't you dare!' His mother is there suddenly, her pale eyes flashing fiery gold. 'Don't want the likes of you talking to him.'

Clara is puzzled. *Likes of her?*

'You say your husband died. We know the truth, don't we?' the woman bites through pursed lips.

And with that, she scoops up her child, who has started crying, picking up on his mother's anger, and stamps away, slamming her door behind her.

Clara sits there stunned, the air fanning her face coolly accusatory. She is reminded, with a painful lurch, of Meg's reaction when she said she was expecting…

*

When Clara wrote to Meg to say she was returning to England, Meg had insisted on Clara staying with her, Fred and nine-year-old Evie until she found her own place.

'This is your godmother, Clara. You were growing in my stomach when I saw her last,' Meg beamed when introducing Clara to Evie – her mother's very image.

Although she had considered stopping nursing after Evie's birth, Meg found she couldn't quite do it and she was still working at St Thomas's. 'Matron Andrews is still going strong at the hospital. She'll be thrilled to have you back.'

'That was a long year away,' Matron had twinkled at Clara. 'Felt like several, to be sure. Glad you're back though. Now, you'll do a training course, Sister Knight, and after, I'll assign you to the wards.'

Between shifts, Meg took Clara house-hunting, Clara in this way discovering anew the city that had been her home in another life when her parents and brother were alive and again after the war when she left her aunt's home.

In contrast to India, the colour, the exuberance, the super-charged brightness, London was weary and grey, and yet full of surprises, with startling, compelling pockets of exquisite, breathtaking beauty.

Eventually she found a ground-floor flat near Meg's home. With its communal garden, and situated near the hospital and shops, it was perfect.

She missed India, the country itself and her loved ones there – Henry, his parents, Rathi and above all, Anand – with a constant, persistent ache.

She wrote to Henry and to Rathi (wondering as she did so if Anand was missing her even a little, if he read these letters she wrote to his wife, hating herself for wanting him to, for writing them to him as much as to Rathi), bright, happy missives that betrayed no hint of her pain. And when their letters arrived, she touched them reverently, smelled them in the vain hope that they had carried, across the ocean, the spice and sandalwood, baked earth and heady vermilion essence of India.

Being in London was like going back in time. Work at the hospital was just as busy as before and it gave welcome structure to her days. In many ways, it was like she had never left.

It was Clara who had changed, fundamentally so. She had journeyed to India a girl and returned a woman.

As her child grew in her belly, Clara worried: *What if he or she looks like Anand? How will people react?*

When the anxiety and the missing got too overwhelming, when clasping her medal and channelling strength did not help, she walked the streets of the city. One day, when even walking until her feet were sore had not eased her anguish, as she was passing the church two streets from her flat, she heard psalms wafting on an incense- and prayer-flavoured breeze and she recalled perching on the cemetery wall in her aunt's village with Dolly, the yew trees sighing over the newly dug graves as snatches of hymns from yet another funeral drifted on the mournful wind, chilled by, tasting of death.

She'd entered the church, sat in a pew, the brassy notes of the organ echoing sombrely in the hushed confines, rainbow patterns of light filtering through stained glass, painting the frescoed ceiling, the myriad of statues, in a golden glow. Her feet rested on bricks beneath which lay centuries-old dead. It was strangely comforting, her own private sorrow rendered small and put in perspective in this hallowed space of death and afterlife, heaven and hell, devils and angels, saviours and demons. She closed her eyes and gave herself to the music.

*

Every fortnight, Meg insisted Clara join her, Fred and Evie for Sunday lunch.

'You're looking peaky, we must feed you up.' Meg bustled about the kitchen while Evie coloured at the table, the scent of boiling potatoes, roasting meat, bubbling gravy, Fred blustering about. Family. Clara would stroke her stomach gently: *I'll create a home for you, even if it's just the two of us, I promise.*

The first time her baby moved, she was at work.

She had felt tiny flutterings, soft as angel kisses, in her stomach as she knelt by a bedside, bandaging a wounded arm. She stood up, touched her stomach. And there it was, a fluttering right under her palm. She had fingered her St Christopher medal as tears started in her eyes. Tears of joy and gratefulness. Tears of ache for Anand, who did not know of his child, and his wife, her best friend, who so desperately wanted a child with him.

I will protect you with my everything, she promised, and her baby responded with what felt like tiny bubbles being blown beneath her hand.

When Clara couldn't hide her bump any longer, she'd told Meg she was expecting. Meg's lips had pursed. She said, 'Ah.' After that, she was distant, not quite as warm. She stopped inviting Clara round to her house.

Matron, Meg and her fellow nurses seemed to have believed her when she told them that she had come back home because her husband had succumbed to illness within months of their marriage. But now they went quiet. The looks they started to give her and her belly, Meg's coolness towards her, no more invitations to Sunday lunch – they were all judging her.

*

Now, the woman's slammed door reverberates in her ears. *Likes of you.* The hatred in the woman's voice. Tears sting. Part of her wants to leave, to go indoors, hide away. Instead she stays on the bench, defiant.

I have every right to be here. She strokes her bump. *I will not cower and hide. I am a mother, bringing my child into this world. If I can't take it, how will I protect my babe?*

She sits there until night arrives, cold and stark with frost-stippled shadows. And only then does she go indoors.

She makes a point of sitting outside every day after that. She will not back down. The other residents gossip among themselves while shooting daggers at her. They will not let their children come close to her. They avoid her bench like the plague.

Only a kind old man limps over to sit beside her, earning vicious looks from the disapproving clique.

'I'm Mr Moffatt. And you're the notorious newcomer who's set our modest block of flats aflame.' He winks at her.

'Ah.' She's glad he's addressing the issue. 'You've heard about me then.'

He pats her hand. 'You've made quite the impression. But don't worry, my dear, none of them are perfect. Why, those who judge, I could tell you a thing or two about them.' He throws his head up to the striped gold firmament. 'A bit of sun. Make the most while it lasts, eh?'

Once you experience the sun in India, Clara thinks with ache and longing, *it pervades your very bones and nothing else comes close.*

Chapter Sixty-One

Clara

Perfect

Clara is on fire and there's no respite.

'My St Christopher medal. It will keep you safe,' her mother whispers.

But the medal too is burning. Pain. Hot. Blinding, raging, roaring, eating her alive.

'Push, Clara,' the midwife urges.

Unrelenting. Throbbing, pulsing, enervating, immobilising. The red-hot scorch of agony.

'One last push, Clara, yes, that's it,' Meg urges.

Her friend's voice is like flowing water, silky smooth, twinkling silver. She sinks into it gratefully. Her baby is coming. She will meet this child she loves with her all at last. Clara clasps Meg's hand and pushes, concentrating all the waning strength left in her.

There is a sudden release from all the desperate pain, followed by a mewling cry. But then… Quiet. An unnatural hush from the adults in the room, only broken by her child's – her newborn's – plaintive wail. Panic grips her.

'What's wrong? Meg?'

The midwife leaves the room, slamming the door behind her.

'Is something the matter with my baby?' Dread crushing her heart. *If there is, it will be fitting after what I did.*

Please not my baby.

Why not? her conscience counters. *Rathi loses her children.*

But I can hear *my child.*

She sits up, wincing, frantically casting about for her child. 'Meg, please, my baby…' Her voice tremulous.

Her friend reaches into the basket Clara had prepared when labour was imminent, cushioned with the softest linen she could find.

Meg places Clara's child upon her chest, against her medal, and her heart seizes up with love.

She has loved, but not like this. This overwhelming tornado of emotion, so heady and fierce, so desperately, painfully joyous and protective, for this tiny little human. A boy. A beautiful boy.

She holds him to her heart, his scrunched-up little face, like a wise old man, his wispy black hair, his tiny fingers and toes, bunched-up hands and minuscule legs windmilling away. He is *perfect*. Then why…

She looks to Meg, who is glaring at her with barely concealed horror. 'What's the matter? He looks fine to me.'

Has she missed something now that this perfect child, who is rooting at her breast, latching now, sucking with all his might, his little gums working, has made her a mother, her heart over-whelmed with a wellspring of love so tender and excruciating and rapturous. Is motherhood dulling her nurse's instincts?

'I cannot believe it of you!' Meg's voice shocked and revolted in equal measure. 'I can get over you lying about having a husband. I don't want to ruin our friendship over it. But this… How could you stoop so low, Clara? The boy's *black*!' The last word a venomous accusation, flung over her shoulder as Meg storms out, leaking its bitter poison into the room, mingling with the scent of blood and pain and new life, tainting it.

Clara's newborn clings to her. Her beautiful child, barely arrived in the world and already condemned because of his colour, his beautiful golden skin branded a sin.

'You are perfect, my boy,' she whispers, her voice quivering with indignation, anger, hurt, pain and, above all, love. She takes her St Christopher medal off, slips it around his tiny neck. 'I will protect you with my all.'

Chapter Sixty-Two

Clara

1938, Curse

It is when her winsome three-year-old – she has named him David for her father – is spat at, the sour spittle barely missing his glossy brown curls, his face crumpling in distress as he turns towards her, puzzled, tears running down his rosy cinnamon cheeks, choking out, between sobs, 'M… Mama, that man… Why did he call me coolie? What does ha-caste mean?', that she makes up her mind.

Her son, her love, her all, cannot stay here. He doesn't belong. He never will. Her forbidden love stamped on his skin, making him stand out, a recipient of hatred, loathing, others' narrow-minded prejudice. She cannot stand it. She cannot bear it. Not any more. Not now *he* is beginning to question, take note, hurt.

They are not welcome anywhere. But she has put up with that. She experienced a little of it when she was carrying him, when people guessed she wasn't married. But not to this extent. She has put up with the doctors, the nurses at the hospital and even Matron treating her like an outcast. With the loss of friendship.

Meg had visited a few weeks after David's birth. She'd looked distinctly uncomfortable as she sat rigidly, her back too straight, her gaze flitting away from Clara's son even as she said, '*I* can see past his colour, but others won't.'

Clara had closed her eyes then, not wanting Meg to see how much her words hurt. *I can see past his colour.* As if her son's beautiful hue was a curse.

'Fred does not want you visiting us,' Meg said and Clara nodded. She squeezed Clara's hand. 'But I'll visit.'

She did not look at or touch David, who squirmed in Clara's arms. She did not mention bringing Evie, Clara's godchild, along and Clara didn't ask. Perhaps Fred had decreed she be kept away as well. Meg must have gone against her husband's wishes to come and visit Clara, the outcast.

Clara doesn't mind *that* much when she is discriminated against. But it is unbearable when they do so to her child. Her heart. Her life.

When he made his entry into this capricious world, she had held her newborn and all the worries she'd had throughout her pregnancy – *what if he looks like Anand, how will he fit in, what will people say* – were pushed aside by the sheer force of her love. *Her* child. This perfect little being. He was created from one stolen night with a man who is not and will never be hers. But this child *was* hers, of her, and she was amazed, astounded and humbled by his existence, his immense fragility, his dainty perfection. She had kissed her little boy, his brown scrunched-up face, his black wisps of hair, his beautiful almond eyes shut tight against the light, his bow lips, his minuscule, exquisite fingers and toes, and promised, *I will protect you with my all.*

And she has tried. But, she understood, the very first time she took him out and people looked at her and especially David with distaste, disdain, loathing, that she couldn't always do so. Their shocked, sneering, hateful reactions made her wonder, anger, hurt and bewilderment ambushing her: *Is this how it will always be, my son judged for his colour rather than for who he is? Will he be at a disadvantage all his life because his roots are branded on his skin? Is this punishment for what I did – taking what was not mine, sleeping with a married man, the husband of my friend – to stand by and watch my son suffer through no fault of his?*

After that, she took care to wrap him up so no inch of golden skin showed, hating herself for hiding his colouring as if it was wrong. How to protect him so he doesn't feel lesser, unwanted, unworthy? Can she?

When Clara couldn't find anyone willing to mind David while she was at work, she gave up working at the hospital, subsisting on her savings, which, although substantial as she hardly spent much in India, and supplemented by the maharaja's jewels and gifts over the years, will go quickly if she's not careful.

She recites her favourite poems, narrates stories, sings to him. As a baby, David's liquid gold eyes would follow her and it was as if he understood her every word. Soon he was talking, sounds at first, then words that didn't make sense and then words that did! Oh, the miracle of him, toddling after her on his hands and knees, then lurching on his little legs, and soon, running from one end of their little flat to the other; his laughter: sunlit celebration, dazzling, energising, beatific, illuminating, incandescent.

She loves every minute she spends with him but is aware that she cannot keep him entertained forever, that soon he will want more, she alone will not be enough, and neither will the confines of this flat, their haven.

I will protect you with my all, she promised her baby. And yet she is beginning to realise she cannot, not always, not from this prejudice against his skin. And that hurts. It flays. It destroys her.

*

One day, when out walking with a swaddled six-month-old David, she'd dropped a coin in the hat of the black man who slept rough on a bench in the park.

'Thank you for your kindness, my dear.' He smiled.

David squirmed, windmilling his arms, and his swaddling slipped – she had not wrapped him securely enough. She quickly covered him up again but not before a passer-by had a good look at him.

'Shame on you,' the stranger hissed at Clara.

Clara bit her lower lip hard and pulled David closer to her. The rough sleeper sighed, shaking his head at the woman's retreating back. And to Clara, warmly, 'You have a beautiful boy.'

Clara had felt tears prick her eyes. Yes, her boy was beautiful. *She* certainly thought so. But this was the first time someone else had acknowledged it, said as much. The man was saying, eyes glinting with the cumulative hurt of many similar incidents, 'I fought for this country. Lost my family and nearly my life.' His voice thick with resignation. 'But now I can't find work and I'm reduced to this.' Waving his hand around at the moisture-laden breeze sighing among the branches – it had just rained, pigeons cooing around them, pecking at the bright green grass. 'It's not so bad. It's people's reactions that get to me.'

When the man spoke next, it was so softly that she had to step closer in order to hear. He smelt earthy, of grass and rain and star-spangled, ice-scattered winter nights. 'He will learn to hate his skin, be ashamed of who he is.'

'Oh!' Startled, she hugged her son closer, making sure once again that he was covered. She wanted to walk away but she was rooted to the spot, a part of her wanting to hear what this man had to say, this rough sleeper who was the only one who had *seen* her child beyond his colouring, who had dared address what others shied away from, clamming up, chilling silences that radiated scorn, judgement.

'You can't hide him forever, his beautiful skin secreted away like a transgression.' The man was gentle, his eyes sparkling with frozen tears from a thousand hurts. 'It chips away at you, you see, the constant treatment as inferior because of the colour of your skin. It undermines who you are, regardless of your education, your profession. You begin to lose your self-worth, you stop seeing yourself as someone worthy and start seeing yourself through their eyes.' His pain, palpable, bleeding.

I will not let it happen to David, she had thought. The boy who had shown her what love could be, the heights it could reach, the width it could span. The child who had given her a new identity as a mother.

'As much as you want to, you can't protect him always,' the man said as if reading her mind. 'It's the world we live in.' He looked at her child, sleeping peacefully in her arms. He swallowed and she could see he was struggling with some great emotion. 'During the war, the worst injuries I received were not physical but emotional, the most painful wounds not inflicted by the enemy but from the racial abuse of my own side.'

Her eyes stung, her voice shaking as she said, 'I will protect him with my all.'

'You'll try.' He sighed and there was a world of pain in that exhalation. 'But you won't be able to, my dear.'

And Clara remembered when, the other day as she was queuing at the butcher's, the swaddle she'd wrapped David in slipped, like it had just now, and the women behind her got a glimpse of her son's skin. The recoil and horror in their faces. The way they looked at her again, judgement hardening their eyes, stone-cold, disdainful gazes stark with loathing. How they had moved away, as if David's colour was catching.

*

When, all those years ago, she and a wounded Anand first crossed paths and he was kept apart from the other soldiers, she should have had an inkling. But she did not put herself in his shoes, think of how he might feel about this casual, ingrained racism.

Perhaps by not asking him how he felt, she too had been guilty, just as much as those who had shunned him because of his skin colour. She never spared a thought for how he might feel; for *she* had never experienced racism directly, only the oblique effects of it from her aunt and Danny when she volunteered to look after Anand. She hadn't given it a second thought until her son was born with skin the hue of conkers burnished by autumn sun.

Now, at three years old, when he should be carefree and unburdened, happy and safe, her son is noticing the racism she has tried so desperately to shield him from. He is starting to feel bewildered and insecure, to hurt and question. Now she can no longer protect him, just as that man sleeping rough on the park bench warned. In her heart of hearts, she knew this, but did not want to accept it.

She was deluding herself. But she cannot any longer. She does not want David to grow up thinking that his skin colour is to be derided. She does not want him to believe the lie that the way everyone treats him is what he is – someone wrong, his colour a curse, his existence a sin.

If this is punishment for what she did, sleeping with the husband of her best friend, it is an effective but extremely cruel one. *She* should be punished. But not, surely, her innocent child, his sweetness and light beginning to dim with the prejudice being directed at him…

What she did was wrong, but *he* is not and she cannot bear that he will be punished for it, her beautiful son growing up believing he is other, different, hated, shunned. She will not stand for it.

Clara has evolved through many versions of herself – her parents' pet, Paul's adoring and adored little sister, wartime nurse, nurse to Henry and to maharanis, miracle Memsahib to the villagers she treated at her clinic and Anand's.

She'd thought nursing was her calling but when she held her son in her arms, she found her true calling: mother. Her son is her life. But if he stays here, he will have only half a life, a life of being mocked and hated. She doesn't want this for him, this much she knows.

What to do?

Chapter Sixty-Three

Clara

Proof

As Clara worries and agonises, two things happen at once. She is at the door of her building, arms laden with shopping, when an older woman, who lives in the flat above and who, like everyone else (except Mr Moffatt, who, bless him, has accepted David as easily as he accepted Clara), has shunned her, enters before her.

Just as Clara is about to follow with David, the woman very deliberately shuts the door in her face, narrowly missing David's small fingers. It is the last straw. She drops her shopping, hears the eggs shatter but doesn't care and runs after her, yelling, 'How dare you?'

The woman turns, hunched shoulders, flinty eyes, flecks of sour spittle speckling Clara's face: 'How dare you? This building was respectable before you and your half-caste desecrated it.'

'He's a child.'

'Disgusting,' the woman mutters and walks away.

Clara is tempted to follow, but David is crying: 'Mama!'

And so she picks him up and manages to navigate her sobbing boy and the shopping into the flat and shut the door. Then she rests her head against the cool wood, holds her son close as he sobs and bites her lip to stop the tears that squeeze out. She will not cry. She is *furious*.

She manages to salvage the remaining eggs and feed her son an omelette. He is full of energy once he's eaten, running about the room, tears forgotten. But she is exhausted, her fury and upset at the woman, at everyone who rejects her son, her worry about how to protect David draining her.

She is overwhelmed by the desire to go to church – she finds peace sitting in there, looking up at the frescoes, rainbow light filtering in through stained glass and dancing on statues of the Virgin Mary with her blue-eyed, blond, perfectly white Jesus, knowing it has survived so much over centuries and will most likely still be there centuries hence.

She clears up in the kitchen, putting away the shopping, wiping the worktops. After a bit she is aware that the flat is very quiet. Where is David? In her upset, did she leave the door open?

The front door is shut. David is standing at the back door, his nose flattened against the glass, peering out at the children playing in the communal garden.

Until now she has managed to keep him indoors. It has been cold but today is the first sunny day of spring and the children are out in full force. Last spring and summer he was too young to want to join in. But now…

'Out,' he says, pointing at the children, his face contorted with longing and plea. 'Mama, please?'

How can she refuse? After all, they are children. They will not have the same prejudices as adults, surely? And so she opens the door and he runs out, delighted. The other children watch him and she watches them. Then they smile and soon they are all playing together. Relief flushes away the stresses of the day, that woman shutting the door in David's face, David's shock. His tears.

She feels it all leave her as she watches her beloved boy play with the other children, his laughter ringing, joyous. She is just about to turn away when she hears the slam of doors and then a mother is rushing out, pulling her child in, followed by another.

'You're not to play with that half-caste, understood?'

The slur tossed like a hateful grenade at her beautiful boy, who stands stunned as his new friends are yanked away, his face scrunched up in distress preparatory to tears. Clara, incensed, rushes outside. David throws his arms around her, buries his face in her skirt.

She turns to the women who are still outside gathering their offspring away from hers. 'He's just a child and was playing happily with—'

'We don't want our children mixing with the likes of him. Have you no shame? You're not welcome here.'

She is shaking with fury but before she can come back with a retort, they march off and she is left with an inconsolable child. Again.

Later, David in bed, the newspaper catches her attention.

Austria was last night officially proclaimed a 'State of the German Reich'. In all countries except Italy and Japan, partners with Germany in the Anti-Comintern Pact, the annexing of Austria is condemned.

The words pulse before her eyes.

She has heard rumbles of a possible war. But nobody believed it would actually happen – not after the devastation of the last. But it will. *It will.* Here is proof. Another war. Bombs. Air raids. Death. Destruction.

No. What she and David are living through now is bad enough. But another war... She is suddenly cold, despite the spring day. Memories threaten to overwhelm her. Waking up an orphan in hospital after the air raid. The orphanage. She shudders at the distressing image of David in an orphanage reviled, ostracised. *No, I cannot let history repeat itself.*

Chapter Sixty-Four

Clara

Innocence

Clara sways on her feet, light-headed, watching her son. And as she breathes in his beautiful, golden perfection, untainted, in sleep, by the dark taunts flung at him, she knows that she will do everything in her power to preserve his innocence, to keep him safe from harm and abuse, even if it crushes and devastates her.

Nearly four years ago when she discovered he was growing inside her, a miracle, a gift, unexpected but oh so welcome and beloved, she had made a decision that broke her heart: to leave the country she loved, the people she loved, and travel here, for she had thought it best for him.

Now she is on the cusp of making another decision in his best interests. It is the hardest, the most painful decision she will ever make, and she wishes with all the pieces of her shattering heart that she didn't have to make it. It will mean parting with the one person who means the most to her. The only meaningful love of her life. It will destroy her life as she knows it, but it will save her son's and that is what matters most.

The *only* thing that matters.

Sitting beside her son, watching him sleep the sleep of the innocent, she picks up her pen and a sheet of notepaper. Her hand shakes as she lifts the pen. She presses too hard on the sheet and it tears.

Her son stirs, mumbles a soft protest. *I have to do this, son, for your sake.* She picks up a new sheet. *Dear Anand,* she begins.

Chapter Sixty-Five

Clara

To the Point

Anand looks just the same as ever. This man whose every feature and expression, every look, she has studied. This man whom she nursed to health and has nursed beside. Her friend. Her love. The keeper of her heart.

The man who broke her heart. Her son's father. The man who would recite poetry in his golden voice after a harrowing day at the clinic as a tropical sun set over a kaleidoscopic sky, several seas and miles away in another lifetime.

She hasn't dared think about him, not even after she wrote telling him about his son. But she can't prevent him taking over her dreams. She can't deny the heartstopping, heartwarming glimpses of him in her child, his smile, the way he cocks his head to look at her, his golden eyes with their myriad expressions.

This man her destiny. Whom she first met as a fledgling nurse, to whom she will now entrust her son.

His son.

His reply had come within days of her writing to him. It was to the point.

No, *why didn't you tell me.* Only

> *I've booked a passage on the SS Ranchi leaving Friday – I've convinced Rathi it is on the maharaja's business. She's going*

*to her mother's to recuperate after her last miscarriage. As
you know from her letters, she's decided to give up trying
for a child and is now actively looking to adopt. She will
be writing to you about my trip to England. In your reply
you can tell her about David and your suggestions with
regards to his origins.*

David.

Her son's name in his father's letter – Anand's first proper
communication with her since that night when they created their
beautiful boy. The way he wrote about Rathi – the love and pain
in every word…

She didn't dwell. She couldn't spare the time or the emotion.
All she could think of was how little time she had with her boy
now that her plan was actually in place. She concentrated on
loving him, learning him by heart even though every bit of him
was written indelibly into every fibre of her being.

Rathi's letter arrived a few days after her husband's, just as
Anand had said it would, telling Clara of his visit to England and
reiterating their decision to adopt a child. Tears stabbing her eyes,
choking her throat, Clara had composed yet another lie – the
most important one yet – to her trusting, beautiful friend whom
she has chosen as new mother for her son, while he climbed all
over her, planting sloppy kisses on her nose, her eyes, her cheeks,
saying, 'Mama, face wet.'

London, March, 1938

Darling Rathi,

It's so wonderful to hear from you.

If you are serious about adopting, there is a little boy here of mixed Indian and British heritage, a beautiful child three years old. His mother delivered him at the hospital where I work. She passed away recently from a sudden illness – I was her nurse and she pleaded with me, before she died, to please make sure her child went to a good family who cherished him.

He has apparently been subjected to racism because of his mixed race and she was very particular that he went to a family that would treasure and not malign him. The boy's father was a visiting Indian academic who only revealed he was married when she told him of her pregnancy. He does not want anything to do with the child as he already has a family.

I've been taking care of the child as I feel responsible for him – he does not have anyone else now his mother's gone and he is really a divine child. Sweet and well behaved and no trouble at all. But obviously the arrangement cannot continue and, as per his mother's dying wish, I have been looking to find him a good home. But it is harder than I expected as there is a lot of prejudice towards dark-skinned children.

If you are willing to take him, and I do vouch for him – he is a healthy, clever, wonderful boy – I can send him with Anand when he arrives here. He will thrive in India and especially in your care, of this I am sure.

With all my love,
Clara

Now here he is. This man Clara has loved for most of her adult life, his gaze taking his child in. Hungrily. Breathlessly. And now his eyes on her face. The expressions there. Love and guilt and friendship and sadness – their entire history in that liquid gaze.

'Why didn't you tell me?' he breathes.

'What would you have done?'

His gaze falters.

'Oh, Clara,' he says, those two words encompassing friendship and pain and everything unsaid, everything hidden, the secret they will keep from the woman they both love, the knowledge of how his hands, those same hands that deftly sliced through human flesh in his role as physician, were oh so tender on her skin.

Once upon a time she had been envious of how Rathi could conduct an entire conversation with her husband, the man Clara loved, with just one gaze that encompassed so much. Now Clara is doing the same. Friendship, hurt, betrayal, history, secrets and promise, a pact sealed by their son, who is regarding this stranger a little shyly but mostly curiously from within the fortress of Clara's arms.

Perhaps anyone who has a long association with someone can conduct silent yet charged conversations the same way. No, not anyone. *I have been intimate with this man. My destiny interwoven with his. We have a child together. He was my friend and more. Always more.*

She clears her throat. She has something to say that cannot be conveyed through a glance. 'You took advantage of me when I was at my most vulnerable.'

She sees him flinch, his face closing up with hurt. It generates reciprocal hurt within her – she has always hurt when he has.

Oh, this man and the complicated emotions he engenders within her. Even now when she thought she had no space for any emotion other than her heartbreak at her impending separation from her beautiful boy.

'I did not see you saying no.'

'I did before, at the clinic.' She sees the memory pulsing alongside guilt in his eyes. 'But that day, I was hurting, grieving Maharani Maya. I was weak and you...'

'You wanted it.'

'You knew I loved you. You led me on.'

He does not meet her gaze, just as after he had slept with her, even as he says, 'I am sorry.' An abashed, embarrassed child caught in a transgression.

I will never catch my own son in one, she thinks, heart splintering even as she hugs her beloved boy closer, his little-boy scent, purity and innocence. 'I wanted you to acknowledge your part in what we did. I do not regret it. I wanted it for so very long. And I have David because of it.' Her voice breaks.

'Oh, Clara. I loved you too, differently.'

Loved. Past tense. *Not in the way I wanted you to. Not in the way you love Rathi.* Again, he does not look at her. Her heart is sundered by the imminent agony of parting from David and yet this hurts too.

He holds out his arms.

Not so soon. I'm not ready. I will never be. But her son, who has only ever known his mother's arms, goes gladly into his father's and grins at her from there. They look complete, father and son. They look right in a way she doesn't with David.

'He is beautiful,' Anand whispers.

Her son is playing with his father's hair, which is so like David's own, although David's curls are touched with gold. It is painful, torturous relief that her son is so at ease with Anand, as if recognising his father at a primeval level.

'Yes.' *I will not get to see him grow into his features, that regal nose, that patrician forehead. What am I doing? Give him back.* 'Love him. Look after him for me.'

'I already do. I will look after him, protect him, with my life. And you know Rathi will love him. She has so much love to give.'

Rathi will watch my son change, become a man. My penance for stealing her husband.

I'm doing right by David, she tells herself, as she has been doing since she made her decision. But it does nothing, nothing, for her pain.

'You're going on an adventure,' she'd told her son as she packed his bag.

He tugged at her hand. 'Mama come too.'

She had turned away to hide her tears. 'I'll come later. You'll be going on a ship. On the sea. It's full of water. You love water.'

'I want Mama,' her boy insisted.

She gathered him in her arms, breathed him in, sugar and mischief. *How can I bear to let you go, my love?* 'I'll come soon,' she lied. 'Until then, this,' she pointed to his medal – her medal, her mother's before hers, 'will keep you safe. When you miss me, hold it and you'll feel better.'

'I want *you*, Mama,' her son cried.

It's best this way, she tells herself, as Anand loads her son's things, lovingly packed and seasoned with her tears, into the car.

'Mama,' her boy cries, clinging to her neck. She commits his smell, the feel of him to memory. The perfect, anchoring weight of her son in her arms.

She kisses him one last time, breathing him in, learning him by heart, although of course every single beloved bit of him is tattooed upon her devastated heart, which beats only for him. Then she gently disentangles his arms from her neck, every instinct in her screaming to hold on, not let go, not do this, handing her love, her heart, her life, her all, to his father.

'Mama!' her son screams.

It takes all her strength to smile and wave, the car blurring as her son cries for her in his father's arms.

She waves long after the car is out of sight, bearing all she loves most in the world, standing beside the deserted road as frosty night settles white and silent and ice-cold as her life without her son in it.

Part Nineteen

India

The Best of Intentions

Chapter Sixty-Six

Indira

1995, Platitudes

Indira breathes in the canteen's smell of sambar and spices, roasting dough and curry and sweet milk. She wonders, when did she and Karan stop saying, *I love you* to each other? When did it start being replaced by a formal: *Take care*? When did they become strangers, dancing around each other, not talking through their emotions but dumbing them down and replacing genuine feelings with platitudes?

'What would you like, Ma'am?'

She blinks.

The lady at the counter is smiling at her kindly. 'There's a deal on the veg thali – two rupees off, and the samosas are fresh, just out of the frying pan. The *semiya kheer* is gone, but there are a few jalebis left. I'd recommend them, very syrupy.' She pats her stomach, overflowing above her sari skirt. 'I've had more than a fair few.' She beams happily.

When Indira returns with far too much food, vadas swimming in sambar, a samosa and a potato bonda with coconut and mint chutneys and several nectary jalebis, her mother looks stricken.

'Is it Bab…?'

'No.' Ma's eyes softening with apology and love. Then, upset clouding them afresh, 'I need to go home. Your dadu… I forgot about him. How could I?'

Dadu, Baba's father, lives with Ma and Baba.

In actual fact, it is the other way round, Ma and Baba living in Dadu's house – Baba, the only son, staying on in his parents' house and looking after them, as per tradition, Ma moving in upon her marriage to Baba.

'Ma,' Indira says, gently but firmly, 'you will wait here and eat this food. I'll go and see to Dadu.'

Her mother manages a weak smile, her face slack with gratitude. 'Take some of this for Dadu. You have the best of intentions, Indu, but I really can't eat it all.'

Part Twenty

England

Two Wars

Chapter Sixty-Seven

Clara

1939–1941, Soulless

'This country is at war with Germany,' Prime Minister Neville Chamberlain announces on 3 September 1939. But Clara is already at war. In her mind, her thoughts, every moment, asking herself, *Did I do the right thing giving my heart, my soul, my life away?*

The week after David left with Anand, Meg had arrived on one of her visits to find Clara broken, lost, grieving, a shell. She had spent the long days and endless nights after David left in bed, unable to get up. Her reason for living gone.

'I sent him away,' Clara had sobbed and Meg had taken her in her arms – the first time she had hugged her since David was born – and allowed her to cry. Meg must have relayed this information at the hospital – Clara never asked – for she visited the very next week with a request from Matron for Clara to return to work.

After Meg left, Clara considered climbing back into bed as she had been doing since David left with Anand. She courted sleep, for then she could dream that her son was with her, she heard his voice calling, 'Mama' while flashing that cheeky, mischievous, irresistible grin. She dreamed of him and grieved anew when she woke to a world soulless without her son.

She was sorely tempted to close her eyes, shut out a world without David in it. But she couldn't keep doing it forever. Her son was safe. He was loved. He would thrive. And perhaps one day, sooner rather than later, she would see him. She couldn't give up.

And so, with a colossal effort of will, Clara opened the door, walked to the hospital and took up Matron's offer, although Matron had shunned her like everyone else when David was born – there was no place for pride when she was missing, hurting. She would give back. Nursing had been her solace after her mother died. It would perhaps in time be so again, although it felt like nothing, nothing could heal the raw wound where her heart had been, the black hole of yearning. Her arms, her body, her soul bereft, lost, wanting.

She worked all the shifts she could. She worked and tried to forget that her son would grow and change without her in his life, every moment without him sheer torture. Tending to the afflicted, the wounded and the terminally ill, seeing the stoic bravery of family members and of the dying themselves was humbling, as always. She was lucky. Her son was alive, well, safe, happy.

She was lucky. *Then why did it hurt so much?*

When Matron insisted she take a break, she walked the streets of this great city. And that was a lesson too. She saw homeless men, desperation etched onto every line on stark faces old before their time, shivering in the freezing winter dark. Children barely older than David, holey shoes and ragged clothes, begging, hawking newspapers, gap-toothed grins in dirty faces.

And again, she thought, *my son is safe. He is loved.*

Rathi writes regularly with updates – she has unquestioningly accepted Clara's lie about David's provenance, believing Clara to be the kind nurse who took in a dying mother's child and honoured her desperate last wish for her son to go to a good family. Clara had worried that she'd suspect something when she saw David with her St Christopher medal but Rathi, bless her, believed Clara's excuse in the letter accompanying David, that he'd grown attached to it and wouldn't settle without it. Clara suspects she's too happy to have a child of her own to query too deeply the whys and hows – her trusting friend. Rathi natters away about David, her love for him evident in every word. Her letters are both blessing and torment.

Clara's son doing all the things she wanted for him, without her in his life. David, whom they've renamed the more Indian-sounding *Dev*. A small death. *Her* son no longer answering to the name, her father's, that she had given him. The second was when Rathi wrote: *He tugged at my hand, pointed at a pistachio barfi and said, 'Want that one, Ma,' as casual as anything. The first time he's called me 'Ma'. The second was right after, when he climbed into my lap, saying, 'Why are you crying, Ma?'*

Clara had set the letter down, gently, and walked outside, breathing in several mouthfuls of bracing air, until she regained her breath and colour, and the nausea eased. She walked until afternoon gave way to evening, heedless of her feet blistering and bruising, and dusk descended on a city being torn asunder by the second war in two decades and the blackout came into effect and the darkness was absolute.

In the velvet awning above, twinkling stars broadcasted defiant hope despite the menace of war. Wide sky, spanning the world, arcing over where, on the other side of a vast ocean, in a beautiful house, its outer walls festooned with bougainvillea, scented with jasmine, fountain gurgling a soothing melody and peacocks preening in the central courtyard, her son slept, calling another woman *Ma*.

Mothers lose sons all the time. They lost sons to the last war and will lose others to this one. I am lucky. My son is alive and well and thriving and happy. I did the right thing. He is safe. He is loved. It should be enough.

A baby's wail like a siren. Clara closed her eyes, her hand upon her heart where the medal no longer rested – babies, children, everything a reminder of her own child. The child no longer hers. Answering to a name different to that she had given him, although in her mind he would always be David – and that's where he'd stay, in her mind, her bruised heart, her anguished soul, loved, oh so much, from afar.

Rathi wrote in her last letter,

> *When are you coming to visit? There's a war on and I know you want to help, do your bit. Anand chided me when I told him I'd asked you to come to India.*
>
> *'I want her to be safe,' I cried.*
>
> *'I do too,' Anand said. 'But she's doing good there. Saving soldiers like she did me. And you know Clara, she faces life on her own terms – she is not one to shy from danger. She will do what needs doing, go where she is needed.'*
>
> *I have copied down what he said word for word – high praise indeed from my husband. You know him...*

Clara paused in her reading, *I do, intimately.*

> *He's not the best at showing his emotions but his regard for you is right up there.*

Clara, I know you want to do your bit. But we, your friends, want you to be safe and, with London being bombed incessantly, so we hear, we worry for you.

You know you're always welcome here. Will you come and visit?

Clara set the letter down carefully. Dusk had descended, the nights drawing in, earlier every day. It was Mr Moffatt's turn hosting his friends – veterans of the last war, too old to take active part in this one although they did their bit as air-raid wardens and firemen. She could hear them reminiscing while despite the wintry chill they played cards on the communal lawn, much to neighbour Maud's annoyance – she'd yelled at them to keep it down a few times. Hawthorn and sweet pea and daphne perfumed the nippy air, accented by the aged soldiers' raucous laughter.

Shadows flirted with the rose-edged grey of evening, the old men's chatter fading as darkness encroached and blackout was imposed, utter and still, broken only by hovering enemy planes heralding bombs, war intruding, relentless.

Tonight, houses would be rent apart and lives destroyed by the orange-winged, smoke-topped, violent ire of the enemy. This city, noisy with air raids, its residents' dreams blazing, choked with smoke, confettied with ash, keening with sirens. If they were lucky, their part of London would be spared and they wouldn't have to trudge to the shelter, the icy night smoking hot and bright yellow as around them the city burned.

Alone in her flat, the utter black of wartime, fraught with danger, warplanes buzzing and droning overhead, Clara composed a reply to her friend in her head that she would never commit to paper. *If you knew the truth, Rathi, you would not invite* me so effusively. You would not invite me at all. For you are mother to my son and you know all about a mother's love.

This is why Anand is dissuading you from asking me to visit, it is nothing to do with regard. If I do visit India, Rathi, I will not want to leave. I will not be able to stick to my resolve of having nothing to do with my son. I will want him back. I'd give myself away – you'd read the truth in my eyes.

Although there's nothing I want more than to gather my son in my arms just one more time.

Chapter Sixty-Eight

Clara

1941, Lucky

'Who would have known we'd experience *two* wars?' Meg shudders. 'I'd have thought we'd learn from the last one.' She is pensive. 'It's the mothers I feel for. They lost brothers and fathers in the last war and now their sons…' Her voice trembles – she is thinking of her son, George, being looked after by big sister Evie while Meg works her shift.

And Clara is thinking of her own, who, if not with her, is always, always in her thoughts. *I am lucky. David is safe. Thriving.* Her mantra since she gave her son away. And yet… Pain flares all the same, stoking the ache of loss.

Three endless, empty years without her child, who is six now, who has lived away from her for as long as he was with her. Three interminable years living with missing, her time with David feeling more real and colourful, more sharply, achingly, vivid than every day since. She has done the best by him but she is undone.

Rathi's letters are full of David. *He loves school, he's started playing cricket and enjoys it. He's an animal lover like Henry.*

Henry… Clara is once again floored by ache. The two boys she loves in a country she loves with people she loves. What is she doing here, all alone, in a war-battered city an ocean away?

*

Anand took him to visit Henry – you heard of course about Captain and Mrs Adams's tragic accident, terrible business. Since then we've been keeping an eye on Henry, who's an extremely able young man – you would be so proud. Henry gave Dev a tour of his zoo and Dev was so thrilled – wouldn't stop talking about it. Now he wants to start a zoo of his own in our courtyard – God help us.

Clara closes her wet eyes, tears leaking regardless, overcome by grief for the Adams, who had, over the years, morphed from employers to dear friends. She hurts for Henry, who must be bereft, losing both his parents at once, wishing she was there to offer comfort and support. Wishing, as she has countless times over the years, that she could take Rathi's place, mother her son and look out for Henry.

Rathi is obsessed, enamoured, in love with Clara's son. It is palpable and swims off the page, her joy, her adoration. To Clara, it is both balm and torture, pleasure and pain. News of her child, that he is loved so very much, is welcome. But it also drives the thought that the more he settles there, the less possibility there will be of him ever—

Don't think that way. You willingly gave him away.

It was so he could have a better life!

But she is so empty, hollow inside. A void that only the sight and touch of her son can fill.

When she is in danger of getting too low, Meg tries to cheer her up. 'Look at you, misery guts,' she teases. Then, softly, 'It does get easier, Clara.'

Meg's husband Fred had signed up at the beginning of the war. He hasn't yet met George – the son he's longed for, conceived the night he signed up, Meg likes to say, a wistful twinkle in her eyes. She knows what she's talking about.

'Does it?' Clara asks.

'Perhaps not, but you get accustomed to the missing, a dull ache in your chest. There always.' Meg sighs. 'It's amazing what the soul can bear. Just ask those mothers who lost husbands to the last war and sons to this one.'

Now, Meg and Clara walk to St Thomas's – when their shifts coincide, Meg calls for Clara as her flat is on the way. The night is calm, the evening breeze icy, tasting of frost.

'It's so suspiciously peaceful. You wouldn't say there was a war on,' Meg muses, then immediately crosses her fingers.

'Aside from the blackout, you mean,' Clara says.

'Oh, I forgot about that.' Meg sighs. 'Funny, isn't it, the things you get used to? Rationing. Blackouts. Air raids. Death. Suffering. All those wounded. Me not knowing where Fred is, his letters arriving once in a rare while with most words crossed out…'

Clara closes her eyes, pain mounting a renewed assault. *Will I ever get used to living without David? Wondering every minute of each day what he is doing, how he's changed, how tall he is, whether his hair is still that unruly mop of dishevelled locks, his eyes gold when happy and the brackish green of muddy pools when upset?*

She looks avidly at every little boy she comes across: *Does David look like this, act like this, laugh with his friends like this, mischievous eyes darting everywhere, tousled hair, clothes torn and muddy?*

She dreams of him and wakes reaching for him, listening for his soft sighs of dreamy breaths, his messy curls, his plaintive voice calling for her: 'Mama.'

Chapter Sixty-Nine

Clara

Ghosts

'Clara, do you believe in ghosts?' Meg whispers, her hand gripping Clara's arm with some urgency, her breath hot and spiced with fear, as they walk past the bombed-out church they encounter daily during their walk to the hospital.

I am a ghost, a shell, for my heart has gone, spirited away into another life that doesn't include me.

St Thomas's is still going strong despite the battering it's endured from multiple air raids. The basement has been converted into underground wards. They've all got used to heating water to sterilise equipment on Primus stoves when the water isn't running (which is more often than not).

When they have to go above ground for any reason, they know to make sure to come back down before the German aircraft, whose constant hovering they've become inured to (along with bloodshed, devastated homes, people sleeping in the streets), stop, as that means a bomb is imminent.

They've all learned to endure – again; the still-fresh memories of the previous war merging and assimilating into this one. They're old hands at rationing and are now accustomed to living with air-raid sirens and traipsing to air-raid shelters.

They've got used to walking home after the night shift, during which they deal with devastation, heartache and death, the torment and wretchedness of war, their steps quickening in the tainted glory of morning, which shows up the rubble, the burnt-ochre slur of blazing desperation, sooty tears and bloodshot agonies, smoke clouds staining the bright new day the ashen navy of darkest midnight.

They walk past firefighters vainly trying to contain fires, of bodies pulled out of smoking debris, of contorted and hopeless faces, a smorgasbord of despair, a stark portrait of the ravage and ruin of war. These near-misses, the constant juxtaposition of death with life, hope with pain, anguish with relief is what Clara has come to equate with war.

And through it all there is the bittersweet siren call of her heart: *I did the right thing by sending David away. He is safe.*

Now, Meg clutches her hand, her face in the pressing dark as pale and washed out as the spirits she's worried about. 'I thought I saw something move in there.'

'I don't—' Clara begins but stops short, for she too has noticed something, a fleeting, darting shadow, out of place among the remains of headstones.

She lets out a little dismayed whine, taut with fear, but it is eclipsed by Meg's high-pitched cry of terror, for a… a *head* has popped out of the sarcophagus that sits, miraculously unscathed, in the rubble of the church's ruins.

'What are you gawping at? Can't a fellow get a little rest around here, even in his own grave?' the head grumbles, in a throaty voice.

And at their shocked expressions, the spectre cackles, long and loud, displaying rotting gums.

Do ghosts have gums? Clara wonders, rooted to the spot.

'Get a move on, I'm not for show,' the apparition complains, as the two boys who were loitering opposite by the entrance to a block of flats come to stand beside Clara and Meg, nudging and whispering even as they gape and point.

'What's going on here?'

Clara and Meg jump at the sudden voice, materialising from the darkness next to them. The boys smirk and the ghost emits another loud and decidedly phlegmy chortle. Do ghosts have phlegm?

'Don't worry, ladies. It's only your air-raid warden, enforcing the blackout,' the voice asserts, puffs of yeasty breath speckling the intrigue-flavoured night. And then, tutting, 'Mr Baggins, how many times do I have to tell you that the sarcophagus is not a suitable place for bedding down in? You're not safe there.'

'Why not?' The man – and now Clara knows he's all too mortal – sniffs. 'If they kill me, I've a ready-made tomb.'

The boys chuckle, their mirth rainbow bright, each sunburst star of a giggle stabbing her heart with a thousand wounds, sweetly, achingly painful, as, suddenly, the sound of her son's joy echoes unbidden in her ears. David's laughter was unconstrained, skittering marbles, dancing sprites, infectious... *Stop torturing yourself*, her conscience hectors. *You sent him away.* The decision, weighing down her heart, emptying her life, leaving hell in its place.

This decision, like mothers who lived through the previous war, and lost fathers and husbands and brothers, standing back as their sons signed up for this one. Insanity or heroism? Perfect lunacy or the sanest decision, the *only* decision in a mad world?

The air-raid warden sighs. 'Come on, Mr Baggins, out you get.'

And to Meg, Clara and the boys, 'Move on, ladies, lads, show's over.'

At the hospital, they part ways, Meg going to the convalescent wing to check on her patients. Clara is just walking to the emergency wing when a sudden violent noise rips the air, shuddering through the hospital.

No.

Her hand rushes to her heart to clasp the medal before she remembers – it's with her son. *If anything happens to me, my darling, I'm sending you all my love.*

She cowers beside the wall, hoping it doesn't collapse on her, thinking of her son, conjuring up his beautiful face so that if the worst happens her last thought will be of him. The venomous hiss and frenzied thunk of bombs splintering the air, rending it with screams, shredding it into vapours, black with smoke, dense with rubble, blazing orange. Rain of plaster and pulverised bricks.

When it is over and she finds she is still breathing, she stands, choked with ash, branded by fire, peering through the dust for her mother. It takes her a moment to understand. That was another war in another life.

She blinks, trying to see through the stinging, amorphous curtain of debris. The Emergency Wing is but a smoking pile of dirt. The nurses' home is no more. Firemen have arrived and are attempting to wade through the burning mess.

Meg.

The thought rouses Clara into action. She runs, heedless, through the scorching wreckage, the bruising ash, tears leaking down eyes assaulted by fiery confetti.

'Where are you going? Take shelter. Bombs are still falling,' a fireman calls after her.

She blindly rounds a corner and feels arms around her, blessedly, gloriously familiar.

'I didn't cross my fingers hard enough,' Meg whispers.

For one brief moment they hug each other and then they run through the blistering earth, death machines hovering above them, persistently dropping their deadly cargo.

More bombs strike just before they reach safety. The noise, deafening, debilitating, reverberating through her very being. The darkness fury-red, blazing bright. Clara feels rather than hears a baby's cries, cleaving her heart.

Earth shattering under her feet. Tremors rocking her, even as she joins the chaos of people seeking safety. The fevered scent of anxiety, the mad, burnt-ash taste of dread. Tears spilling out of gas masks and trembling on folds of parchment skin, on wizened necks. Boiling debris flung at their bodies. Billowing rings of smoke, the orange-topped, grasping yawn of sizzling blue flames, choking everything in sight.

The heat. Oh, the ash-spiked, blistering, scorching heat. Is this the end? *I love you, David.*

Fumbling through smoke, stumbling upon rubble. The acrid odour of burning, the creak and groan of buildings collapsing, the screams and cries that accompany doom and destruction.

And just like that she is a child again, confused, cowering, unable to make sense of this sweltering, fiery, breaking-apart world, her hand, sweaty and slick, slipping from her mother's.

No. No.

She holds onto Meg and they stumble into the shelter, the fire licking at their heels, the world cracking and splitting, flinging grit and navy ash, smoke claiming the breath from them.

Clara stands shivering in the shelter, the heat of the explosion leaving her cold with fear. When the all-clear sounds, she and Meg go back up. Dead bodies are being pulled out of the crumbling remains of devastation that was once a building hosting ordinary lives during extraordinary times.

Homes razed to the ground, lives extinguished with little warning. How many times has she watched this and thought, *we're spared?* This time she had been convinced she would be one of the casualties. Her heart is rent by a little boy, his clothes torn, face blackened, singed by smoke, sobbing over his mother's body, the firefighters holding him back, trying to offer consolation and failing, and she wonders if it is madness to spend what limited time she has left here on earth separated from, aching for her child.

Life is so fragile, so very short; she was spared today but she might die tomorrow or the day after. Just now, when she was convinced she was going to die, her one wish was to see her son and she had conjured him in her mind's eye. But the picture she has of him is three years out of date.

Chapter Seventy

Clara

Shroud

Clara goes to church, the familiar hymns soothing, and lays her dilemma at God's feet. The church has been bombed, half its roof gone, the sky, blue and cloudless, plastering the holes, contrasting with the broken, soot-stained bricks, the ruin and the rubble, prayers drifting right to heaven without the hindrance of roof tiles, golden arcs of glorious sun angling down like bounteous blessings.

Birds startle as the choir bursts into song, wide-arced shadows silhouetted against the gilded firmament, wings flapping frantically as they take flight, as below them the congregation kneels, rustle and creak and sigh, on scarred pews.

All these people, on intimate terms with suffering, reeling from loss, many, like her, who have lived through one war and are enduring a second. Praying in a bombed-out church, praying even when they know the next moment is not certain. Praying on hungry stomachs. *I made a decision to give away my child. But now, when all around me is death and devastation, I realise I cannot live without him. I want him in my life. Please show me what to do.*

A shaft of sunlight angles through the sky-ceiling and falls upon the congregation, haloing them in golden light just as the choir crescendos to *Hallelujah*.

Darkness descends, a gloomy shroud over a devastated city. She's at home, alone, wondering if an air raid is imminent. They cannot relax. If anything, they've learned to be vigilant, always prepared for attack. But…

This terrible war has to end sometime. And if it does, when it does, and if she survives it, given the precious, fragile, capricious nature of life, she'd like to be with her son. That's what she'd like more than anything in the world.

Chapter Seventy-One

Clara

1943, Casualties

Clara is at the hospital, changing dressings, checking temperatures, soothing and comforting. Meg has not been to work this past week; she is tending to George, who's ill with the flu. After her shift, Clara will drop in on them, see if there's anything they need.

George, at three – the age David was when Clara last saw him – usually an inexhaustible bundle of concentrated energy, has been listless this past week, clingy and teary. *Is David like this when he is ill? Does he cling to Rathi, his cheeks flushed, his body floppy yet restless, soothed only by her reassuring murmurs, her loving caresses?*

'Sister Knight, there you are.' Matron appears dishevelled and not her usual calm self. 'There's been an air raid in Munster Road and they're bringing in the casualties now and I need you to…'

She's misheard, hasn't she?

'Where?' Clara asks, one hand going, out of habit, to her heart, where her St Christopher medal used to rest.

'Munster Road, why…?'

Please no.

'Do you know anyone…?' Matron seems to make the connection even before Clara whispers, 'Meg and George.' Evie is with the WRNS, stationed in Dartmouth.

Matron's face is ghostly white.

Clara is flying to the emergency ward to check the casualties they're bringing in, Matron on her heels, praying, *Not my friend and her son, whom his father hasn't even met yet. Please.*

Chapter Seventy-Two

Clara

Too Still

Clara doesn't recognise the bloodied mess that is her friend until she hears a soft, barely-there whisper, 'Clara.' And her heart, which has been desperately fearful, stills before beating again faster. Meg, her whole body bruised and battered, her bleeding hands clutching…

No. It can't be. It cannot. But in Meg's eyes, bereft of light, of spark, she reads the truth. 'Meg, we'll take you into…'

'Too late, Clara,' Meg whispers.

'No.' Clara is fierce, even as her gaze is drawn to George, in Meg's arms, looking for all the world like he's sleeping. But he is too still, pale as dew on the underside of a leaf. George so full of life, now devoid of it.

Resolutely she pushes grief aside. Time enough later. Now she will save Meg. Her friend's eyes bright with pain stop her. And her words, spoken with great difficulty: 'You kept your child safe. I failed.'

'Don't give up, Meg. It's not over yet.'

'I can't Clara. It's… too much.' Meg clutches her lifeless son to her chest.

'Please,' Clara begs.

'Go to India, to David.' Each word is arduous, spoken through several agonised gasps. She chokes, her voice fading. 'Tell Fred and Evie…' She coughs up blood, smiles softly, 'I love them.'

Meg's eyes close, her arms wrapped tight around her dead child.

Chapter Seventy-Three

Clara

The Valley of the Shadow of Death

Two nights later, another air strike. If there's one thing Clara has learned during these interminably long and endless years, it is this: War does not respect grief. It does not discriminate. It does not give pause.

Clara is at home, sitting in the dark, mourning her friend and her son, missing her own, when the air-raid siren sounds. Matron insisted she take some time off: 'You cannot work all hours, it's not healthy.'

'I'm fine.'

'Everyone needs a break, especially you, especially now when…' Matron swallowed, the loss of Meg, palpable, sorrow-infused, between them.

'But Matron, the only place I'm able to function is here.'

Matron unbending. 'You can do the morning shift. Now go home and get a good night's rest.'

The siren bleats and Clara smiles humourlessly. *So much for rest, Matron.*

She hears the rush of footsteps outside, the shuffling and rustling and pounding as people make their way to the shelter. She pulls on her coat and is at the door when… A strangled cry. The tumble of a body thudding down the stairs.

She flings open the door. Maud – the neighbour who almost shut the door on David's fingers, the last straw that prompted Clara to write to Anand – is lying in a crumpled heap outside

Clara's doorway. She has a gammy leg, Clara has noticed before, and in the rush to get down the stairs and to safety, she must have slipped. Her eyes are foggy with pain as Clara squats beside her.

Clara can see Maud isn't going anywhere soon – her ankle bone is jutting out of fragile skin, the whole area swelling rapidly. She knows it's best not to move her – she will need to be seen to by one of the doctors at the hospital. But she can't leave her lying on the cold floor of the communal corridor in that uncomfortable position.

As carefully as possible, Clara helps her into the settee in her flat, Maud wincing and trying not to cry out; she is in desperate pain.

'Thank you, er…'

'Clara Knight.'

'Clara,' Maud whispers, her gaze clouded by agony, 'Go to the shelter. Leave me be.'

Clara looks at this woman who had been so nasty to her son just because she had deemed his skin colour unacceptable, unworthy. Her son's face crumpling with distress as the door shut in his face, almost upon his hand, his sunflower eyes confettied with tears.

She sees a bitter old woman, crêpe skin, lined face clenched with pain, eyes bleary with it. She sets about making Maud as comfortable as possible, rummaging in her nurse's bag for something for the pain.

'You're not going to the shelter?' Maud asks.

'No,' Clara says.

Maud surprises Clara by taking her hand, her grip flimsy, frail. 'But why?' She takes a breath. 'When I was so horrid to you and especially your son.'

Her beautiful son, mentioned by this woman. Clara recoils, pulling her hand out of Maud's grasp. Outside, the footsteps are quieting as the last stragglers leave for the shelter. The building quiet in a way it never normally is. Ominous. There's always sound, the stamp of occupation. Now as the last of the footsteps die away, silence that is resounding in its emptiness.

Bang! The whole building shudders.

'Please go to the shelter,' Maud says. 'I'll be alright here.'

If I die tonight, David, know that you are loved. If I'm spared, I'll come to you.

'I…' Maud swallows. 'I'm sorry I was so rude to you and your son. He was just a child, an innocent.'

Anger flaring as, once again, David's hurt expression as Maud shut the door in his face, nearly catching his fingers, appears in her mind's eye. Maud's eyes shine, the sheen of tears. 'I've seen you pining. He completed you.'

Clara bites her lower lip hard. But the pain is nothing compared to the fire raging in her heart.

Another loud bang. Clara cowers, sorely tempted to abandon this woman, run to the shelter. *I'm crazy for putting myself at risk, staying with this woman who was horrible to David. But if I left her here, alone and in pain, I would never forgive myself.*

Maud is reciting verses from the Bible. 'The Lord is my light and my salvation; whom shall I fear? The Lord is the stronghold of my life; of whom shall I be afraid?'

Their building shakes again and again. It is rent by tremors, the navy scent of smoke, the hot orange taste of fire, the rumble and thunder of buildings collapsing nearby. *If I survive tonight, I will go to India, to David. I have let other people's petty prejudices dictate my life. No more.*

Throughout the bombardment, the scent of smoke and ruination, the terrible sounds of buildings crumbling, their own shaking, Maud's voice, tremulous with age, taut with pain but never wavering as she chants Bible verses, strangely soothing.

'Even though I walk through the valley of the shadow of death, I will fear no evil, for you are with me; your rod and your staff, they comfort me.'

When the all-clear is given, Clara arranges for an ambulance to collect Maud.

'Thank you, my dear.' Maud smiles at Clara through agony-suffused eyes as she is hoisted gently onto the stretcher. 'War is the great leveller, bringing sharply to the fore what really matters. Love. It is *all*. Spending time with family when you have that luxury, for time is limited, scarce. You don't know what's around the corner.' Maud takes a pain-seeped breath. 'I have nobody left. You do. God bless you and your son.'

Part Twenty-One

India

Vortex

Chapter Seventy-Four

Indira

1995, A Ferocious Temper

'Your baba will be alright,' Dadu says, patting Indira's hand. 'The medal will protect him, as it has done all these years. It rests right next to his heart, upon it. It will keep him safe.' Dadu speaks with great conviction, nodding to himself.

Indira is at her parents' home, she and Dadu sitting side by side in the central courtyard around which the house is built. Darkness has fallen and from the kitchen come scents of bubbling rice, rising dough, frying spices, caramelising sugar, the soft murmur of voices – the maid, Sindu, has brought one of her daughters along; they are sleeping over tonight in Ma and Baba's absence.

'The medal, Dadu?'

'Once, when he was around eleven, we travelled to the beach. He loves the water and wanted to swim. A huge wave pulled him under, wrenched his hand from mine. The terror in his face as he was swept away, the current too strong for him to swim, mirrored mine. The Arabian Sea, it has moods, a ferocious temper. "Baba!" he cried. That tone of voice, the desperation and plea and fear – I'll never forget it.' Dadu shudders. 'I tried frantically to get to him, but eddies of the same current that had swept him away were pushing me back. I thought he was gone then.' He swallows. '"Your medal," I shouted. "Hold on to it. It will keep you safe."'

'What happened next?' Indira whispers, picturing her father as a child, flailing, caught up in a maelstrom, unable to break free, his father unable to reach him. Thinking he's going to die, salty waves swamping his mouth, choking, the water he loves now his enemy, holding him prisoner, pulling him under...

Her heart rent with feeling for her father who wasn't her father then, just a boy, barely older than Arun. *Her* beloved boy. He should be here in the next couple of days. And Karan.

Karan.

'A fishing boat was there, suddenly, beside him, materialising as if from the vortex of the eddy itself,' Dadu is saying, a small smile playing on his weathered face as he recounts the story. 'The fishermen pulled him out of the whirlpool. I nearly collapsed with relief.' Dadu's eyes shining in the dusky rose twilight glow. 'Afterwards the first thing he said was, "It saved me, just as you promised, Baba."' Dadu beams, his teeth shining yellow in the gloaming. 'He was wearing only his swimming shorts and the medal. It is his lucky charm and his protection. The St Christopher medal.'

Part Twenty-Two

India

Haunted

Chapter Seventy-Five

Clara

1943, This Time Around

This time around there is no maharaja, no maharaja's physician and no zenana. In fact, Clara is lucky to be on board a ship travelling to India. All passenger ships have been requisitioned to be troopships. Clara was fortunate to get a pass as a nurse, aiding the ship's physician, an old, nervous man who startles at the smallest sound or disturbance and is convinced they will be torpedoed at sea.

'It's happened several times before. I was supposed to be the physician on board the ship taking evacuees to Canada, but couldn't because I was ill. Narrow escape, my dear.' He shudders dramatically. 'What a tragedy that was! So many children dead…'

He stops short upon seeing Clara's expression.

'I'm sorry, my dear.'

'Excuse me.' Clara walks away, steadily she hopes, to her small cabin – a space so tiny that if she stretches her hands, they bump into the walls. But she's grateful for the privacy, a door she can close to shut out the world. She appreciates it all the more because the men do not have even this small privilege, sleeping in bunks, and hammocks where bunks aren't available, most of the cabins having been knocked down to accommodate more troops.

Once she has closed her door and is well and truly alone, she is sick, over and over, the physician's unthinking words reverberating in her head: 'So many children dead.'

It is a very different journey in many ways. Blackout is observed even on board; after dark, no lights can be shown and loud noises are to be avoided, as noise travels through water. The men Clara tends to all wear the same expression: haunted, radiating pain even when smiling, not quite able to forget all they have seen, hide everything they have lost, which shines from their eyes even – especially – when they are relaxed, at ease.

Like Clara, they carry themselves carefully, as if they will shatter if they let go.

Part Twenty-Three

India

Love

Chapter Seventy-Six

Indira

1995, A Great Lady

'St Christopher?' Indira asks. 'But Dadu, you're a devout Hindu.'

'Clara isn't.'

'Clara?'

An expression Indira has never seen on Dadu's face, touched with pain: reminiscence, admiration, nostalgia, regret and… love? 'A great lady.'

He is quiet, lost in musing.

After a bit, Indira prompts, 'Dadu?'

'Ah…' For a moment, as his eyes try to focus, Indira notices her grandfather struggle to place her. Then he smiles but there is ache in it, a wealth of feeling. 'The medal – it's Clara's.'

The gentle evening is suddenly sundered by screeches: an almighty uproar from the direction of the henhouse. The maid and her daughter run, flustered, tucking in sari pallus, pushing back tendrils of hair, bare feet stabbed by stones, anklets jangling.

Indira stands, nearly toppling her chair in her hurry to join them, but Sindu calls, breathless, 'It's alright, just a rat snake setting upon the toads that live in the hibiscus bushes by the henhouse. The hens thought it was coming for them.'

Once her breath has steadied, twilight breeze fruity and mellow upon her face, Indira ventures, 'Dadu, who is this Clara?'

'An admirable woman. When she was but a girl, she saved my life.'

And suddenly his face crumples. He places a hand on Indira's, fragile, crêpe-paper touch pressing. 'She *must* be told. I cannot believe why this didn't occur to me. When Rathi... when she was alive, I didn't... They wrote to each other. Rathi didn't know, of course. It would have broken her. But now...'

'Dadu, you're not making sense.'

Her grandfather's eyes shine with fervent zeal. 'Indu, I need to tell Clara about Dev. She should know.'

'But...'

'The medal will keep Dev safe, as it has done all his life.' He places a tremulous hand, wizened with age, upon his heart. 'I know it here.'

'Dadu...'

'His mother's medal will protect him.'

'Dadu,' Indira is exasperated. 'You said it was Clara's medal.'

'It is.'

'But you said...' Indira stares at her grandfather. 'You said...'

'Yes,' her grandfather sighs. 'Rathi never knew. But Rathi is gone and with Dev in hospital, now, Clara should know. She will want to be here.'

Part Twenty-Four

India

Quit India

Chapter Seventy-Seven

Clara

1943, All Grown Up

India.

Clara breathes its many hues, its bright, eye-wateringly spicy exoticism, its ability to reach deep inside you and shake you alive.

How she loves it, this country that houses her heart, her love, her child. She opens her mouth and takes a deep breath of sun-roasted, dust- and spice-flavoured air and tastes longing.

Clara hasn't told Rathi and Anand she is travelling to India. But she did write to Henry, who is waiting at the port, a tall handsome man, the image of his father, well built and tanned, dashing in the colours of his regiment.

'Look at you, Captain Henry Adams.' She smiles, her heart filling as she breathes him in, this man who was the little boy she adored.

'You look just the same, Nurse Knight.' He holds out his hand for her to shake.

'Oh, don't be formal with me, Henry.' She pulls him into a hug. 'And now that you're all grown up, it's Clara.'

'You'll always be my Nurse Knight.'

She wipes away a tear and changes the subject. 'You are the picture of health.'

'But for my limp. I was to be in Burma but...' He shrugs, sporting that irresistible grin she loves. 'Glad I'm here to receive you.'

'That limp is from when you shot a lion with your last cartridge and saved members of your regiment. Recipient of the Victoria Cross. I'm so proud of you, Henry.'

'It grieved me so, Nurse Knight, to shoot that beautiful, majestic beast,' Henry says gravely.

And Clara laughs, feeling lighter already, revelling in the white-hot sun of this country she's missed, reunited with a grown man who was the little boy she loved and about to be reunited with her very own little boy, her missing heart. 'Henry, you haven't changed a bit. How is the zoo?'

'Growing. I've several subedars to look after it,' he says proudly.

'Oh, Henry.' She is overcome by affection for this wonderful young man whom she first met as a sickly child.

'Nurse Knight, it is a pleasure to see you. I've missed you.' He is a boy again.

'I've missed you too, Henry.'

Chapter Seventy-Eight

Clara

Temperamental

India appears, on the surface, just the same as before – no evidence of the war that has levelled Europe here. No hovering enemy flying machines with their lethal cargo, no blackout curtains or dropping bombs, air-raid sirens, the scorch of smoke, the keens of pain, the stamp of death, the haunting ghosts of lost loves. No gaping holes where buildings should be, the debris left in the wake of fire and destruction.

But… the same expressions: desperate, hopeless, disenchanted, tired, although on brown faces and not white.

'There *is* a war on,' Henry says, 'An entirely different one to that raging in Europe. It is war against the English, against us, we who have colonised this country for centuries.'

When they join the road leaving the city, there's evidence of the war Henry was talking about, their car surrounded by Indians bearing placards, chanting, 'Quit India.'

'Gandhi has been arrested,' Henry says, gently negotiating the car through the protesting, but non-violent crowd. 'People are angry.'

'Oh.'

'They keep on, despite police driving them away, arresting them.' He sighs. 'They say prison is no object, as Gandhi is there anyway. They want us to leave,' he is melancholy, 'and they'll get their way when the war is over.'

'Will you leave?' Clara asks.

'This is my home. My parents are buried here. I'm not going anywhere.'

The protestors fall away and there is only the long road, red dust rising in a cloud.

'Do you see Anand and Rathi?' she asks, casually.

'Often. Their little boy is delightful,' he says, unprompted, a smile on his face. 'He loves animals too, adores my zoo. The questions he asks! Reminds me of myself at that age. You'll love him.'

I already do, with my everything.

'I'm sure.' She keeps her voice neutral. 'I haven't told them I'm here. Wanted to surprise them.'

'Yes, you did say in your letter.' He looks at her, his gaze perceptive. 'Why?'

'I'd like to see the expression on Rathi's face when I surprise her.' She tries to keep the fear and the barely contained anticipation from her voice.

'Ah, she'll be pleased, she's always talking about you.' Then, smiling, 'The maharaja is still going strong.'

'He is?'

'He's very worried about the future of kings and kingdoms when India becomes free.'

'Have you had dealings with him?'

'Not personally. But by all accounts he's a good, if temperamental, ruler.'

The village and its surrounds appear, just the same as ever, a bubble frozen in time. Hay-topped huts mushrooming from the earth, interspersed with shops, colourful, tented awnings selling everything from knick-knacks to sweetmeats, sneeze-inducing mounds of spices to bangles glittering kaleidoscopic in the sun.

Henry points to a huge, modern building at the base of the hill. 'Nurse Knight, your legacy.'

'*My* legacy?'

'That clinic you started grew and grew, people coming from all the surrounding villages, sometimes walking for a whole day! Father made provision in his will for a new building to accommodate all those desperate people and hence the hospital.'

'Your father's legacy.'

'Yours first and foremost. If you hadn't started it, it wouldn't be.'

Tears fill her eyes.

'I've taken over the outhouse that used to house the clinic. It is now my zoo headquarters.'

'Oh, Henry!' Tears chased away by chuckles. Henry has always been able to make her laugh.

The car climbs up the hill and then they are at the house, regal and majestic, the grounds pristine and immaculate as ever. Such wonderful memories associated with this house, these grounds, seeped in wistfulness, tinted mauve gold.

Clara blinks, and there – the ghosts of their former selves, innocent times. Henry's clear musical voice, chiming joy, ringing with laughter, 'Another lap, Nurse Knight.' Clara running smack into Anand when he arrived with summonses from the maharaja.

'Remember when I made you run laps when you got a sentence wrong in Hindi?'

She blinks, mouth flooding, tasting of nostalgia. 'I was recalling exactly that! I thought I'd forgotten the language, but as soon as I set foot on Indian soil, heard it spoken, it returned to me!'

Up close, the house is just the same as in her dreams, sprawling and beautiful, smelling of spices and jasmine and dust and sun. She takes a deep breath as she treads on the cool marble floors.

'I almost expect to see your mother in the rocking chair on the veranda, your father with a glass of whisky in his hand beside her.' Then, softly, 'I'm sorry about the accident, Henry. You must miss them so.'

'Yes. Thank you for your kind letter when it happened, Nurse Knight.'

She nods.

'We had some good times.' He smiles.

'We did.'

Chapter Seventy-Nine

Clara

Endless

Clara hardly sleeps that night, although Henry has kindly put her in her old room and it is just as it was. Comfortable bed with mosquito net and ceiling fan. The scent of jasmine and sun-baked earth. But she counts the hours down to morning, watching milky, rose-tinted dawn part the blackout drape of night, for this is the day she will see her son after being away from him for five long years. Five years, and yet these eight hours until morning feel interminable.

At breakfast, Henry nudges puri bhaji and a platter of tropical fruit towards her. 'Nurse Knight, as I recall, this was one of your favourite breakfasts.'

'Thank you, Henry.' She is touched that he has remembered.

There is no rationing. Instead a cornucopia of the juiciest fruit: mango, pineapple, guava, papaya and watermelon. A rainbow on a plate.

There's also chapati with egg korma and spicy *chole* with puffy *bature*, toast with butter and cheese, scrambled eggs, sweet milky kheer dotted with cardamom and cashew and glossy gold gulab jamun swimming in syrup.

She's missed it, not only the food but also the feast of a spread with no thought to rationing. But she cannot eat, her stomach in knots of anticipation with no space left for sustenance. She will be sustained when she has her child in her arms again, she will feast upon him.

After breakfast, Henry is apologetic, 'I'm sorry, Nurse Knight, I've got to go into town on business for a few hours. Will you be okay?'

'Of course. Don't you worry about me, Henry.'

'What plans for today?'

Her heart beats wildly in her chest, yearning for its reciprocal echo, which it will be reunited with in just a couple of hours, if that.

'I thought I'd surprise Anand and Rathi.'

'Today is a public holiday, so you'll meet little Dev as well. Take my car.'

'Are you sure?'

'Positive.' Henry smiles. 'I'll take the subedars' jeep. Give Anand, Rathi and Dev my love and invite them round at the weekend.'

'Thank you, Henry.'

'Pleasure, Nurse Knight.'

Chapter Eighty

Clara

False Pretences

Henry's chauffeur is taciturn and it suits Clara perfectly. She couldn't make small talk if she tried. She looks out of the window, breathing India in, reacquainting herself with its myriad, kaleidoscopic moods. The bustle of the village, the pungent flavour of perspiration and drains, the sizzle of hot oil, the aroma of boiled rice and rising dough and frying chilli.

Colour scalding her avid gaze – *this is my son's world* – sequinned saris and dark, glittering eyes, bright yellow, fiery orange, potent red mounds of spices, fisherwomen hawking fish, glimmering silver scales, mangy dogs, scrawny cats and scrawnier cows, white-gold sky, dazzling heat, busy liveliness, life going on while hers is on pause.

The music of laughter, a child's kittenish cry. *My child.* What will she say? How will she bring it up? *He's my son. I want him back.* No, she can't do it. Not like that.

Can she do it at all? To her friend? To Anand? When she palmed her son off to Rathi under false pretences. But then she thinks of all the mothers with their children dead, some in this war, some in the last, their brothers and fathers and husbands lost too. The exquisite, precious, ephemeral, flimsy fragility of life.

Does she want to spend the rest of her life longing? Thinking of what might have been? Wanting. Yearning. Empty. Her son, his features stamped upon her heart, her body remembering how it was to hold him.

*

The car turns a corner and then they are crossing the bridge that spans the river that runs through the town on the outskirts of which is Anand and Rathi's house.

On the bank of the river she sees a family. A father, mother and child. The child is in shorts and he runs to the water, his hands up in the air, face lit up in glee, torso bare except for a medal. She can't see from here, but she knows it is scarred silver, slightly burnt and tarnished.

He jumps in the water, sending up an arced spray of dazzling silver. He laughs, a tumbling waterfall of cascading giggles. The mother laughs along with him. She opens her arms, holding out a towel, and he runs into it, shaking his wet hair, spraying her. She holds him, still laughing, dropping kisses upon his wet face, his dripping chest.

'Stop,' Clara manages as the car turns off the bridge, fingering her own chest where the medal used to rest.

Beneath her hand, her heart beats, too fast, aching, wanting, yearning. The driver pulls to the side of the road that adjoins the riverbank, baked earth lending a gold haze to the torpid air. They are close enough to the family now so as to hear them, yet far enough away to afford them privacy.

She looks on as the mother – *the mother* – opens a tiffin box and feeds the boy, her mouth opening in satisfaction at every morsel the child eats. The father looking on, affection and love. The tableau of the perfect, happy family. She sits in the car, watching, oblivious to the sun's relentless gaze.

After he's eaten, the boy carelessly runs a hand across his face, his mother laughingly admonishing, 'That's not cleaning your face! That's spreading germs all over it!'

The boy grins at her and then he's off, running to the water, jumping and splashing, and then along the riverbank, nearly all the way up to the car. The medal catches the light, glinting silver against his burnished torso the colour of sun-ripened conkers. He squats down almost right next to the car.

Look at me, she thinks, prays, pleads, clasping her palms together to stop them shaking.

Fierce, desperate desire igniting her cheeks, drying the moisture there in salty tracks. The humid air sighs languid and lethargic, a dusty yellow haze. *Look at me, please.* But he does not.

He is fixated by a bug; he picks it up carefully and runs back, his little legs windmilling like they used to do in another country in another life with another mother. Now, they take him away from her, to the woman he thinks of as his mother. He opens his hands, shows her the bug.

'That's a big one,' she says. She is completely absorbed in him.

But the father is looking up now, at the car. Into the car. Right at her. Eyes she knows intimately startling in recognition, flashing fear and warning. The boy looks up too, follows his gaze. His eyes the colour of cinnamon-dusted cocoa, so like his father's.

She pulls her hat down to cover her face, roughly swipes at the tears erupting from her eyes. The sun shines, bright gold and merciless, bearing witness from a fiery sky.

'Drive, please,' she says to the chauffeur, her voice spliced by tremors as if beset by an earthquake.

The chauffeur turns, looks curiously at her. But her hat is shielding her face and she is looking down at her clasped hands. The car starts up.

She does not look back, although she hears the boy ask, his voice clear as a sunlit dawn heralding a glorious summer's day, 'Who's that?' and Anand's reply, bright with relief (even after all these years she can read his every expression, identify every cadence and tone shading his voice), to his son, her son but hers no longer, 'Just a passer-by, son. Now show me what you have there.'

Chapter Eighty-One

Clara

Just A Passer-By

Just a passer-by, she thinks, as she asks the chauffeur to take her back to Henry's.

Just a passer-by. As she packs her things. Leaves a note for Henry. Prepares to leave India, this country she loves that hosts her love. As she leaves *her* son, to his – happy – life. The life he knows, with parents he knows and loves.

She longs, more than anything, to be with him just one more time – he is so tantalisingly close. But if she were to stay on, visit Anand and Rathi and David, invite them round to Henry's, she wouldn't be able to pretend to be *just* a family friend, she would give herself away. And it would disrupt her son's life. She can't. She won't, even though it destroys her to be within touching distance and yet… and yet leave without touching him, holding him, her heart.

She makes her final decision that day – one she will not go back on, having realised how selfish she was to come here. She decides to be 'just a passer-by' in her son's life.

Five years ago she made a decision that she believed was the best for her child. To send him away from a country at the brink of war, a country where he was treated as a second-class citizen, to send him away with his father, to a new life in a new country with a new mother. But when she saw the devastation wrought by war, when she was surrounded by death, when she survived so many near-misses, she thought she was spared for a reason.

To mother her child – he belonged with her. And she came to claim him.

But he is happy. He is loved. He has two parents who love him. He has an established, secure, content, *great* life without her in it. He is living the life she wanted for him. She cannot destroy it. She cannot claim it, claim him and upend his life, devastate him and the woman he believes is his mother, hurt him, take away all he knows. She cannot do it to him, much as it devastates her to leave without having met him, touched him, held him, filled that yawning ache of wanting.

And so she leaves even as her hand, from years of habit, goes to her heart, stroking the place where her medal used to rest. *Stay safe, my son. Stay well.* Her son is not hers and will never be. But, he is happy, he is well. He *is*.

She returns to England. Alone. Carrying in her heart an image of her son, long-limbed, happy, a water-splasher, a lover of bugs. His smile. His wide eyes, his zest for life, medal glinting silver upon his sun-bronzed chest. A snapshot for a passer-by in his life.

Part Twenty-Five

India

Exceptional Circumstances

Chapter Eighty-Two

Indira

1995, Family Friend

Families! Indira thinks, as what her grandfather is saying finally sinks in. *Complicated. Rife with secrets languishing for decades.* 'Does Baba know?'

'Not that Clara is his mother. Only that she is a family friend.'

'And she was?'

'Rathi's best friend.' Dadu sighs.

Indira is shocked. She who has prided herself on being unshockable, a modern woman. 'Who is Baba's father?' she asks, prepared for anything.

'What do you mean?'

'Just what I said.' Indira is sharp. 'I've just learned that Daadi was not Baba's mother, that her best friend is.' She takes a breath to compose herself, then asks, again, 'Who is his father?'

'I am,' her grandfather, with his nearly bald head, his aged, wrinkled body, says.

Oh, my!

Her sweet, guileless grandfather, or so she thought, revealed to be the worst sort of man, sleeping with his wife's best friend—Wait a minute…

As if he has read her mind, he says, looking at the jasmine bushes gossiping in hushed whispers with the creeping shadows, which angle closer, the better to eavesdrop, 'It was just the once, sixty-one years ago.'

At least he's not a serial adulterer.

'And although nothing excuses it, they were exceptional circumstances…'

'So they all say,' Indira says dryly.

'I've regretted cheating on Rathi every day since. And Clara, I… Afterwards…' Here, Dadu's voice wavers, '…I was not kind.' There's sadness and regret, pain and atonement in his voice.

'Where *is* Clara?'

'In England.'

Indira assumed she couldn't be shocked further. But she *is*.

Do I know my family at all?

Chapter Eighty-Three

Indira

Doing the Best

'Clara did it willingly – gave him to us. Rathi couldn't... she couldn't carry to term,' Dadu says.

Sitting in the susurrating darkness, Indira imagines how she'd feel to live without Arun, have him call another woman *Mama*. 'How could she...?'

'She thought she was doing the best by our son.'

'Surely the best thing for a child is to be with their mother?' Indira says this and thinks of her grandmother, who died a year ago from cancer. Her kind, gentle grandmother who loved so much and so completely. Indira had been a prickly child, shying away from affection. But she too had fallen under her spell.

And yet, she had failed her grandmother, not able to spare the time to visit even when she knew she was dying...

Guilt biting, blue-black, but her thoughts centring, once again, on what her grandfather has revealed, trying and failing to make sense of it. Her grandparents together were *right*. They fit. She cannot picture this Clara. Her grandfather with Clara... Creating a child. Indira's father.

'You loved Clara?'

He pats Indira's hand gently. His voice when he speaks is taut with regret. 'Rathi was the love of my life. But I loved Clara too, differently. I admired her. Cared for her. She was my friend.'

There's ache there, wistfulness, affection, great sadness. What might have been.

Indira leans back in her chair, breathing in night jasmine and spices, secrets, betrayal, pain and love, all the ingredients knitting families together in complex, entwined, wounding, loving, devastating bonds.

There is so much to each of us, multiple selves within us, she thinks. *I'll talk to Karan. He cares for me. I've always known this for he's shown me in a myriad of ways. But I... I have neglected to convey how much he means to me. I need to do so, show him I care, tell him I need him, that I love him. He loved me once. Does he love me still?*

Chapter Eighty-Four

Indira

Prayer

Indira leaves Dadu at home with Ma's kindly maid, Sindu, and returns to hospital hoping that Baba is out of surgery. But Ma is still in the same chair, her hands clasped together in prayer. The lights in the waiting room have been switched off, the shadowy room appearing sinister, unwelcome, dirty yellow bars of light angling in from the corridor playing on sallow faces, sunken eyes, trepidation mingled with hope.

Indira slips into the seat beside her mother. In the navy-tinged gloom, her mother's skin is purple, new lines seem to have sprouted on her face in just a few agonised hours.

'Is Dadu okay?' her mother asks.

Indira thinks of her grandfather's words: 'His mother's medal will protect him.' His shocking revelations.

Now is not the time.

'He's fine,' she says. 'In any case, Sindu and her daughter are staying the night.'

Her mother smiles gratefully, her eyes soft in the darkened room, glowing dark chocolate.

'Mrs Goel?' A doctor, finally, calling for Indira's mother.

Ma stands, her hand going to her heart. Behind them, a child sniffles and is soothed by its mother. Indira tries to read the doctor's face. Is it just weariness slumping his shoulders, pulling down the corners of his mouth, or something else? He's standing against the light, so she can't quite read his eyes.

Please.

She thinks of her grandfather's conviction: 'The medal will keep Dev safe, as it has done all his life.'

'It was touch-and-go for a while but he's made it. You can see him as soon as he's moved into the ICU.'

And now, Indira blindly turns to her mother, who is also turning to her, both of them collapsing in each other's arms. *There's something to be said for hugs,* Indira thinks, exhilarated, light-hearted, grateful. *I should give them more often. The medal,* she thinks, *it kept Baba safe. I have my chance now, to show him I care. To show how much I love him.*

Chapter Eighty-Five

Indira

Diet

'You can go in now,' the doctor says.

Indira's father is in bed, swamped by machines. He looks diminished, wiped out, *old*.

How close we came, Indira thinks. She hangs back, trying to wipe her face of the painful shock of seeing him like this, to contain the tears that stab and sting with prickly condemnation: *He could have died without knowing how much you love him. He could have died without knowing his real mother.*

He could have died.

Indira has always dismissed her parents' bond as boring, lacking passion, energy, that vital spark that nurtures relationships. The spark that she has just realised is missing from her own relationship with her husband.

But now, she notes how tenderly her mother looks at her father, how he manages a smile for her, his eyes shining, 'I'm sorry. I gave you quite the fright, didn't I?' His every word is an effort.

'You did, *jaan*.' Her mother gently takes her father's hand.

They *never* touch in public, not even in front of their daughter. Indira, feeling like a voyeur, suddenly distinctly uncomfortable – something she has never before felt when with her parents – experiences a blast of shame for having judged their gentle relationship.

How could I have thought their love was any less? There is such tenderness, a whole private conversation in the looks they give each other, in that soft touch, in the way her father squeezes his wife's fingers to reassure her.

'Your daughter says we're to put you on a diet,' Ma announces with a watery smile.

Her father looks at Indira, his face lighting up. He is wan, weak, a pale shadow of the Baba she knows. And yet… that glow. *It's not too late.*

'You came, Indu.'

'Of course.'

'Your work…'

It says something about Indira that her father has just returned from near death and this is the first question he asks of her. She has given the impression that her work is important above all else. That has to change, starting now…

'Let's hope they manage without me a few days without everything falling apart.'

Her father's eyebrows rise. Before, it would have riled her; she'd have taken offence, thinking he was condemning her, judging her to be too focused on and bigging up her contribution to her job. But now she notices the tears he's trying to hold back. He's touched and aiming to direct attention away from his emotion.

Tell him you love him. Before she can speak, her father blinks his tears away. 'What's this nonsense about a diet?'

And they all burst out laughing, joy, relief, celebration, love.

Chapter Eighty-Six

Indira

Subterfuge

'Karan called while you were with Baba. He and Arun are arriving later this afternoon,' Indira's mother says as she prepares to leave for the hospital. Now that Indira's father is out of the woods – although he has to stay in hospital for a few days while they monitor him – Indira has managed to convince her mother to have a break every so often, come home, freshen up while Indira sits with him.

Now they're swapping: Indira has come home and Ma is preparing to return to Baba. And although Ma's face is weary from the stress of Baba's illness, lines pulling her eyes and lips down, she smiles, genuinely happy at her grandson's imminent arrival. 'Your baba will recuperate quicker when his grandson's here. Our Arun is a balm for our souls.'

Indira takes in her mother's obvious joy and thinks, *Why haven't I brought Arun more often? He loves coming here.*

Arun enjoys playing in the courtyard and the vast grounds around the house, a luxury after the cramped confines of the city. He loves the fuss his grandparents make of him, unable to deny him anything, her father indulging in subterfuge to supply his grandson with sweets, sugary drinks and other contraband: 'I'm just going to stretch my legs,' his pockets bulging upon his return.

Or, 'I'm taking Arun to watch the youngsters playing cricket, see if he wants to join in.' Buying him ice cream from the new bakery that had opened round the corner more like. When they got back, Arun smelling chocolatey, with telltale brown smears on his T-shirt where the ice cream had dribbled: 'How was the cricket?'

Arun sharing a conspiratorial glance with his grandpa: 'I didn't want to take part.'

Arun thrives in his grandparents' and great-grandfather's company and even his perpetual colds are less in evidence. So why has she not brought him more often?

When Arun started school, her parents had offered to look after him in the holidays and Karan was all for it – having lost his parents a few years ago, he looks upon hers as his own. It was Indira who vetoed the plan. She wanted to be around, manage, keep an eye, and so she enrolled Arun in that crèche he hates instead.

I must learn to relax, to let go. I cannot control everything all the time. In wanting control, I've made Arun's holidays a misery and have denied my parents the joy of their grandson and my grandparents their great-grandson.

It is already too late with Daadi, who adored children and was besotted with Arun. If something had happened to Baba, I'd never have forgiven myself, having begrudged him time with his grandson. Life is precious and I should be prioritising my time right, with those I love at the top.

Indira couldn't get away from home quickly enough, choosing an engineering college so far from home – her excuse: it was one of the best in the country – that it justified not returning for weekends and short breaks. And after, she was too busy establishing her career to visit her parents.

Truth is, they've always irritated her with their lack of ambition, their contentment with living simply. They don't aspire for more, better, and it has frustrated and annoyed her. How can they live without something to aim for? What kind of life is that? A fulfilling one, she sees now. They are happy. They've always been so. Content in what she's always thought of as their 'small' lives.

Indira thought she'd feel fulfilled once she became CEO. But since getting there, she's had to work even harder to show herself worthy of it. And in the course of doing so, she's lost so much. Her husband's love? *No.*

She didn't plan for a husband or children. Then Karan and Arun came along. Her husband and son changed her. She thought she was invincible. They made her vulnerable. She was practical. They made her sentimental. They flayed her heart open. They made her *care*. And now, she's determined to win back her husband's love if it's the last thing she does.

Chapter Eighty-Seven

Indira

Raised in Song

'Clara saved my life during the First World War,' Indira's grand-father says. He and Indira are in the courtyard, in the shade of the jacaranda trees, flowers in resplendent bloom, their scent heady, fecund.

Her mother has returned to the hospital but not before cooking up a feast, all of Indira's favourites: warm, ghee-dotted rotis and fluffy phulkas, pea pulao and mushroom rice, aloo gobi and saag paneer, dhal and baingan with gulab jamun, kheer and kulfi for afters, her preferences – the aubergine not too mushy, the aloo gobi without mustard seeds, cashew nuts in the kheer but no raisins – carefully remembered.

Birds twitter in the branches above them and from the kitchen the musical chime of Sindu's anklets, her voice raised in song, not in tune yet entirely unselfconscious, as she goes about her chores. Sitting beside her grandfather, Indira breathes in the gritty-sweet air, as, in a voice tremulous with age and emotion, he tells her of Clara, his son's mother.

'I knew Clara cared for me, and I… I thought Rathi had left me…' His voice is a lament. Sorrow and love. 'Clara was upset about Maharani Maya and I…' He swallows. 'I regret how I behaved after. I was angry with myself, and it made me so brusque with her…' His voice layered with regret.

It astounds Indira afresh that this man beside her has lived through two world wars, that he was a maharaja's physician. And

Clara, choosing to care for a sick Indian soldier, nursing him to health in the face of prejudice and scorn, and, later, spurning a maharaja's advances, yet keeping in his good books and becoming nurse to the zenana.

I thought what I do, standing up to older male directors who are angling for my downfall every day, was brave. But it is nothing, nothing *compared to what Clara faced…*

The taste of cinnamon-spiced, stewed tea and drenched-in-syrup, just-out-of-the-frying-pan golden jalebis, which Sindu had brought out a few minutes ago. When Dadu finishes, they are both crying. They are a pair, she and her grandfather, holding hands and bawling in the courtyard while crows call among the palm fronds and mangoes ripen in the indolent sunshine.

'You look like her,' Dadu says, sniffing.

'Oh?'

'Along with her looks, you have inherited her fierce passion, her unflinching determination to see things through.'

'I have?' Indira is inordinately pleased to be compared to a woman who had faced down a maharaja.

While her parents were thrown by Indira's ambition, Dadu has always been supportive of it, applauding, proudly, 'You're just like your grandmother.'

Indira had been puzzled. Daadi was a housewife, she was clever but not aspirational. *Now* she understands.

'When racism was directed at her son she couldn't bear it, she had to do something. So she gave up her claim on him. It takes great love to willingly let go of the one you love for their sake. To live each day without them, knowing they're living a life you're not a part of. How hard it must be… And yet she did it.'

Tentatively, Indira pats Dadu's hand, and he clutches it as if it is his lifeline.

And Indira thinks: *Why have I kept my distance for so long? Why have I lived like this, pushing away those who care for me? Clara had only her son and she gave him away because she loved him. I have been blessed with so much love. Yet I haven't appreciated it, revelled in it, too busy in my pursuit of success and accolades from people who do not matter.*

Chapter Eighty-Eight

Indira

Fraying Seams

Dadu pats the pockets of the coat he always wears, which her mother has tried to prise from him to wash but which he refuses to relinquish.

'It reeks,' her mother sighs.

But Indira likes it. It smells of her grandfather, musty and grave – all the years he's lived worn into its fraying seams.

From an inner pocket that Indira did not even know was there, he pulls out a long, tattered packet, which he deposits into her palm.

Somewhere in the orchard a cashew drops with a splosh, the liquor tang of overripe fermenting fruit. Flowers nod in the dappled breeze, green and gold shadows dancing on umber-bronzed earth.

The packet gapes open, revealing pages of notepaper covered in dense writing.

'The letters Clara wrote to Rathi. Her number is in there somewhere. Please will you find it for me?'

She squeezes Dadu's hand. 'I will. I have time before Karan and Arun arrive.'

Chapter Eighty-Nine

Indira

History

Indira scrolls back through the letters – so many, spanning several decades, her grandmother having kept every one. Clara's handwriting changing over the years, clear and precise at the beginning, spindly and wavering towards the end, the earliest dated 1934. *1934!* It is very worn, almost as creased as Dadu's skin and just as fragile. Purple ink fading on the yellowed paper musty with age. It carries the pungent lavender scent of old memories and nostalgia.

She gently touches Clara's words, entranced, the past in the room with her, feeling its gravity, its solemn weight; history suddenly rendered real, immediate. Half a century since the Second World War ended, nearly that since India won freedom from British rule, but when Clara wrote this, the world was nudging into war and India was still a British colony. Indira is amazed and humbled as it strikes her afresh how much her grandparents and Clara have lived through, the history they've experienced and helped shape.

She doesn't have time to read all of the letters and so she just glances through them, getting an insight into the friendship between these two very different women, each strong in their own way. Clara quietly determined, her questions about her son understated yet insistent, giving nothing away, and yet, once you knew she was his mother, her love palpable in every word, hidden ache, secret longing.

She finds Clara's number in one of her last letters to Rathi, a few months before Rathi's death.

'Dadu.' Indira is barely able to contain her excitement.

Her grandfather startles from where he's been dozing in his chair.

'Oh sorry, I didn't notice…'

He raises a hand, quieting her. It is trembling, and not from old age. His mouth quivers. 'Tell me.'

'I've found her number.' Indira waves the precious sheet at him. His entire body smiling. 'I knew you'd find it.'

He holds out his hand and she hands him the letter with Clara's number.

'You'll call?' Indira asks.

Dadu nods, a determined look in his eyes. 'She'll want to know. I meant to write to her after Rathi died, knowing she yearns for updates on Dev, but I was floundering… Grief…'

'Yes.' *I wasn't there when my grandmother was dying and for my grandfather when he lost his wife. From now on, I'll try to live my life without regrets, putting loved ones first. Like Clara did, living without her son despite aching for him, because she thought she was doing the best by him.*

'Can you also be there when I call? I can't hear very well at the best of times and this is important…'

'Of course,' Indira says, touched by her grandfather's request. 'But shouldn't we speak to Baba?'

'It will be a shock, might put a strain on Dev's heart. We *will* tell him, once he is home and recovering. But I really think Clara needs to know *now*. You see, until now, he has been fine, living the safe and secure life she wanted for him. But this…' Dadu's eyes shine.

'Of course.' Indira pats her grandfather's palm.

And that is when she hears the car.

Chapter Ninety

Indira

Brave

'Mama!'

Indira is waiting, arms open wide, and Arun runs into them. Her beloved little boy. She gathers him to her, breathes his sweet mischief and candy scent and thinks, *How could you bear to give your son away, Clara? How could you live without him all these years? How could you endure knowing he was turning to someone else for succour, comfort, calling another woman Mama? I admire you. You put love above all else. I will too, from now on.*

'Are you feeling okay, my love?' she asks, revelling in Arun's little heart beating against hers, his downy cheek pressed against her neck.

This is what it is important, this feeling of completeness right here. This won't last, Arun wanting hugs from me. I need to cherish it, enjoy his childhood now and not wonder where it went when it's far too late. I need to find a balance between work and life. This is what my parents tried to tell me, but I always took it as criticism and we'd end up arguing.

'I am. They said I was very brave. They gave me a lolly. Now I can eat all the ice creams I want without getting a cold.'

'We'll see about that.' She laughs, dropping kisses upon his beautiful face.

Why isn't it this easy with adults? Why is there restraint, second-guessing, hesitation? Why can't I unthinkingly open my arms and hug my loved ones, like I'm doing my son?

'I dreamed about my favourite great-grandson who under-went an operation and was so courageous about it all, and here he is!'

'Grand-dadu!' Arun wriggles in Indira's arms, wanting to be let down so he can greet his great-grandparent.

'You definitely deserve ice cream,' Dadu says.

Before, Indira would have grumbled, admonished Dadu, but now she smiles as her son cheers, 'Yay!', jumps out of her embrace and into Dadu's.

'Oof!' Dadu doesn't have to pretend to look winded. 'I'm an old man and you're growing so tall and strong that you almost knocked me down.'

Arun preens, standing up to his full height, which comes to a stooped Dadu's waist. 'Here, hold my hand, Grand-dadu, I'm a brave boy, the doctors at the hospital said so.'

'You are the strongest and the bravest, my *jaan*, my heart.' Dadu takes his great-grandson's kindly proffered hand. 'Now, your grandma has stocked the freezer with kulfi because she knows you like pistachios and also coconut and mango ices.'

'Can I have all three?'

Now, Indira interjects, 'One, Arun!'

'Yay!' Her son cheering her concession.

'Come.' Dadu links arms with his great-grandson. 'You can choose your ice cream and then we'll see the kittens.'

'Kittens?' Arun glows, hopping from one foot to the other in excitement.

'Yes, didn't I tell you? The cat had a whole litter and they're in the courtyard…'

Indira watches them walk into the kitchen to choose Arun's ice cream, great friends despite nine decades separating them, one who has lived through two world wars and the immense turmoil following India's independence from British rule and partitioning into Pakistan, another who will usher in a new century in five years' time.

And now she turns. She has put off this moment, strangely nervous at facing her husband, the person with whom she should by rights be most at ease. He looks the same as always, perhaps a little tired, a day-old stubble on his chin. But he does not behave the same as he would have done once, taking her in his arms, telling her he loves her, how much he's missed her.

In the early days of their relationship, he would hug her after any amount of time away, even half an hour. 'Now I can face anything,' he'd murmur against her hair and she'd laugh, swatting playfully at him.

She opens her mouth, but it is dry, tasting blue, words having somehow evaporated upon her tongue, and so, instead she smiles at him.

'I'm so happy your baba is—'

She doesn't let him finish, leaning into him, resting her head upon his shoulder, in the crook of his neck. He smells the same as always: ginger and musk with a hint of tiredness. It is the first time she can recall that *she* has initiated a hug.

But he is a stranger, standing stiff in her embrace. She raises her head to look at him. He arches his eyebrows at her. No hint of a smile, no give of his shoulders, no softening of the rigid set of them. Tears threaten, salty bitter, and she is tempted to pull back.

But she doesn't. *This is on me. I need to show him that I love him, I want him, I need him.*

It has always been Karan doing the pursuing, Karan making the sacrifices, Karan offering hugs and saying, *I love you.* He is standing very still. She wraps her arms tighter around him, rests her head against his chest, feels his heart beat. 'I… I'm sorry I left it all to you, the burden of maintaining our relationship.'

She hears his voice start as a rumble in his chest. 'It was not a burden, initially.'

Her heart sinks. 'But it became one?'

'I got weary of giving and giving.'

'I'm sorry. I realise now, I took you for granted.'

'You did.'

'Is it too late?'

'Do you want it to be?'

'No, never, you're the only one for me.'

And now, he wraps his arms around her.

'Then it isn't,' he says into her hair.

She lifts her head, kisses him.

It is blessing and gratitude and thanksgiving and love.

Afterwards, 'I love you,' she says.

'I've been waiting forever for you to say that to me first just once.' He smiles.

'Are you going to make me wait then?' she asks.

'I should, shouldn't I?'

'Say it,' she whispers, 'please.'

'I love you, Indira, it's only ever you. You know that.'

'I was sure and then I wasn't. It broke me.'

Gilded rays of playful sun slant through the emerald awning of tree branches above them, dazzling the dust motes suspended in the baked air, setting them on fire, a red-gold haze. The drone of bees and buzz of flies. The song of birds nesting in the banana and coconut fronds.

'Mama, Baba, come and see the kittens,' their son calls, his face and clothes smeared with cream and flecks of pistachio – he chose kulfi, of course. 'Can we take one home with us?'

And together, they follow their son.

Part Twenty-Six

England

Safe

Chapter Ninety-One

Clara

1995, The Call

The call arrives on a Saturday when Annie is visiting. Some part of Clara has been expecting it – she does not have premonitions as such, but all this week she hasn't slept well, waking with her heart beating wildly in her chest, aching, breaking, has dreamed of her brother, her parents, her husband, all the lost. Of David. *David.*

Even her granddaughter's visit, which she looks forward to, has not dulled the unease.

Clara's grandchildren are very good to her, Annie and Charlie taking turns to visit every other Saturday. Annie is content to potter in the garden with her, while Charlie attends to any bits and pieces that need fixing.

The phone rings just as Annie breezily enters the cottage, bringing with her the fragrance of outdoors: glittery frosticles, ripe apples, falling leaves, barbecued meat and autumn smoke, overlaid with Annie's flowery perfume.

Clara is in the kitchen switching on the kettle and reaching for the oven gloves to take out the scones she has baked, the room toasty and sweet with the scent of rising, raisin-studded dough. The oven gloves drop to the floor as she deposits a shaking hand upon her heart.

The phone sounds like an air-raid siren, the same shrill urgency, portending doom. Last night, she'd dreamed of war, dropping bombs, blazing buildings, shattered lives, disaster. She woke gasping, sure the medal had scorched her heart even as her hand was wrenched from… Not from her mother but from her son.

'Mama,' he cried. 'Mama.'

She woke wheezing, choked, tasting fire. Wet with perspiration, sweating all over like the hot flushes so many years ago now. Her heart ached. Literally. The place where the medal had rested, from when her mother gifted it to her during the air raid nearly eighty years ago until she bequeathed it to her son, throbbed and pulsed with urgent ache.

The phone rings, incessant, ominous. She is rooted to the spot, so Annie answers.

'Hello?' Annie says. Then, 'Nan, it's for you.'

An old man shouting down the line in a tremulous voice, 'Clara?'

Her heart stabs viciously, the pain breaking her. Annie notices and helps her onto a chair.

'Anand? Please tell me he's alright.'

'He is.'

She can breathe again, the pressure upon her heart easing. Her mouth tastes bitter, of salty relief. 'Thank goodness.'

'He had a heart attack.'

Her hand not holding the phone clasps the phantom brand of the medal upon her chest, which hurts. It hurts.

'The medal kept him safe,' Anand says.

Clara's hand rests over her heart, the David-shaped hole in there.

Chapter Ninety-Two

Clara

The Tune of a Much Younger Woman

Afterwards, in Clara's kitchen fragrant with baking, caramelised sugar and risen dough, Annie offers her a tissue, which disintegrates at once, and another, and another. An ordinary day made extraordinary by a phone call encompassing decades and distance, time and history. Worry, fear, hope, anticipation.

'Nan,' Annie asks, eyes wide and anxious, 'are you alright?'

She cannot answer.

Clara returned from India without her son, defeated, brokenhearted and alone, to a country being razed by a brutal war that showed no signs of easing. She went back to working at St Thomas's Hospital. By trying to allay the suffering of others she could escape, briefly, the pain of her own wounded heart. She learned, once again, to live with the ache of missing, joining the ranks of the barely living on intimate terms with death. The eyes of everyone she saw as haunted as her own, by the ghosts of their beloved lost.

Eventually, she met a man, also scarred by war, who had lost his wife and was struggling to bring up his children. He had moved into Maud's flat while Clara was in India. During the nights when she wasn't on duty, when each hour dragged with missing, memories of her son torturing her with their poignant perfection, hearing her neighbour pace as he tried to ease the wailing of his twins was another form of exquisite persecution. She had finally knocked on his door.

'I'm sorry,' he said, bloodshot eyes desperate, one sobbing child on each shoulder, 'they want their mother and I just won't do. My wife, she... she popped out to the shops and a bomb...'

He swallowed, and she had gently touched his hand to show she understood. She had held out her arms and he had handed her his sobbing children. They looked at her with huge wet eyes, shocked out of their crying by this soft woman's chest against which they were snuggled, and, holding them, their warm weight, the pain that hammered relentlessly at her had briefly eased.

The man – Charles, an engineer, a reserved occupation, and thus exempt from conscription – was extremely grateful. And so, each evening, after her shift, she'd help soothe his little ones and in this way the clamouring of her heart for her own little one was ever so slightly alleviated.

Neither Charles nor Clara could bear the indulgence of romantic love, they had lost too much, were too damaged for that. Although when they decided to get married, it was a marriage of convenience – the twins were attached to Clara and vice versa – it had evolved into a steady, enduring love born of companionship, regard, mutual respect and their fierce and protective love for the twins.

She missed David every moment of every day. She endured and celebrated Rathi's letters, cherished them even as they devastated her. She talked to David all the time in her head, sent him her love and best wishes. And all the while she busied herself being the best nurse, mother and wife she could be. Eventually grandchildren came along, all the complicated, wonderful ties of family, a life she had not expected, but was grateful for.

With each passing year, as she grew older and more frail, as, after losing her husband, she had to swallow her pride and accept the help her grandchildren so kindly and lovingly offered, she tried to resign herself to dying without seeing her son.

'You are loved,' she whispered each night before sleeping, touching her heart where her mother's medal had nestled and which she hoped now rested against his. 'You are loved, David.'

And now, her heart aflutter, alive with hope at the same time as it is floored by anxiety, dancing to the tune of a much younger woman within her frail chest.

'I can't hear you very well. Age, you know,' Anand had said. 'I'll hand you over to Dev's daughter, Indira.'

Dev's daughter. Her granddaughter.

'I'd like to see him,' she had said.

'You are very welcome,' Indira said, immediately, unhesitatingly.

You are very welcome. She had been waiting a lifetime to hear those words.

'Does he know?' Clara asked.

'Not yet. His heart…'

Her hand upon her own heart, which beat for him. Her son. 'Don't tell him on my account, please. I'd like to see him and I'm happy if that is in the guise of Rathi's friend.'

After all these years, what did it matter who he thought she was, as long as he was well, and she could see him, touch him, learn him by heart once more?

Chapter Ninety-Three

Clara

Modern-Day Royalty

This time again the journey to India is very different to her previous two. No travelling by sea, taking days, Clara's emotions up one moment, down the next, much like the rollicking movement of the ship, a tidal welter of feeling: hope and anticipation about finally reuniting with David, worry about what to say to Rathi, guilt at breaking her friend's heart, the betrayal and the deception. No encounters with maharajas and invitations to join harems, no visits to an exotic menagerie in a travelling zoo.

Nevertheless, travelling by aeroplane affords its own encounters with modern-day royalty.

'That's Ian Botham, the famous cricketer, Nan,' Annie nudges as they walk past first class. 'And that's Amitabh Bacchan, an Indian movie star – he was in the Indian newspapers I've been reading to prepare for our trip!'

Annie sounds extremely giddy. She's been so since Clara finally explained what the phone call was about and said tentatively, 'I'm going to India, Annie, but you know, I've always travelled with your granddad in recent years and I…'

Annie had taken Clara's hands in hers, looked into her eyes. 'Nan, of course I'm coming with you. I wouldn't dream of letting you travel all that way alone. And in any case…' Here, her voice rising in a shriek, 'It's always been my *dream* to visit India!'

Annie's mother, Clara's daughter Ellie, had insisted on paying Clara's fare: 'Your Christmas and birthday present from me this year, Mum.'

Annie had marshalled her brother Charlie to drop them at the airport and to water Clara's plants while they were away.

'You're a star. What would I do without you?' Clara says gratefully as they settle in their seats.

'You'd have managed just fine, as you have all this time without your son,' Annie replies.

Clara tears up, looking out of the plane window at men hauling luggage into the hold. 'Now, I'm finally meeting him,' she whispers, still unable to believe it, one hand upon her heart. The flight feels endless, each moment dragging even as she marvels that the journey is now just nine hours!

It takes less than a day to reach India, that is all the distance between her son and herself – nine hours and a lifetime of unspoken, withheld and yet overflowing love.

So heartbreakingly close, so accessible, and yet separated, upon her instigation, by decades of heartache and pain and missing.

Part Twenty-Seven

India

Happy

Chapter Ninety-Four

Indira

1995, A Benture

Indira's father is in the courtyard in his rocking chair, ostensibly reading the newspaper – an excuse to get a little shut-eye. He's been so since he came home from hospital, tiring easily, talking one minute and asleep the next. But, on the whole, he's improving, having established an exercise regime – walking each morning, yoga in the evening.

'I'm fitter than I ever was,' he gloated the previous evening and in the saffron glow of the lamps in the courtyard, he did look almost his normal self. 'Soon I'll carry Arun on piggyback everywhere and not be breathless once.'

Ma's laughter accompanied his boast, sounding like the music of celebratory drinks splashing in overfilled glasses.

They've waited, they've watched and now, they've decided they must tell him – he appears strong enough to withstand a shock. In any case, Clara is on her way, although she's assured them she's happy to be Rathi's friend to him – she just wants to see him again.

Karan and Ma know now too and it feels conspiratorial keeping it from Baba, but as Clara did when she gave her only son to Anand and Rathi, they've rationalised that they're doing what they think best for him. And it's not that they'll keep his parentage from him forever, only until he is well enough to take it, which they've decided he is now.

Indira, Karan and Dadu arrived in the courtyard armed with the freshly squeezed salty-sweet lime sherbet her mother has made using limes from the orchard, with the plan of breaking the news to Baba when Ma joins them (she's chopping fruit for Baba to sweeten the blow he might experience – he is on a strict diet, no fried or oily foods, which he has submitted to resignedly), only to find him dozing.

Sindu is sweeping the dust in the seating area beside the merrily burbling fountain – a thankless job as a sudden gust of breeze just spreads it all over again. Indira sits beside Karan and it is like old times, during the early years of their marriage when they would visit her parents and sit talking in the courtyard, her mother plying them with potato bondas, kebabs, bhajis, jalebis and sweet spiced tea.

Her mother's chickens are pecking at the earth, the cat – the mother of the kittens that have Arun so smitten – watching them from where it is sprawled upon the mossy brick surround of the fountain, the water shimmering and spilling radiantly in the sunshine.

Arun is off on a 'benture' – his word for 'adventure'. He's in the copse of coconut, tamarind and mango trees, digging for worms and centipedes with the stick Dadu has shaped into a spear for him. She can hear his laughter wafting on the mango-flavoured breeze as he chatters away to his posse of kittens, who seem to have imprinted upon him.

It will be a task to try to dissuade Arun from bringing all the kittens along when they return home, something that, along with work, feels very far away. Why on earth did she think work so important? Why did she rush, rush, rush all her life, when taking a pause, just *being*, is so wonderfully pleasant?

Right at this moment, although she is worried about how Baba will take the news they are about to impart, she is happy. Her loved ones beside her, her son playing, his joyous starburst of laughter gilding the afternoon. This is what life is about.

The scent of fruit and spices, sweet and cloying. Bhajans playing softly on the sound system inside. Her mother humming along as she chops and prepares the fruit – in her element now her husband is out of hospital and getting better, her daughter visiting with her husband and son.

Familiar smells and sounds and rituals, unchanged since Indira's childhood, and there is comfort in that. Why did she never appreciate her childhood home, always set on running away, as far as she could go, both distance-wise and in her ambitions? *I will never settle for this*, she'd decided, feeling only derision for her parents.

But she is finding out that what she thought was lack of ambition was actually contentment. They are fulfilled, she understands now, happy with each other and in the life they've made together. It is she who, she is realising, has never really relaxed enough, except in these past few days, to be truly happy. She is beginning to understand that life is not a competition but a journey to be enjoyed.

The previous day, her father had taken her hand: 'I'm so proud of you, all you've achieved, who you've become. I don't think I've told you this.'

She had been waiting all her life to hear these words from him. 'I thought you were disappointed by my refusing to marry someone you chose…'

'We were set in our ways. I was happy with your mother, who was my parents' choice, and I wanted the same for you.' His eyes glowing with warmth and love. 'I should have trusted you. I couldn't have chosen better myself.' He smiled gently, patting her hand. 'Your mother and I, we just want you to be happy. I admit we— I don't always put it across well.'

She was overwhelmed by his words but now they were talking openly she wanted to lay bare all the grievances festering within her. 'I thought you wanted me to give up work.'

'I didn't want you to lose sight of what was important, that's all.'

'I was in danger of doing so. Not any more,' she'd said, smiling at him.

Indira's grandmother died yearning to see her and Arun – Indira regrets this sorely. She has decided anew that she will not have any regrets with regards to her parents or grandfather. From now on, she'll bring Arun to visit them regularly. She will not let her relationship with Karan flounder again. She will revel in her son, make memories with him that he will look back on and cherish. Clara didn't have the luxury of watching her son grow and change; Indira *does* and she will no longer take this for granted.

Ma comes to the courtyard, bearing a plate of freshly sliced mango, watermelon, papaya on one palm and a plate of guava sprinkled with chilli powder, the way Indira likes it, on another. 'I wanted to make samosas, but…'

At this, predictably, Baba startles awake, sitting up in his chair. He adjusts his glasses, which had fallen down his nose, and smiles upon seeing his family gathered around. 'Did someone say samosas?'

'Your wife said she'd have made some but we have to endure fruit salad because of you. Couldn't you take better care of yourself?' Dadu says, a twinkle in his eye.

'But this diet is no hardship, for my wife's cooking makes even diet food taste delightful,' Baba says, smiling tenderly at Ma.

He's changed since the heart attack, more open with his emotions, holding his wife's hand often – in front of all of them, something he never did before – telling her how lucky he is, how blessed. Indira is not the only one who's taken stock since her father's heart attack; it appears he has too.

Ma blushes, hiding her face in her sari pallu, while Sindu stops sweeping to hoot and cheer, 'You said it, Goel-ji.'

Spurred on, Baba says, 'My wife is one in a million.'

Sindu stuffs two fingers in her mouth and lets out a piercing whistle, which makes the chickens scatter and the cat pause in the act of lovingly licking its paws.

Arun comes running, his clothes and face spattered with dust, the army of kittens following, waving his stick like a sword. He looks at Sindu in great admiration. 'Show me how you did that, please?'

And it is as Indira watches Sindu teach Arun to whistle, both of them squatting on the just-swept patch of ground, the kittens gambolling around them, the cat snoozing unconcerned on the mossy velvet fountain surround, the chickens pecking at the earth a safe distance away, birds calling from among the trees, the water of the fountain gushing in starry abandon, that she has her epiphany about what to do next, now that she has realised what's important and what is at stake if she doesn't change her ways.

Chapter Ninety-Five

Indira

Talisman

'The heart attack was my body telling me to take early retirement, just as I planned,' Indira's father says, biting into a chilli-seasoned guava slice. Then, gently stroking the medal resting on his chest, 'It was this that saved me.'

Indira's grandfather catches Indira's eye, his gaze prompting, *This is the opening we were looking for.*

They've decided that Indira should be the one to tell him.

Ma: 'I'll get emotional.'

'Me too,' Dadu agreed. 'You're level-headed and matter-of-fact, Indu. You'll do it right.'

I hope I do, Indira thought. She, who had faced down directors twice her age at board meetings, was nervous. For nothing mattered as much as this. This revelation would change how Baba thought of himself, it would upend the very core of who he was. *I need to get this right.*

Indira's father is saying, of the medal, 'It has magical powers.' His eyes twinkle with reminiscence. 'It helped me through my exams. It soothed me when I was upset or worried. Just holding it has always made me feel better.'

It is time. Indira feels speared by three pairs of eyes, urging her on. And yet, she worries. Will this set him back? She reads his features, trying to decipher in them what she now knows, as she has tried with her own face in the mirror since she discovered the truth about her father's mother. The eyes everyone says are like her father's – light for an Indian, amber gold. The hair, her father's and hers, more gold than brown, lightening to a dark blond in the sun.

Indira's mouth is suddenly dry, her words come too fast. 'It belonged to Clara.'

'Ma's friend, yes.'

'Ah, about that, Baba. We've something to tell you...'

Dadu closes his eyes. Ma worries the pallu of her fiery orange sari, twinkling with sequinned silver stars along the border. Karan squeezes Indira's shoulder, offering quiet reassurance.

'Yes?' Her father's gaze, mildly curious, upon hers.

She can't do it. She can't come straight out with it. Indira has climbed the rungs of her company to become its youngest ever, only woman CEO. She hasn't reached that position by being kind. She's sacked men and shouted at others. She's never been at a loss for words. Until now.

'What's wrong?' Her father sounds anxious, lines creasing his forehead as his face scrunches in worry.

Karan meets her eye, nods gently.

She swallows, and, taking a deep breath, she begins to tell her father the true story of his origins.

Chapter Ninety-Six

Indira

Fantasy

Afterwards, they sit, Indira's mother on one side of Baba, Indira on the other, Karan beside her and Dadu facing them, hands linked, tears garlanding their faces.

'That's why I'm so light-skinned when both Ma…' He hesitates, then appears to arrive at a decision, for he continues, addressing Dadu, 'Ma and you are so dark.' Then, in a voice that is the same shade of soft purple as the dusk enveloping them in its perfumed embrace, 'I had a recurring dream as a child. I… I'd dream of a woman. I could almost but not quite picture her. I sometimes heard her voice. She had soft soothing fingers and she sang exotic lullabies and recited poetry to me.' He sniffs. 'I'd wake yearning for something I couldn't name. More often than not, my pillow was wet – I had been crying.'

'You never told us,' Dadu says softly.

'I somehow knew not to. I knew it would make you upset. And I didn't want to think about her – it hurt. I'd stroke my medal and it would soothe me.' He swallows. '*Now* it makes sense. It was my mother – I remembered her, but only in my dreams. And when I held her medal, I felt comforted.' Awe shining in the caramel grey eyes that Indira is sure are a legacy of the mother whose love he has experienced all his life via his dreams. 'As I grew older, they were not as frequent, but I sometimes still dream of her.'

Her father smiles through his tears. The little boy who used to dream of the gentle touch of a fantasy woman, singing lullabies and reciting poems that disappeared with dawn, shining through her father's middle-aged face.

'That is the power of love, I suppose. My mother's love haunted me in my dreams. I sensed, somehow, that she was there. I was yearning for her, even though I didn't *know*. When you told me just now, it was fantastical but it also made perfect sense. It's as if I've been waiting for her all my life.'

'Oh, Baba.'

Her father reaches across, cups Indira's face, gently. 'Love. It is the most important, the *only* important thing. It transcends time and memory. I remembered my mother, dreamed about her without knowing it. I always knew I was loved, I had this almost tangible impression of love.'

'There is one more thing to tell you. She's coming here, Baba.'

His hands clasped around his medal, fresh tears budding and trembling like the season's first flowers in his overwhelmed eyes. Mosquitoes hover, crickets chant, the evening breeze, weary but sweet, caresses their faces.

Dadu speaks up, his voice quivering with emotion, 'Indira found her number in Rathi's correspondence. We called to tell her about your heart attack. She wanted to see you, she was willing to be introduced as your mother's friend, if we decided not to tell you.' Dadu pauses. 'We were worried, you see. Your heart…'

'My heart feels whole for the first time I can recall.' Baba's voice is an awed whisper. 'I've always felt there was something important missing, even when I got married, even when Indira was born. I never felt wholly complete. Now I understand why.'

'Why're you all crying?' Arun asks, climbing onto Indira's lap. Her son is covered head to toe in dust, he smells of sun and earth and vegetation and mischief.

'Happy tears, my love,' Indira says.

Arun scrunches his nose. 'Adults are funny,' he pronounces firmly. 'I only cry when I'm hurt and sometimes not even then because I'm very brave.'

They all laugh wetly in the gathering dusk, fragrant with love. Indira gathers her son to her, dust and all, and thinks of Baba's words: *Love. It is the most important, the* only *important thing.*

'Time for your wash, son,' Indira says.

'Can't I stay here with all of you a little longer?'

'You heard your mother, son,' Karan says.

'*Please*, Mama? If you agree, Baba will too for he can never say no to you.'

They all laugh some more even as Karan sighs, 'That's true.'

'Grand-dadu, Dadu, Daadi,' Arun announces grandly. 'Do you know, Mama is the head of a big company, she is bossy with everyone, even sometimes with Baba, but *never* with me.' Arun's voice bright with pride. 'Mama always says I'm the only man who can boss her around.'

The courtyard rings with the chuckles of her family. In the softly settling velvet dark, Karan's hand finds hers. *Arun knows I love him. He knew even when I was working all the time.* Again, her father's words: *Love. It is the most important, the* only *important thing.*

Arun turns to her. 'Mama, you're the only one crying now. Are these happy tears as well?'

'Yes, my love.' She deposits wet kisses on her son's dirty, beloved face, tasting gratitude, juicy sweet.

Chapter Ninety-Seven

Clara

Gilded Warmth

India is busier than Clara remembers and yet, in many ways, unchanged. The profusion of colour, scents, languages. The kaleidoscopic saris, rainbow spices, bangles glimmering in the bright white sun. A fiery assault on the senses.

Clara had left India devastated, destroyed, defeated. She hadn't dared to indulge or nurture the hope that she might return. But here she is after having been away more than fifty years, feeling welcomed into this transcendent country that houses her son, enveloped by its gilded warmth, the brilliant rainbow embrace of anticipation and promise.

Her son lives in the same house where he was conceived and it is like coming full circle, returning to the place where she was so welcome and happy, where her son has grown up, living the life she wished for him, bestowed upon him by sacrificing her own time with him.

Chapter Ninety-Eight

Indira

Potent

Indira waits beside her parents, grandfather and husband, Arun, on another 'benture' in the courtyard, Sindu keeping an eye on him.

They had worried for nothing – if anything, her father has recovered even faster since being told of Clara.

'Most people have two parents,' he marvelled. 'I've been lucky enough to have three.' He's been determined to get back to how he used to be, more so now Clara is arriving. 'I don't want to worry her. I want her first glimpse of me after so long apart to be gratifying, not upsetting.'

'Baba, she's seeing you after having loved you from afar all these years; it *will* be gratifying.'

Nevertheless, he's been going for walks around the courtyard, morning and evening, accompanied by Arun and the litter of kittens.

Indira's father cannot stop pacing, so anxious that Ma is moved to lay a gentle hand on his shoulder and say softly, '*Jaan.*'

He smiles at her, his gaze so tender that Indira wonders, once again, how she had ever questioned the love between her parents. Just because theirs is a calm love, no fizz or frills, doesn't mean that it is any the less potent for it.

Dadu in contrast to Baba stands very still, his hands clasped together, the lines on his face taut with tension. Indira wonders what is going through his mind. Is he recalling the night he spent with Clara that created their son? His friendship, and his wife's, with this woman?

'I loved Clara too, differently. I admired her. Cared for her. She was my friend,' he had said, wistfulness, regard, sadness colouring his voice the kaleidoscopic rainbow of a summer evening.

Karan holds Indira's hand, offering silent comfort. She has discussed the idea that germinated when watching Sindu teaching Arun to whistle with him – bringing her considerable experience in management to a non-profit organisation helping women and children in need – and he is all for it.

'I… I'd like to base it near here, so we can visit Ma and Baba and Dadu regularly.' She'd looked at him, not sure what he'd say to this. It would mean moving, upheaval.

'I've always wanted to move closer to your parents but never suggested it because of your job,' he said softly.

She exhaled, tasting relief and gratitude – she was so lucky in her husband. 'Your work?'

'We've been thinking of expanding to other parts of India. I could head the branch here in town. And Arun has only just started school, so he can switch easily. He'll love visiting his grandparents every weekend.'

She took a deep breath, tasting possibility, promise, her mind buzzing with plans.

'And this way, we solve the problem of how to dissuade him from bringing that whole litter of kittens with him – we can convince him this house is best for they have space to roam and he can visit every weekend.'

She grinned and went into his arms, resting her head against his heart, hearing it beat in synchrony with hers.

'We'll make it work,' he whispered before leaning down to kiss her.

Indira had thought she was brave and daring, rising to become the only woman CEO of her firm. But the most daring, the bravest thing, she has come to realise, is to love fully and completely, throwing yourself open to pain, vulnerable to loss. Knowing there will be hurt but loving anyway.

Like her father said, 'Love. It is the most important, the *only* important thing.'

'They're here,' Indira's mother says and they turn as one to the gate, which they've left open. The taxi turns in to the drive, a cloud of red-gold dust mushrooming in its wake.

Her father stops pacing, transfixed by the advancing car, hope and anticipation playing a tableau upon his face. Her mother beside him, offering comfort and strength. Indira's grandfather stands even straighter, his hands clasped so tightly together that the knuckles stand pale as soldiers, bloodless white.

Karan squeezes her own hand and it is then that she realises she is crying, for all that has been lost, all the missing years, sadnesses and sacrifices, and for the reunion that is about to take place.

Chapter Ninety-Nine

Clara

Perfect Rhythm

Clara sits up as straight as her aged body will allow as they advance up a drive lined by lime trees, the tart citrus scent sharpening her anticipation. The drive is new – well, new since she visited last, so it could be sixty years old for all she knows – but the house up ahead is just as she remembers, warm red-gold and welcoming. She can see several people standing by the house – an older man, a middle-aged couple and another younger couple.

The older man holds himself as straight as the stoop of his shoulders will allow. His thick head of dark locks is now a few sparse grey strands. His face is lined with experience. But his eyes are the same, aglow with warmth, if anything even brighter, shining out of his weathered face. Anand. The wounded soldier she nursed back to health. Her friend. Her first love. The father of her son.

The younger woman carries herself with a confidence – pushed-back shoulders, chin lifted assertively – that makes her appear taller than she is. Her hair tumbles down around her elfin face, a glorious mass of brown curls glinting gold in the sunlight. Her face... Looking at her granddaughter Indira's face is like seeing a younger, prettier version of Clara herself.

And now, her gaze is drawn to and arrested by the middle-aged man, who has been walking up and down but comes to a stop as the car approaches. The man she last saw cradling a bug on a riverbank on a blistering hot afternoon, the man she last held as a little boy of three. A man for whom her heart beats, despite the distance and years and lies and love separating them.

She is not aware of Annie opening the door and helping her out of the taxi, of her granddaughter paying the driver, the exchange that follows as the woman standing beside David – Dev – insists *she* will pay.

'You are our guests; please, let me.'

'I'm happy to be paid by both of you,' the taxi driver laughs, cheekily.

But Clara is not aware of any of this, as she is transfixed by the man in front of her, whom she has loved and longed for and missed, whom she *knows* despite never having laid eyes on him since that hot afternoon more than half a century ago when she decided to allow him to live the life she had chosen for him.

He is looking at her and in that look – hope and love and wonder – she knows he knows who she is to him.

She walks up to him, one hand on her heart, where her mother's St Christopher medal, that she bequeathed him, used to rest and with the other, she strokes, very gently, his cheek, the tears she finds there, perfect jewels.

'David, my heart,' she says and he envelops her in his arms.

And for the first time in fifty-seven years, she hears and feels his heart beating beside hers, alongside hers, in perfect rhythm.

Chapter One Hundred

Clara

Poetry in Motion

Her son.

'Mama,' he says, and his voice is just as she imagined, poetry in motion, liquid gold. 'I've felt your love all my life. Here.' He touches the medal, her mother's medal, resting upon his heart. 'Thank you,' he whispers, 'for your sacrifice. I've had a wonderful life.'

'I can see that.' She smiles.

'I used to dream of a woman who sang lullabies, narrated stories and recited poetry to me; who loved me. I remembered your voice, your touch, your love. I dreamed of you, experienced your love, felt loved, all my life. And now, here you are.'

He felt loved all his life.

All these years, this distance, ache, regret, loss, yearning, missing.

He remembered me.

She smiles through her tears, heart replete, overflowing with gratitude and joy and love. 'Here I am.'

A Letter From Renita D'Silva

I am hugely grateful to you for choosing to read *The War Child*. If you enjoyed it and would like to keep up to date with all my latest releases, just sign up at the following link. Your email address will never be shared and you can unsubscribe at any time.

www.bookouture.com/renita-dsilva

What I adore most about being a writer is hearing from readers. I'd love to know what you made of *The War Child* and I'd be very grateful if you could write a review. It helps new readers to discover my books.

You can get in touch with me on my Facebook page, through Twitter, Goodreads or my website.

Thank you so much for your support – it means the world to me.

Until next time,
Renita

 RenitaDSilvaBooks

 RenitaDSilva

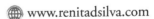 www.renitadsilva.com

Acknowledgements

I would like to thank all at Bookouture, especially Maisie Lawrence – you are amazing and I feel incredibly lucky and beyond privileged to have you as my editor. Thank you for your advice, kindness, patience and insight. You are the absolute, absolute best.

Huge thanks to Jenny Hutton, editor extraordinaire. I am so grateful to you for homing in on the story I wanted to tell. I cannot thank you enough. Thank you, Jacqui Lewis, for your eagle eye and wonderful suggestions during copy-edits for this book. Thank you, Jane Donovan, for proofreading this book. A million thanks to Lorella Belli and all the team at Lorella Belli Literary Agency for your untiring efforts in making my books go places.

Thank you to my lovely fellow Bookouture authors, especially Angie Marsons, Sharon Maas, Debbie Rix, June Considine (aka Laura Elliot), whose friendship I am grateful for and lucky to have. Thank you to authors Manuela Iordache, Chris Babu, Janet Rising, June Arnold for your wonderful friendship and support.

Thank you to all the fabulous book bloggers who give so freely of their time, reading and reviewing, sharing and shouting about our books. I am grateful to my Twitter/FB friends for their enthusiastic and overwhelming support. An especial thanks to Jules Mortimer, Joseph Calleja and Sandra Duck, whom I am privileged to call my friends and who are the best cheerleaders one could wish for.

A huge thank you to my mother, Perdita Hilda D'Silva, who reads every word I write; who is encouraging and supportive and fun; who answers any questions I might have on any topic

– finding out the answer, if she doesn't know it, in record time – who listens patiently to my doubts and who reminds me, gently, when I cry that I will never finish the book: 'I've heard this same refrain several times before.'

I am immensely grateful to my long-suffering family for willingly sharing me with characters who live only in my head. Love always.

And last, but not least, thank you, reader, for choosing this book.

Author's Note

This is a work of fiction set around and incorporating real events.

I have taken liberties with regards to the Indian setting, picking characteristics, such as food, vegetation and customs, from different parts of India to fashion my fictional villages and cities; the areas I have set them in may not necessarily have places like the ones I have described.

I have also moved certain events around – for instance, St Thomas's Hospital was bombed several times during the Second World War, well into 1944, the worst of the bomb damage occurring during the Blitz, between September 1940 and May 1941, but the Westminster Wing (Emergency wing in the main text) did not necessarily get destroyed during the raid I've mentioned. In this and other events, like the air raid on Munster Road and Clara's street in 1943, I've employed artistic licence for the purposes of the story. There is no Munster Road near St Thomas's, no Burnham Road housing an orphanage; I made them up.

Clara encounters Belgian refugees on her journey to Aunt Helen's in 1917, but most had arrived and settled in England by then.

I apologise for any oversights or mistakes and hope they do not detract from your enjoyment of this book.

Lightning Source UK Ltd.
Milton Keynes UK
UKHW041551110821
388611UK00001B/36